PRAI...

W9-CSX-241

Redemption, Kansas

"Has everything a truly good Western novel should have—a gritty, likable hero, action as explosive as a Colt .45, a page-turning plot, and prose as smooth and swift as a good saddle pony. It's no wonder he is considered one of the genre's best writers. A crackling good story that will have me reading more Reasoner."
—Bill Brooks, author of *The Messenger*

"A Western novel with characters you care about and a crackerjack plot. If anybody asks you who's carrying on the heritage of fine traditional Westerns in the vein of Louis L'Amour and Elmer Kelton, tell 'em James Reasoner's the man." —Bill Crider, author of *The Wild Hog Murders*

"A twisty, fast-paced, stay-up-late-and-read-till-mornin' saga of the West. Grand stuff!"
—J. Lee Butts, author of *And Kill Them All*

"James Reasoner knows how to tell a story. He has produced a suspenseful, extremely satisfying page-turner, with a hero who is strong-willed but very human. This book reminds me, once again, of why I became a James Reasoner fan."
—Troy D. Smith, Spur Award–winning author of
Riding to Sundown

"A wonderful book, wonderfully told. James Reasoner has the gift of words, telling a fast-paced story that reaches into the hearts of his characters . . . and his readers."
—Frank Roderus, author of *Ransom*

"A fast-paced cowboy tale written with the flair of a master. If you've never read a Western by James Reasoner, pick this one up. You won't put this novel down until you've finished it, and you'll be ready for more."
—Larry D. Sweazy, Spur Award–winning author of
The Cougar's Prey

Berkley titles by James Reasoner

REDEMPTION, KANSAS
REDEMPTION: HUNTERS

REDEMPTION: Hunters

James Reasoner

BERKLEY BOOKS, NEW YORK

THE BERKLEY PUBLISHING GROUP
Published by the Penguin Group
Penguin Group (USA) Inc.
375 Hudson Street, New York, New York 10014, USA

Penguin Group (Canada), 90 Eglinton Avenue East, Suite 700, Toronto, Ontario M4P 2Y3, Canada
(a division of Pearson Penguin Canada Inc.)
Penguin Books Ltd., 80 Strand, London WC2R 0RL, England
Penguin Group Ireland, 25 St. Stephen's Green, Dublin 2, Ireland (a division of Penguin Books Ltd.)
Penguin Group (Australia), 250 Camberwell Road, Camberwell, Victoria 3124, Australia
(a division of Pearson Australia Group Pty. Ltd.)
Penguin Books India Pvt. Ltd., 11 Community Centre, Panchsheel Park, New Delhi—110 017, India
Penguin Group (NZ), 67 Apollo Drive, Rosedale, Auckland 0632, New Zealand
(a division of Pearson New Zealand Ltd.)
Penguin Books (South Africa) (Pty.) Ltd., 24 Sturdee Avenue, Rosebank, Johannesburg 2196,
South Africa

Penguin Books Ltd., Registered Offices: 80 Strand, London WC2R 0RL, England

REDEMPTION: HUNTERS

A Berkley Book / published by arrangement with the author

PRINTING HISTORY
Berkley edition / February 2012

Copyright © 2012 by James Reasoner.
Cover illustration by Dennis Lyall.
Cover design by Diana Kolsky.
Interior text design by Kristin del Rosario.

ISBN: 978-0-425-24608-5

BERKLEY®
Berkley Books are published by The Berkley Publishing Group,
a division of Penguin Group (USA) Inc.,
375 Hudson Street, New York, New York 10014.
BERKLEY® is a registered trademark of Penguin Group (USA) Inc.
The "B" design is a trademark of Penguin Group (USA) Inc.

PRINTED IN THE UNITED STATES OF AMERICA

10 9 8 7 6 5 4 3 2 1

To the Western Fictioneers

Thank heaven, my boys, for a land which is blest
With a frontier so boundless and free,
So drink to the hunters and drink to the West,
And pass the "red liquor" to me.

From a verse printed in the *Dodge City Times*,
September 29, 1877

Chapter 1

The loud rumble jolted Bill Harvey out of a sound sleep. Instinct made him jerk upright and throw the blankets aside. He groped for his boots. The herd was stampeding, and Hob would need every hand he could get to bring the panic-stricken cattle under control.

Bill was on the verge of panic himself. Where were his blasted boots? *Where was the ground?*

Suddenly there was nothing under him for a dizzy second. Then with a painful impact, he landed on something hard. Pain stabbed through his torso and made him gasp.

"Bill?"

That sweet voice didn't belong to any cowboy on Hob Sanders's cattle drive.

Bill opened his eyes and looked up just as light flashed around him. He caught a glimpse of a young woman's face surrounded by blond hair tousled from sleep and realized that she was looking down at him over the edge of a bed.

The light lasted only a second before flickering out. In the darkness, the young woman said, "Bill, what in the world are you doing down there on the floor? Did you fall out of bed?"

The rumble came again. But it wasn't a stampede, Bill told himself as his sleep-drugged brain finally figured out what was going on.

It was thunder.

"Sorry," he said. "I guess I was dreaming. I heard that thunder and thought it was a stampede."

"You thought you were back on that cattle drive?"

"Yeah, I reckon I did. I was lookin' for my boots."

Eden Monroe Harvey laughed. "Once a cowboy, always a cowboy, I suppose." She reached down to offer him a hand. "Let me help you up."

Bill took his wife's hand to brace himself as he pushed up to a sitting position. He put his other hand on the bed and climbed to his feet. He was wearing the bottom half of a pair of long underwear, but that was all.

Outside, lightning clawed through the Kansas sky again. The brilliant glare lit up the room, giving him another look at Eden as she sat in the bed wearing a white nightgown. There was nothing fancy about the garment, but she sure made it look good.

"Are you all right?" she asked as he lowered himself to the mattress beside her. "It hasn't been that long since you had that cracked rib, you know."

Bill wasn't likely to forget being shot, and on the very day he and Eden were supposed to get married, to boot. But the wedding had taken place a few days later, and he had healed up just fine.

Since then he had enjoyed a couple of months of wedded bliss. It had been pretty doggone blissful at times, too.

He turned to her now and said, "I'm fine. It jarred me a mite when I landed on the floor, but no harm done."

"You're sure?"

He slid an arm around her. "Positive."

"Bill . . ."

"I just figured since we were both awake already . . ."

Outside, the thunderstorm continued to whoop and holler its way across the Kansas plains and the town of Redemption. When Bill was little and thunder had rumbled, his ma always said it was the tater wagon rollin' over. A fella sometimes remembered the damnedest things at the damnedest times, he thought.

Then he stopped thinking about anything except the beautiful young woman in his arms. He closed his eyes as he kissed her and drew her closer.

The burst of silvery light from the electrical display in the heavens reflected off the piece of metal lying on the small table next to the bed.

It was a tin star, and it belonged to the marshal of Redemption.

The cannons were roaring again. Ward Costigan felt the earth tremble underneath him as the bombardment resumed.

He wondered if the Rebs were launching another attack. Be just like those secessionist varmints to come charging out of the night, screaming those devil yells of theirs.

Costigan reached out in the darkness and fumbled for his rifle. He couldn't find it.

With a huge whumping sound, one of the artillery rounds landed near his tent and shook the ground again. He had to get out and hunt a hole, otherwise he was liable to get blown to bits. The next shell might land right on top of him.

He got onto hands and knees and shoved himself out of the tent, slipping and sliding in the mud outside as he tried to get to his feet. Rain lashed at his face. The Confederates were attacking in the middle of a storm, damn their hides!

Costigan jerked his head from side to side as he searched for the enemy . . . or for a place to hide from those terrible explosions. A shell went off with a blinding flash and a huge peal of sound that pounded against Costigan's ears. He clapped his hands over them and fell to his knees.

Nowhere to run, no place to hide. All he could do was wait for death to find him, as it had found so many of his friends and comrades.

So many bodies, broken and bleeding, blown apart by

artillery, riddled by musket fire, ripped open by bayonets . . . Costigan hunched forward in the rain, and the drops flowed together with the tears rolling down his weathered cheeks.

"Costigan! What the hell you doin' out here in this storm? Better get back in your tent before you drown or get struck by lightnin', you dang fool!"

Costigan lurched to his feet. He didn't have his rifle or his old cap-and-ball pistol, but a heavy-bladed knife rode in a sheath at his waist. He snatched it out and lunged at the indistinct figure that loomed up in front of him.

"I'll gut you, you filthy Reb!"

The man let out a startled, frightened yell and made a desperate grab for Costigan's wrist. He caught it and twisted the blade aside before Costigan could sink it into his belly.

Costigan felt a wave of despair. He expected a shot to smash the life out of him at any second now.

Instead his opponent stuck a foot between his ankles and tripped him. Costigan sprawled on the wet ground.

The man landed on top of him, driving a knee into Costigan's belly. He pinned Costigan's knife hand to the ground and yelled, "Stop it! Stop fightin' me, Ward! It's me, Dave McGinty!"

After a moment the words began to penetrate Costigan's brain. Dave McGinty . . . The name was familiar. He was . . . he was . . .

McGinty was a buffalo hunter.

And so was he, Costigan thought.

Panting for breath, hard rain sluicing into his upturned face and threatening to drown him, Costigan managed to say, "Lemme go, Dave. I'm all right now."

McGinty kept him pinned down. "You sure about that? You came mighty near stickin' me with that knife."

"Yeah, I'm sure. Let me up."

McGinty released Costigan's wrist and climbed off of him. Costigan rolled onto his side and coughed and choked from the rainwater that filled his nose and throat. He lay there for several seconds.

"Let's get you back in your tent," said McGinty. He bent and got his hands under Costigan's arms. McGinty wasn't very tall, but he was broad and incredibly strong. He lifted the taller, rangier Costigan without much trouble.

Costigan scrubbed his hands over his wet face. It didn't help much in the downpour. When these summer thunderstorms sprang up in Kansas, they could dump a lot of water in a short period of time.

"Come on, Costigan," McGinty urged.

Costigan stayed where he was. He couldn't believe he had been so lost in his dream—or his memories—that he'd been so convinced he was back in the war.

For a few minutes there everything had been so vivid. He looked down at the knife in his hand, seeing lightning reflect off the blade, and turned to McGinty to ask, "Dave, did I just nearly kill you?"

McGinty laughed. "You came a lot closer than I like to think about. Did you really think I was a Reb?"

"Yeah. Yeah, I guess I did."

"That was more than ten years ago, Ward. You got to forget about it. I have."

The glare from a burst of lightning washed over McGinty's round, bearded face. Costigan saw the look of concern on his friend's features. He sheathed the knife and put his hand on McGinty's shoulder.

"I'm sorry, Dave. I didn't mean to—"

Costigan stopped short and his fingers tightened on McGinty's shoulder as another flash lit up the edge of the camp. A figure stood there, near one of the hide wagons.

Costigan got a good look at the man, even though it only lasted for a heartbeat. He saw the buckskins, the hawk-like face with streaks of war paint across it, the eagle feather sticking up from the black hair slicked down with grease.

"Indian!"

McGinty twisted free of Costigan's grip and whirled

around to look. His hand went to the heavy revolver holstered on his hip and pulled it out.

"Where?" he asked. The lightning flash had already faded, and darkness covered the prairie again.

"Over there by the wagons," Costigan said.

"How many?"

"Just one."

"Did you get a good look at him? Was he a hostile?"

"He was painted for war," Costigan said. "I'm sure of it."

For a moment, McGinty didn't respond. Then he said, "I hate to say it, but you were sure I was a Rebel, too, Ward."

"You think I imagined that Indian?" Costigan didn't know whether to be angry that McGinty didn't believe him, or scared because he knew, deep down, there was a possibility he *had* imagined the painted warrior.

"Hell, I didn't say that. Let's go take a look."

The two buffalo hunters moved toward the wagons. The rain had let up a little, and the thunder and lightning were starting to move off.

There was still enough lightning for them to see where they were going, though. When they reached the parked wagons, they looked around.

"I don't see anybody," McGinty said.

Neither did Costigan, although a part of him hated to admit it. He rubbed his eyes and shook his head.

"Mind you, I ain't sayin' he wasn't there," McGinty went on. "I just don't know."

"But if he was here, he's gone now," Costigan said.

"Yeah, looks like it. I'm gonna wake up some of the boys anyway. I think we need to stand a better watch the rest of the night, just in case there's any trouble skulkin' around. I was takin' my turn, that's how come I saw you out stumblin' around in the storm."

"I'm sorry, Dave. I never meant to—"

"Forget it," McGinty said. "Hell, most of us who lived through that war saw a lot of things we can't forget but wish we could. Go get some more sleep, Ward. You'll feel better in the mornin'."

Costigan wasn't sure about that, but he hoped McGinty was right. He was a little nervous about trying to go back to sleep.

Most of the time, nightmares didn't plague him. Tonight, what with the thunderstorm and all, everything had come together just right to get him mixed up in his head. He'd heard the thunder and thought it was artillery, and once that started, the rest of it just tumbled along like rocks rolling downhill.

"Good night, Dave. Be careful. Keep your eyes open."

"Don't worry. My eyes are gonna be wide open."

Eyes wide open, Costigan thought as he stumbled toward his tent. Eyes staring in death, lifeless but still haunted by the stubborn refusal to accept what had happened.

He had seen so many like that.

Ward Costigan crawled into his tent. Water had seeped into it and soaked his blankets, but it didn't matter since he was already drenched from the rain.

He lay there and thought about that stark figure he had seen standing by the wagons, and a shiver went through him. He tried to tell himself it was because he was wet all over and even a summer night could be a mite chilly out here on the plains.

Morning couldn't come soon enough to suit him.

Chapter 2

The storm moved on during the night. Rain had been rare enough lately in these parts that the streets of Redemption, Kansas, were almost dry by morning.

Only a few puddles remained as Bill walked from the Monroe house toward the marshal's office and jail. He had a slight limp that would stay with him the rest of his life, the result of a steer goring his left leg during an actual stampede, not an imagined one like the night before.

Odd though it might seem, he couldn't help but feel grateful to the ornery old brindle steer that had gone after him. If that injury hadn't happened, Hob Sanders, the trail boss, never would have left Bill behind to recuperate in Redemption. Bill never would have met and fallen in love with Eden Monroe, and he never would have taken the job as the town's marshal. It was a lot of responsibility for a young man in his early twenties, but he was learning to handle it.

No, without that old brindle steer, he'd be back in Texas by now, just another shiftless cowboy waiting until the next drive to the railhead. Broke, too, more than likely. He probably would have blown all his wages in a drunken bender once the herd reached Dodge City.

Benjy Cobb was sweeping the boardwalk in front of Monroe Mercantile when Bill got there. Cobb, who was small and shiftier-looking than he really was, worked part of the time at the store for Perry Monroe, Eden's father, and part of the time as the swamper in Fred Smoot's saloon.

Perry Monroe had been wounded in the same fracas that left Bill with a busted rib, and he'd had to hire someone to help out in the mercantile. So far, Cobb was staying sober and doing just fine in the job, as far as Bill knew.

Bill gave Cobb a friendly nod and said, "Mornin', Benjy. Quite a storm last night, wasn't it?"

Cobb leaned on his broom and returned the nod. "It sure was. When that thunder went to crashin', it sure gave me the fantods. Sounded like the world was comin' to an end."

Bill didn't mention how he had mistaken the thunder for a cattle stampede and fallen out of bed as a consequence.

"But I reckon we needed the rain," Cobb went on. "Been mighty dry lately."

"Yeah. How's Perry this morning?"

Cobb lowered his voice as he answered, "Kind of crotchety, if you ask me. Said he didn't sleep well last night. Probably because of the storm."

Monroe had been up and gone from the house when Bill woke up this morning. That wasn't unusual. His father-in-law liked to get to the store early and get ready for the day.

Hearing that Monroe had been awake some during the night made an uncomfortable feeling come over Bill. A young, recently married couple sharing a house with the wife's father could be an awkward situation at times.

Because of that, Bill and Eden tried to be discreet, but it was difficult. Bill hoped Monroe hadn't overheard anything he shouldn't have.

What it amounted to was that he and Eden needed a place of their own. He made up his mind to talk to her about that the first chance he got.

"I'm sure Perry will be in a better mood later," Bill said. "I'll be seein' you, Benjy."

"All right, Marshal. So long."

It still seemed odd to him when somebody called him "Marshal," Bill thought as he moved along the boardwalk and then crossed the street toward the jail.

The badge pinned to his blue bib-front shirt was a constant reminder, of course, but it still hadn't completely sunk in that he was the law in Redemption.

The idea that he might wind up packing a star had never even occurred to him until a few months earlier. He supposed he would get used to it sooner or later.

Redemption didn't have a night deputy, so the office stayed locked up when Bill wasn't there. So far that had worked out all right. People knew where to find Bill if they needed him.

He took the key from the pocket of his jeans, unlocked the door, and went inside. His flat-crowned brown hat went on a nail next to the door, which he left open because it was a little hot and stuffy in the office.

Despite the heat, he went over to the potbellied stove in the front corner of the room and started a fire so he could boil a pot of Arbuckles.

If the town continued to grow, he would have to give some thought to hiring a deputy. Mayor Roy Fleming and the rest of the town council might not be too fond of that idea, after what had happened with the last deputy, but Bill figured he could bring them around if he had to. If he was all right with hiring some help, they ought to be, too.

Once he had the coffee brewing, Bill did some sweeping of his own, like Benjy over at the mercantile. He didn't mind the work. The townspeople had a right to expect the marshal's office to be clean. He worked for them, after all.

He started at the back, in the empty cell block, and swept toward the front, eventually pushing the dirt and dust out the front door, onto the boardwalk, and into the street. With that chore done and the coffee still brewing, he took his hat off the nail and set out on his morning rounds.

Quite a few people were out and about by now. Bill saw Eden going into her father's store.

She worked there part of the time, too. Later in the morning, she would go back to the house to prepare lunch for him and Perry Monroe, then deliver those meals to the mercantile and the marshal's office.

She hadn't appeared to notice him when she went into the store. He happened to be standing next to an empty hitch rail, so he leaned on it and contemplated things.

Eden would have to take things a mite easier once she was in the family way, he told himself. She might balk at that, because she liked to stay busy all the time.

Of course, she wasn't expecting yet and there was no way of knowing when, or even if, she would be, but the possibility cropped up in Bill's mind from time to time.

Growing up, he'd never given any thought at all to having kids someday. His own family life hadn't been that good. If anybody had asked him a year earlier if he wanted children, he probably would have said not just *no*, but *hell, no!*

A lot of things had changed when he met Eden, though, and that was one of them.

Hoofbeats broke into his musing and made him look down the street. Bill straightened in surprise as he saw the riders coming toward him.

About twenty of them, he estimated, all wearing dust-covered blue uniforms with yellow stripes down the trouser legs. The man in front wore a black hat, and the rest of the men sported stiff-billed caps.

What was a cavalry patrol doing in Redemption?

The best way to find out was to ask them, Bill supposed. He moved out into the street, stepping around a couple of muddy places that couldn't be called puddles anymore.

The officer leading the troopers held up a hand and signaled for them to halt. A grizzled sergeant riding behind him relayed that order in a bull-like voice.

Bill wasn't all that familiar with the army's insignia. He thought the officer was a captain, but he wasn't sure. He nodded to the man anyway and said, "Howdy."

The officer studied Bill, his haughty gaze lingering on the tin star. Bill felt his temper shortening. He didn't cotton to being stared at like that.

He kept a lid on his anger, though, and waited for the officer to speak.

Finally, the man asked, "What town is this?"

"Redemption," Bill replied. It seemed to him that even an army officer ought to be smart enough to know where he was.

"And you're the local law, I take it?"

The officer's voice was crisp, even curt. He was from back East somewhere, Bill decided. Folks here in Kansas talked faster than Bill did with his Texas drawl, but they were still a lot more leisurely than this fella's clipped speech.

"That's right," he said in reply to the man's question. "Marshal Bill Harvey."

"I'm Captain Timothy Stone, in command of this patrol from Fort Hays. Could I have a word with you in your office?"

"Sure," Bill said. He wasn't going to turn down a request from the cavalry. He turned and gestured up the street toward the jail. "It's right along there."

Captain Stone nodded. He turned to the noncom and said, "Sergeant Hutton, order the men to dismount and water their horses." Stone glanced at Bill. "I assume it's all right for my men to use the town's well?"

"Go right ahead."

Stone swung down from his saddle and turned his horse over to the sergeant. He clasped his hands together behind his back and fell in step beside Bill as they started toward the jail.

"Are you injured, Marshal?"

"You mean the limp?" Bill asked. "Old injury. It's fine, and it doesn't slow me down much."

"I suppose not, or the citizens wouldn't have entrusted you with the job of maintaining law and order."

Bill didn't like Captain Stone very much. He tried not to jump to conclusions about folks, but Stone struck him as the sort of man who didn't care what people thought of him, and because of that he didn't mind rubbing them the wrong way.

Despite that, Bill wasn't going to let the feeling get in the way of doing his job. It would be best to cooperate with the cavalry if he could, no matter what they wanted.

He ushered Stone into the office. "Coffee's ready," he said as he hung his hat on the nail. "Care for a cup?"

"No, I think—" Stone stopped, appeared to think it over, and said, "Why not? Thank you, Marshal."

Maybe he wasn't such a bad sort after all, Bill thought. He went over to the stove, used a thick piece of leather as a potholder, and filled a tin cup for each of them with the hot, black brew.

Stone took his cup, sipped, and nodded in approval. "That's very good."

"An old chuckwagon cook taught me how to make it," Bill said.

"You were a cowboy before you became a lawman?"

"For most of my life." Bill smiled. "Becoming a star packer was next thing to an accident. I never planned on it."

"Well, fate holds many surprises in store for all of us, I suppose."

Bill propped a hip on the corner of his desk, blew on his coffee, and drank a little of it. "What can I do for you, Captain? By the way, feel free to take your hat off and have a seat if you want to. That old sofa's pretty comfortable if you can avoid the busted spring."

"No, thank you, I'm fine," Stone said. "As I mentioned, we're on patrol from Fort Hays. The commanding officer sent me and my men out to visit all the settlements in this part of the state and deliver the news."

Bill frowned and gave a little shake of his head. "What news?"

"Why, that the savages have commenced another round of depredations, of course." Stone sounded genuinely surprised that Bill hadn't heard about it. "You need to be aware that Redemption may be attacked at any moment, and all of you may well be murdered in your beds."

Chapter 3

The thirsty prairie had sucked up most of the water overnight, so as long as the drivers were careful, the hide wagons shouldn't bog down, Ward Costigan thought as the group of buffalo hunters got ready to move out the next morning.

His sleep had been restless, and because of that, weariness gripped him this morning.

Dave McGinty hadn't mentioned anything about Indians around the campfire during breakfast and neither had any of the other men, so evidently McGinty was still the only one who knew about Costigan's nightmare and the phantom Indian he had seen.

Costigan was glad McGinty had seen fit to keep his trap shut. Some of the other men might have ridden Costigan about what happened, and that would have led to trouble.

Costigan did notice that before the wagons were hitched up, McGinty wandered over to them, apparently aimlessly, and had a good look around. Maybe McGinty was searching for moccasin tracks.

If that was the case, he was bound to be disappointed. That downpour would have wiped them out.

The Indian might have left some other sign, but Costigan knew that wasn't true, either. He had already been over there himself and looked for anything out of the ordinary.

"Mount up, men!" Colonel Bledsoe called out.

He wasn't a real colonel, not since the end of the war, but he'd continued using his rank and nobody had ever told him he couldn't. He owned the outfit and hired the shooters, drivers, and skinners, and he'd been making good money selling hides for the past seven or eight years, first in Abilene and now in Dodge City.

William Bledsoe was a big man, wide through the shoulders, with a sweeping handlebar mustache and bushy eyebrows. The rest of his head was as bald as an egg. Even on a hunt, he wore a suit, tie, and derby hat.

Costigan didn't like the colonel. Bledsoe was loud, arrogant, and a bully. He liked to tell stories about his exploits as the commander of a Union cavalry regiment during the war, and he expected the men who worked for him to listen attentively and tell him what a dashing hero he was.

Costigan felt more like spitting every time the man was around. But Bledsoe paid good wages, no doubt about that, and he cut his men in for a share of the profits when he sold the hides.

The party had eight shooters, twelve skinners, and six drivers, one for each of the five hide wagons and one man to handle the supply wagon. If need be, some of the skinners could drive, and the drivers could be pressed into service as skinners if the kill was really good. The shooters didn't do anything but shoot.

Costigan was a shooter.

Riding snugly in sheaths strapped to his horse were a pair of Sharps .50-caliber rifles, the weapon people called the Big Fifty. They carried the thirty-inch barrel, and Costigan had modified the sights himself, adding a scale that could be raised for precise sighting.

Rifles like that weren't cheap, but they were perfect for hunting buffalo. Costigan had two of them so that when the barrel of one got too hot during a long day of killing, he could set it aside to cool off while he used the other rifle.

Costigan had a Henry rifle, too, a repeater that he usually carried with him across the saddle when the hunting party was on the move. Some of the men had extra rifles in the supply wagon, but to Costigan's way of thinking, those weapons wouldn't do anybody any good if savages jumped them and the men were cut off from the wagons. It could happen. Costigan liked to plan ahead, even if he wound up never needing those plans.

Thinking like that had kept him alive through the war, after all, when a lot of other men had died.

The buffalo hunters moved out. The previous afternoon, the herd they had been following had begun shifting slowly to the west. Costigan knew he and the other men wouldn't have any trouble catching up to the great shaggy beasts.

When they did, they would find a hillside or a bluff several hundred yards away from the herd, preferably downwind, and set up their firing stands there. The distance and the wind would keep the buffalo from noticing the shots that were killing them.

The creatures were so stupid, hundreds of them might fall before they realized anything was wrong. And although hundreds of them might have died the day before, they had no memory of that. Every day was a new day for a buffalo.

Every now and then, Costigan caught himself feeling sorry for the animals. They hadn't done anything to deserve death except having hides that people found valuable.

But there was another way to look at it, Costigan told himself at those moments. The buffalo hadn't done anything to deserve death except for being born.

That was enough, for them and for every other living creature.

McGinty rode up alongside Costigan. "What say we go do some scoutin'?" the shorter man suggested.

"You in a hurry to get to work?"

McGinty grinned. "The more we shoot, the more money we make."

"Can't argue with that," Costigan said with a shrug. He nudged the big roan gelding he was riding into a trot.

Colonel Bledsoe was leading the way, of course. He always had to be out in front. McGinty lifted a hand and waved to the colonel as he and Costigan rode past.

"We'll find those great hairy critters for you, Colonel!" McGinty called.

Bledsoe didn't call them back. Costigan was grateful for that. He was glad for an excuse to get away from the wagons. They stunk, and so did the drivers and skinners.

When you were elbow deep in blood, guts, and hide so much of the time, it was pretty much impossible to get the stench off of you. The smell soaked permanently into the boards of the wagons, too. Sometimes not even all the air in the huge open skies of the plains could disperse it.

"Nobody was talking about Indians this morning," Costigan said once they were well away from the rest of the hunting party. "What did you tell the men you rousted out to stand extra guard duty last night?"

"Told them I thought I caught a glimpse of a pack of wolves during that storm," McGinty said.

Wolves nearly always avoided men unless they were starving, but every now and then, maddened by the smell of fresh meat, a pack would attack a hunting camp. So McGinty's story was a reasonable excuse for waking some of the men.

"You could have told them what I saw," Costigan said. "It would have been all right."

"Didn't really matter. The thought of some lobos lurkin' around probably kept them more wide awake anyway."

Costigan grunted. "Maybe so. But I'm not crazy, Dave. I know what I saw."

"Sure. I never doubted it."

McGinty might say that, but Costigan wasn't completely convinced he was telling the truth. The two of them had been friends for several years. Of course McGinty didn't want to believe that Costigan was seeing things.

But why would one Indian come sneaking up to the

camp like that and then disappear? It didn't make any sense.

Unless the Indian was trying to see how many men were in the group, so he could go back and tell the rest of the war party and they could plan their attack.

Back in the sixties, when the hunters had first started coming out here to the plains after the war, the Pawnee and the Cheyenne had put up fierce resistance to that unwanted incursion into their hunting grounds.

Sometimes a single shooter would go out with one wagon and a couple of skinners, and almost inevitably those brave but foolish gents wound up scalped and mutilated. Even larger groups were attacked, too.

Over time the hunters had learned that parties numbering at least a couple of dozen well-armed men were usually safe. The Indians had tried to attack those groups, too, but the men were good shots and had long-range rifles, and their accurate fire took a deadly toll.

The cavalry had stepped up its patrols as well. Taken together, those things meant that the danger from an attack by the savages had gone down considerably.

The threat still couldn't be ruled out, though. Earlier this summer, a veritable army of Indians had wiped out Colonel George Armstrong Custer and the Seventh Cavalry up in Montana.

If enough of the Indians down here on the southern plains ever got together like that, there was no telling what they could do. A party of buffalo hunters wouldn't stand a chance in hell against them, that much was certain.

"Look at that dust up ahead," McGinty said. "We've found 'em, Ward."

Costigan nodded. "I think you're right."

Because the buffalo herds moved so slowly, they didn't really kick up a cloud of dust. But that many hooves shifting around produced a thin haze that hung in the air when there wasn't much wind, like today.

It was easy to miss seeing that haze, but experienced hunters were able to spot it. Costigan and McGinty needed to make sure they had found their quarry, though, so they rode on until they would see the vast brown stain across the landscape.

Ten years earlier, the big herds might include millions of buffalo, and when a herd like that was on the move, a man could sit on a hill and watch them sweep past all day without the shaggy tide ever coming to an end.

A decade of hunting had reduced those numbers, but a good-sized herd could still have thousands of the beasts in it.

This herd had been about fifteen thousand strong when they started thinning it out, Costigan estimated. The hunting party had killed several thousand since then, but there were still a lot of buffalo out there.

The two men reined in atop a gentle rise and sat there for a moment looking out over the grazing herd. McGinty said, "The colonel and the wagons aren't much more'n a mile behind us. We better get back and let them know what we found."

Costigan nodded and started to turn his horse.

He stopped as all the breath seemed to go out of him. He felt like he'd been punched in the chest hard enough to stop his heart from beating.

In a choked voice, he struggled to say, "Dave . . . look over yonder to the north."

Another bluff lay in that direction, maybe a quarter of a mile away. Costigan could see clearly the three men who sat there on horseback, unmoving. Even though the three figures were too far away to make out any details, Costigan recognized their watchful attitude.

"Son of a bitch," McGinty said softly under his breath. "What do you think, Ward? Are they gonna jump us?"

"It would be three against two, and we've got Sharpses and Henrys. They'd never get close to us, and they're bound to know that."

"Yeah, three against two," McGinty said, "unless there's five hundred more of the red-skinned varmints right on the other side of that ridge."

Costigan's shoulders rose and fell in a shrug. "If there are, there's not much we can do about it."

McGinty tightened his grip on his horse's reins. "Let's make a run for the wagons," he suggested. "It'll be a good race. Those Injun ponies are fast."

"Hold on. We'll go back to the wagons, but we're not gonna make a run for it. Let's just take it nice and easy."

Costigan heeled the roan into a walk. McGinty followed suit on his dun, but his eyes were big with fear.

"You think we can fool 'em into believin' we didn't see 'em?"

"I'm not sure we could fool those old boys about much of anything," Costigan said. "They know we spotted them. And now we're letting them know that we're not afraid of them."

"Who says we ain't scared of them?"

"Well . . . they don't have to know it."

Costigan watched the three Indians from the corner of his eye as he and McGinty rode back toward the rest of the hunting party.

The colonel and the wagons had been pushing on the whole time, and Costigan knew it wouldn't be long before they came in sight.

Before that could happen, the three watchers wheeled their ponies and disappeared. McGinty heaved a sigh, then said, "I shouldn't be relieved, should I? They could've just gone back to fetch the rest of their bunch."

"Or it could've been just the three of them out doing some hunting of their own," Costigan said. "Let's not borrow trouble, Dave."

"I don't have to borrow it. It usually comes up and drops right in my arms without me even askin' for it."

Not today, though, Costigan thought. The Indians were gone, and he had a hunch they wouldn't be back.

At least not right away.

But even though he was calm outwardly, on the inside he heard the sounds of battle, the screams of dying men, the rumble of artillery like the pounding of distant drums.

The smell of blood filled his nostrils, and it didn't come from the buffalo he would kill today. As it had for years, death rode at his side like a boon companion.

As they came in sight of the wagons, Dave McGinty blew out his breath and said, "Son of a gun. We made it. I don't know about you, but I could sure use a drink."

Costigan didn't say anything.

Some memories all the booze in the world couldn't banish.

Chapter 4

For a long moment following Captain Stone's pronouncement, Bill could only stare at the officer. When he was able to speak again, he said, "Savages? Depredations? What are you talking about, Captain?"

"The Indians, of course. The Pawnee, to be precise. They're on the warpath."

"I hadn't heard anything about it."

"That's why we're here," Stone said, with the air of a grown-up patiently explaining something to a child.

"From what I've heard, there hasn't been any Indian trouble in these parts for a long time. I don't think they've ever attacked the town itself."

"Possibly not, but a Pawnee war chief named Spotted Dog led a sizable contingent of warriors off the reservation several weeks ago, and since then they've raided several ranches northwest of here and even attacked a train. Patrols are out looking for them, and eventually they'll either be forced back to the reservation or wiped out. But in the meantime it was deemed necessary to alert the civilian population, so my men and I were assigned to that task."

Stone didn't sound too happy about it, either, Bill

thought. The captain probably would have rather been commanding one of those patrols that was actually searching for the renegades.

For a cavalry officer, winning a battle was the fastest and easiest way of advancing his career.

To give himself a chance to think, Bill took several sips of the hot coffee. He didn't know how to handle the threat of an Indian attack. He had figured his main responsibility as marshal would be to break up the occasional bar fight and throw the drunken brawlers in the hoosegow to cool off overnight.

There might be outlaws to deal with from time to time, too, but a Pawnee war party . . . that was a military matter.

"Captain, you're gonna need to talk to the mayor and the town council and tell them about the Indians. They're the ones who'll have to decide what to do about this."

"Whatever preparations they decide to make are none of my business. I've done the job I came to do. You can pass along the information to whomever you choose."

"Wait just a minute," Bill said. "They need to hear this from you."

Stone sighed in what sounded like exasperation. "Very well. If you can assemble those individuals quickly, I'll speak to them. But I don't have a lot of time to waste, Marshal. My men and I need to move out as soon as we can. We have other communities to warn, you know."

Bill set his half-empty coffee cup on the desk and started toward the door. He reached for his hat.

"I'll go round 'em up right now," he said. "The town hall's across the street, a couple doors down from Monroe Mercantile. I'll tell the council members to get there as fast as they can."

"In the meantime, I'll check on my men and horses," Stone said.

Bill hurried out of the office. He headed first for the bank, where he knew he would find Roy Fleming, who owned the establishment and was also the mayor of Redemption.

Mason Jones, the head teller at the bank and the only one who appeared to be working at the moment, didn't have anybody at his window, so he gave Bill a friendly nod.

"Morning, Marshal," he said. "Come to make a deposit?"

"Hate to dash your hopes, Mason, but I need to see Mr. Fleming."

Jones nodded toward the closed door of the bank president's office. "He's in a meeting. Probably be best not to disturb him right now."

Bill wasn't sure some business deal could be more important than the prospect of a Pawnee war party attacking the town, but at the same time he didn't want to get on Fleming's bad side. As mayor, he was Bill's boss, after all.

"As soon as he's through, could you tell him to come over to the town hall right away? I'm getting the council together for an important meeting."

Jones's eyebrows went up. A worried look appeared on the man's narrow face.

"Another gang of outlaws isn't about to attack the town, is it?" he asked.

"No, nothing like that," Bill said.

Not outlaws. Just hostile Indians.

Bill didn't like keeping the information from the teller, but Mason Jones was a notorious gossip and would spread the news all over town if he got a chance. Bill didn't want that happening until he found out how the council wanted to proceed.

"Does this have something to do with those cavalrymen who rode into town a while ago?"

"Just tell Mr. Fleming what I said, would you, Mason?"

"Of course," Jones replied with an offended sniff.

Bill hustled out of the bank and started toward the law office of Judge Kermit Dunaway. The judge was Redemption's justice of the peace and wasn't an official member of the town council, but he was part of the inner circle of the town's leaders and would be in on any decision, anyway.

Bill nodded distractedly to people who greeted him on the street. He couldn't stop thinking about the Indians.

Where he grew up down in south Texas, around Victoria and Hallettsville, Indians hadn't been a problem, although some of the old-timers still talked about the Long Raid back in the forties, when a large band of Comanche had come down from their home in northwestern Texas and marauded all the way to the Gulf of Mexico, leaving death and destruction in their wake.

But even though he hadn't lived in constant fear of such an attack, like everybody else in Texas he had heard plenty of stories about the atrocities carried out by the Comanche elsewhere in the state.

He didn't figure the Pawnee were as bad as the Comanch', but he was sure they were plenty dangerous. The idea of a war party rampaging through Redemption, setting fire to the buildings and murdering and mutilating the citizens, filled him with both dread and anger.

Such a thing wasn't going to happen while he was marshal, he vowed to himself. Not if he had anything to say about it.

Bill went up the stairs on the outside of the hardware store. Judge Dunaway had his office on the second floor of the building. He answered, "Come in," to Bill's knock.

The judge was at his desk with his coat and beaver hat off and his shirt collar loosened. Papers were scattered in front of him and he had a pen in his hand. He was a heavyset man with a broad, florid face and graying red hair. When he was conducting a trial he could be pretty intimidating, but now as he looked up at Bill he wore a friendly expression.

"Come in, Marshal, come in," he said in a hearty voice. "What brings you here on this fine morning?"

"I'm not sure how fine a mornin' it is, Judge," Bill said. "Can you come down to the town hall for a few minutes? I'm getting the council together, and as justice of the peace I figure you ought to be there, too."

Dunaway's bushy red brows bunched in a frown. "That sounds like there's trouble."

"Could be. But I'd just as soon wait until everybody's together to lay it all out."

Dunaway considered for a moment and then nodded. "All right." He started to get up but stopped while he was still in his chair. "Is there any chance I might need to be armed?"

Bill thought about it and said, "Might not be a bad idea, Judge."

Dunaway opened a drawer in the desk, reached in, and brought out a small pistol. He stood up and tucked it into the waistband of his trousers.

"I'll be along," he said.

Bill nodded and left the office.

In short order, he paid visits to the livery stable run by Josiah Hartnett, Leo Kellogg's tailor shop, and the shed where Charley Hobbs made saddles, holsters, and other leather goods. Hartnett, Kellogg, and Hobbs were all members of the council, as well, and although they were curious, they agreed to come to the town hall for the meeting.

That just left Monroe Mercantile. Bill's father-in-law, Perry Monroe, had been appointed recently by Mayor Fleming to serve out the remainder of the term of a councilman who had passed away.

Bill had waited until last to visit the general store because he knew it was going to be almost impossible for him to keep the truth from Eden. If she asked him what was going on, he wouldn't have any choice but to tell her.

Other than a couple of local ladies looking through the bolts of fabric stacked on a table, Perry Monroe sitting on a tall stool behind the counter, and Benjy Cobb sorting out some harnesses that had gotten tangled up, the store was empty. Eden must have gone back to the Monroe house already to prepare lunch, Bill thought.

"Hello, Bill," Monroe greeted him. "If you're looking for Eden, she's not here. She left a few minutes ago."

"I figured as much, sir. And it's really you I came to see, Mr. Monroe."

"Oh? Why's that? And I reckon you can start calling me Perry any day now, you know, since we're related and all."

Perry Monroe was big, barrel-chested, and had a long white beard like an Old Testament prophet. Bill figured the odds of him ever being comfortable calling his father-in-law by his first name were pretty slim. Right now, though, that wasn't exactly important.

"There's an emergency meeting of the town council about to start in a few minutes," Bill said. "I'd sure appreciate it if you could go down to the town hall. Benjy can watch the store, can't you, Benjy?"

Cobb nodded eagerly. "I sure can, Mr. Monroe," he said. Bill knew that Cobb was trying to stop drinking so much, and right now he seemed completely sober.

Monroe frowned. "What's going on, Bill?" he asked. "What's this meeting about?"

Bill glanced at the two customers. The ladies were trying not to look like they were listening, but really they were hanging on to every word, he thought.

"It's just some council business," he said. "I'll explain when everybody's there."

"I'll bet it has something to do with those soldier boys," Cobb said. "Are they gonna build a fort here, Bill? Is that it?"

"Not that I know of," Bill answered honestly. Although a fort would be a handy thing to have around. It would certainly make the town safer from Indians.

On the other hand, a fort would mean a lot of soldiers who would get drunk, get in fights, and get in trouble when they were off duty, which would mean a lot more work for the local law, namely him.

Anyway, it didn't matter because the army wasn't going to build a fort here. They weren't even going to leave any troops here temporarily. Captain Stone had made it clear that he and his patrol would be moving on as soon as they could.

That meant if the Indians *did* show up, the citizens of Redemption were going to be on their own.

Monroe came out from behind the counter in the rear of the store, untying his apron as he did so. He tossed the apron on the counter and said to Bill, "All right, let's go. Have you talked to the other members of the council yet?"

"Yes, sir."

"So I was the last one, eh? Probably wise of you, son. If Eden had been here, she would have wormed the truth out of you with no trouble at all."

"Yes, sir," Bill agreed. "I sure know it."

It took them only a moment to head down the boardwalk to the town hall. As they did, Bill looked across the street and saw Captain Stone talking to the sergeant. The troopers were sitting or standing on the opposite boardwalk, taking a few minutes of ease while they had the chance.

The other members of the council were already in the town hall, sitting at the long table where they conducted business and talking among themselves. They fell silent and turned curious looks toward Bill as he came in with Perry Monroe.

"Thanks for comin' on short notice like this," Bill told them.

Mayor Fleming, round-faced and usually filled with a politician's natural affability, didn't look happy at the moment. He said, "I hope this is important, Marshal. I was discussing some business matters with a gentleman who plans to establish a new grain warehouse here in Redemption."

"Yes, sir, Mr. Mayor, I think it's mighty important," Bill said. "I'll be right back."

"Wait a minute—" Fleming began.

Bill ignored him and went outside. He trotted across the street to where the soldiers were and said, "The council's ready for you, Captain Stone."

The officer nodded. "Good. We've already spent too much time here."

Bill had to hurry to keep up as Stone crossed the street

with a brisk, long-legged stride. That made Bill's limp more pronounced, but it didn't slow him down. He was right behind Stone when the captain entered the town hall.

"Benjy was right," Perry Monroe said when he saw the blue-uniformed officer. "This does have something to do with the cavalry."

Bill performed some quick introductions. "This is Captain Timothy Stone," he told the council members. "Captain, this is the town council of Redemption."

"Gentlemen," Stone said with a grave nod. "I'm here to deliver an important message from the commanding officer at Fort Hays. A Pawnee war party has left the reservation, and there's every possibility that the savages may attack your town and attempt to massacre everyone in it."

Chapter 5

Remembering the dramatic way Stone had announced the reason for his presence in Redemption earlier in the marshal's office, Bill realized that the fella liked to cause a stir. Stone probably enjoyed the way the council members stared at him speechlessly for a few seconds, then erupted with excited questions.

Stone allowed the hubbub to continue for a few seconds, then said, "Please, gentlemen, please. I can't deal with such confusion. Who's in charge here?"

"I am, I guess," the banker said. "My name's Roy Fleming. I'm the mayor of Redemption."

"Well, Mayor Fleming, I suggest that you act as spokesman for the group. If you have questions, you may direct them to me, but I warn you, my time is limited."

"Limited!" Fleming exploded. "You mean you're not going to stay here and protect us from those savages?"

"No, my orders were to visit the settlements in this area, along with the farms and ranches, and warn the inhabitants of the possible danger. Now that I've done that here, my men and I will be moving on shortly." Stone glanced resentfully at Bill. "We've already stayed longer than I intended, thanks to your marshal here."

"I figured you ought to hear the news from the captain himself," Bill said.

"But . . . but what are we supposed to *do*?" Fleming asked. "What do we tell people?"

"I suppose that's up to you," Stone said. "You can inform the rest of the citizens of the situation or not, as you choose."

"We can't just not let them know they're in danger of being scalped," Josiah Hartnett said.

"Then tell them. Perhaps you can form a militia or something like that."

"God Almighty," Charley Hobbs said. He was a small, wiry man with thinning gray hair. "This is gonna be worse than when those outlaws attacked the town."

"Wait a minute, wait a minute," Judge Dunaway put in. "Captain, is there any actual evidence that those savages are headed this way?"

Stone shook his head. "Not really. According to the reports, they're ranging rather far and wide across the western half of the state. We don't know where they are at the moment or where they might strike next."

"Then there's no reason for us to panic," the judge said as he leaned back in his chair. "They may not be coming in this direction, and even if they are, the army may have them rounded up and back on the reservation before they ever get here."

"We can certainly hope so," Fleming said. He took a handkerchief from the breast pocket of his coat and blotted the beads of sweat that had popped up on his forehead. "The judge is right. We need to stay calm."

"But we need to be ready for trouble," Perry Monroe said. "That business with Norris, Rakestraw, and those other owlhoots proved that."

Bill picked up one of the chairs, turned it around, and straddled it. He was glad his father-in-law had spoken up.

As much as Bill felt at home here and liked the people

of Redemption, he knew they had a tendency to be complacent. He had seen the evidence of that with his own eyes when he first came here and found the town living in the grip of terror because of a string of mysterious killings.

Even when it became obvious who was behind the murders, people hadn't taken action until they absolutely had to . . . and to be honest, Bill knew he himself was responsible for a lot of that. Born and bred in Texas, he didn't have it in him to let anybody run roughshod over him.

"What do you suggest we do, Captain?" Leo Kellogg asked. Small and nimble-fingered, Kellogg had that in common with Charley Hobbs, but unlike the saddlemaker, who was a lifelong westerner, Kellogg was from Philadelphia. Bill knew from talking to him that Kellogg had a certain thirst for adventure at odds with his mild appearance. That was what had led the tailor to come west.

"I already told you, form a militia," Stone said. "Assign men to stand watch outside of town. Make plans to establish defensive positions in case of attack. Didn't any of you men serve in the war? Do you have no military experience whatsoever?"

"I was in the Union army," Hartnett snapped, "and so was Perry here."

"I was a colonel in a Georgia regiment," Judge Dunaway added. Bill hadn't known that about the judge. "We know something about fighting, Captain."

"Then I suggest you put your knowledge and experience to good use." Stone nodded curtly to the council members. "Good day to you."

"You're leaving, just like that?" Fleming said.

"I have my orders."

With that, the captain turned and strode out of the town hall, leaving a worried silence behind him.

After an uncomfortable interval during which the soldiers mounted up and rode out of town with a clatter of hoofbeats and shouted orders from the sergeant, Fleming cleared his throat.

"What do you think? Should we form a militia like the captain suggested?"

"I'm not sure there are enough men in town we can count on to follow orders and work together," Hartnett said. "It could just make things worse. They might start mistaking each other for Indians and get trigger-happy."

"We have to do something," Kellogg insisted. "I think we should send a letter to the commander at Fort Hays formally requesting protection."

Monroe shook his head. "Wouldn't do any good. The army's already stretched too thin out here, what with most of the cavalry being sent up north to chase the Indians who wiped out Custer. I agree with you, Leo, we need to do something, but we can't let ourselves get stampeded into it."

Bill sat there listening while the council members tried to hash things out. Finally, Judge Dunaway said, "We're forgetting that we have our marshal here, too. Bill, what do you think we should do?"

"You're asking the wrong fella, Judge," Bill said. "I never fought Indians in my life."

"None of us have," Hartnett said.

"But I never even saw very many until I helped drive that herd across Indian Territory with Hob and the rest of the boys, a few months ago. I'm just learnin' how to be a lawman. No offense, but you gentlemen knew that when I hired on to be marshal."

"But you're in charge of maintaining law and order," Kellogg said. "If we form a militia, maybe you should be in command."

Bill's eyes widened in surprise. "No, sir!" he said. "I mean, well, you'd be better off with the judge givin' orders, or Mr. Hartnett or Mr. Monroe. They've got a heap more experience at such things than I do."

"We're getting ahead of ourselves again," Fleming said. "The first thing we need to decide is whether to tell the citizens."

"I vote no," Kellogg said. "It'll cause a panic if we do."

"And I say we can't keep it from them," Hartnett responded. "We have no right to pretend that we're not all in danger."

Hobbs said, "Maybe we aren't. Maybe the judge is right and those redskins won't even come here. I reckon there's a better chance of that than there is of us bein' attacked."

"We can't keep it a secret," Monroe said. "I'm not saying we *shouldn't*, I'm saying we *can't*. A lot of people saw those troops ride in. Some of them probably talked to the soldiers. We can't be sure nothing was said about the Indians. Even if there wasn't, folks are going to be worrying and asking questions." He looked around the table. "You really think those of you who are married are going to be able to keep this from your wives? And I'm including you in that, Marshal. I know how persistent my daughter can be when she wants to know something." Monroe cleared his throat. "She's, ah, forced me to admit things I rather wouldn't have."

Fleming sighed. "Perry's right. We're going to have to make an announcement. It'll be up to you, Marshal, to maintain order and keep things from getting out of hand."

Bill nodded. He knew the mayor was right, even though he wished there was some other way to handle this.

At that moment, the situation got even worse. The door of the town hall opened, and Eden walked in.

"Mr. Cobb told me there was some sort of emergency council meeting going on," she said. "What's wrong?"

Monroe glanced at Bill, as if to say, *What did I tell you?* He said, "Go back to the store, dear. This is council business."

"Business that involves my father and my husband," Eden said.

Bill stood up and walked toward her. "Your father's right," he told her. "We're just about done here—"

"No, I can tell that something bad has happened. What is it?"

"Look around," Monroe said. "I don't see anything to worry about. Do you?"

"I certainly do," Eden replied without hesitation. "I see all of you sitting around looking gloomy and scared, like we're about to be attacked by wild Indians or something—"

She stopped short and her eyes widened at the looks of surprise on several of the council members.

"Wait a minute," she said. "Is . . . is that true? Is that why those soldiers were here? Redemption is going to be attacked by Indians?"

"We don't really know that—" Bill began.

"But it's possible? We're all in danger?"

Bill saw the fear in her blue eyes and knew, as he had known all along, that he wasn't going to be able to lie to her.

"Some of the Pawnee are on the warpath," he said. "That's why Captain Stone was here, to warn us that they might be headed in this direction. *Might*," he added, emphasizing the word. "We don't know where they're going to turn up next or what they're gonna do."

"But don't worry, Eden," Mayor Fleming said. "We're going to be ready if those savages show up here. If they're looking for a fight, the good citizens of Redemption will give it to them!"

Bill saw the doubt in the eyes of Monroe, Hartnett, and Judge Dunaway. The three council members with military experience weren't convinced that the townspeople could fight off an Indian attack.

To be honest, neither was he.

But as he looked at Eden, resolve grew inside him. Her beautiful blond hair was never going to decorate the lance of some Pawnee warrior.

He turned to look at the council again. They were right: he was the marshal here. It was his job to keep the settlement and all of its citizens safe.

"Go ahead and call a meeting of everybody in town," he said. "If we're gonna have to fight, we'd better start getting ready."

But at the same time, he was hoping desperately that the Pawnee would pick somewhere else to go on their next rampage.

Chapter 6

"Three Indians are hardly anything to worry about," Colonel Bledsoe declared with a dismissive snort when Costigan and McGinty told him what they had seen. "Such a small group would never dare to attack a large party like ours."

"Yeah, but like I told Costigan, there could've been five hundred more of the varmints waiting on the other side of that hill," McGinty said.

"If that was true, why didn't they kill you?" Bledsoe wanted to know.

"Maybe because they planned on following us and finding out how many men there are in our bunch."

Bledsoe scowled, clearly not liking what Costigan had just suggested. "You believe they're going to come back with reinforcements?"

"I believe there's no way to predict what they'll do," Costigan said. "We won't know it until they do it."

A stubborn look came over Bledsoe's beefy face. "Well, by God, that herd's right over there, and I'll be damned if I'm not going to take some more hides. Set up the stands."

Costigan nodded. He dismounted, and McGinty followed suit. The other marksmen swung down from their saddles and gathered around the supply wagon to take out their shooting stands.

Some men preferred elaborate folding tripods to support and steady the heavy barrels of their rifles. Others made do with just a forked stick they could drive into the ground. As long as it did the job, it didn't matter.

Costigan had made his own stand, carving it out of a piece of oak. It was as thick as a man's wrist and slightly more than six feet long. He had bolted a couple of metal prongs on the bottom so it was easy to drive into the ground. Instead of the two legs at the top forking into a Y, he had fashioned them into a more gentle U-shape that cupped the barrel of whichever rifle he was using. It was fancier than some, not as much so as others.

Costigan didn't care about any of that. The stand did a good job for him, and that was all that mattered.

He set up on the edge of the shallow bluff Bledsoe had chosen. The bluff rose about six feet over the surrounding terrain. Out here on these plains, that was enough height to give the shooters a good view of the herd several hundred yards away.

Costigan slid one of his Sharps from its sheath and un-wrapped it from the layers of oilcloth and buckskin in which he had rolled it. The barrel and the breech had dull gleams to them, but Costigan hadn't polished them to a high shine. They wouldn't give off much of a reflection this way.

McGinty put his stand about fifty feet to Costigan's right. The men were strung out along the bluff at similar distances. The deafening reports of the guns would be bad enough without them being closer together.

A gentle wind touched Costigan's face as he placed the barrel of his rifle on the stand, settled the butt against his shoulder, and leaned his cheek against the smooth walnut of the stock.

The wind brought the strong, musky scent of the herd to him, and that was good. It would carry the smell of powder smoke away from the great shaggy beasts, as well as helping to muffle the sound of the shots.

The shooters chose their targets. They liked to pick off beasts on the outskirts of the herd and gradually work their way in. Less chance of spooking the others that way.

As Costigan raised his sights and settled them on one of the bulls, he heard a rifle boom farther along the line. A second later one of the other men fired.

Satisfied with his aim, Costigan squeezed the trigger. The Sharps roared and kicked against his shoulder. Costigan's firm grip kept the recoil under control.

The gray powder smoke that erupted from the barrel drifted back over his head, and as it cleared he saw the bull he had targeted still standing there stolidly.

Costigan was patient. He knew he hadn't missed.

A couple of seconds later, the buffalo took a step. Its short front legs buckled under its immense weight. The animal tipped forward, then rolled slowly onto its side. It didn't move again.

Those buffalo were so big they had to be dead for a little while before they realized it.

Costigan worked the lever that also formed the trigger guard and opened the breech. He took out the empty shell and replaced it with a fresh cartridge from a pouch that hung at his waist from a shoulder strap.

He didn't have to take the Sharps off the stand to reload. The process took only a few seconds. Costigan had done it countless times and could have reloaded in pitch darkness, even if he was only half conscious.

Other shots blasted, and more of the buffalo collapsed under the onslaught of lead. Almost unbelievably, the rest of the herd continued to graze peacefully.

When Costigan had first heard that buffalo would just stand there oblivious while their fellows were dying all around them, he had found it difficult to comprehend how any creatures could behave that way. He'd had to see the grisly spectacle with his own eyes before he fully accepted it.

His second shot brought down a hefty bull. He reloaded and fired again, then again and again and again. The day became a blur of noise and smoke and the Sharps's recoil against his shoulder.

The rifle's long, heavy barrel grew warm and expanded slowly from the pressure of the lead missiles traveling through it. Costigan knew from experience when the barrel got too hot for him to continue using the weapon. To keep from damaging the Sharps, he set it aside and unwrapped the second rifle.

By the time that one had heated up, too, the first Sharps would be cooled off enough to use again. All the buffalo hunters switched weapons like that during the long hours of slaughter.

Meanwhile the skinners sat on the ground or the wagons and waited for their turn. Later, when the smell of spilled blood finally became bad enough and the tiny brains of the surviving beasts began to figure out that something might be wrong, the rest of the herd would drift away. That was when the wagons and the skinners would move in.

As far as Costigan was concerned, there wasn't a worse job in all of creation than skinning buffalo. The skinners had to cut through those thick hides, peel them off the gory carcasses, and load the stinking, blood-dripping things onto the wagons to be hauled back to the main camp.

There wasn't enough money in the world to pay him to be a hide skinner, Costigan had often thought as he watched the men at their work.

Like any other task performed over and over, killing buffalo became routine. Costigan's mind wandered. He didn't have to think that hard to load, aim, fire, and load again while another of the shaggy beasts collapsed.

His thoughts went back to the Indians he and McGinty had seen earlier, and to the savage he had glimpsed during the thunderstorm the night before, as well.

Were the Indians stalking them, the same way he and his companions stalked the great herds of buffalo? There was a certain similarity, after all, between the Indians taking scalps and the skinners ripping those buffalo hides from the carcasses.

To the Indians the scalps were trophies, though, symbols of their victories over their hated enemies.

Buffalo hides were . . . just business.

"Ward! Hey, Ward!"

Costigan raised his head. McGinty was calling him. He looked over and saw the smaller man pointing.

"Over yonder!"

One by one, all the guns fell silent. Costigan turned to look where McGinty was pointing. He saw a dark, irregular blur moving over the prairie and recognized it as men on horseback. The riders were probably a mile away, maybe more.

Bledsoe stomped up. "Is that them?" he demanded. "By God, is that the savages?"

"I'll take a look," Costigan said.

He lifted the Sharps down from the stand and placed it on the oilcloth he'd left lying on the ground nearby. He went to his horse and reached into the saddlebags, pulling out a telescope.

During the war, he had used the brassbound spyglass to look for Rebs, and he had carried it with him ever since. Now it served other purposes.

Costigan walked to the edge of the bluff, extended the telescope, and brought it to his right eye. He peered through the lenses and searched for the riders he had seen a moment earlier only as a vague mass.

When he found them, the figures seemed to leap into focus. Indians, all right. They wore buckskins and rode ponies with no saddles, only blankets. A few carried rifles, but most seemed to be armed only with bows and arrows.

Even with the telescope, Costigan couldn't make out many details at this distance, but he didn't think the Indians were painted for war.

Nor could he make a reasonable estimation of how many of them there were in the group. More than twenty, probably less than a hundred. That was as much as he could narrow it down.

One thing he felt fairly certain of, though, was that the Indians weren't interested in him and his fellow buffalo hunters. He lowered the telescope.

"Indians, all right, Colonel," he told Bledsoe, "but they're not coming this direction. From the looks of it they're circling well around the herd . . . and us."

One of the other shooters, a man named Browne, spat and said, "Probably tryin' to get behind us so they can ambush us, the filthy redskins."

Costigan shook his head. "I don't think so."

"How do you know what they're thinkin'?" Browne challenged him.

"I don't," Costigan admitted with a shrug. "But I didn't see any war paint on their faces."

A dark, thin-faced man named Tolbert said, "From what I've heard, they only paint themselves up just before they're about to attack."

"That's right," Bledsoe agreed.

Costigan wanted to ask Bledsoe just how much experience he'd had fighting Indians. As far as Costigan was aware, the answer was none.

But arguing with a blowhard like the colonel was a waste of time and energy. He turned back toward the Indians and lifted the telescope again.

Costigan watched the distant riders through the instrument until they vanished into a fold between two small hills well off to the northwest.

"They're gone," he announced.

"They could come back," Bledsoe said. "And by God, while we were talking, the herd's started to move. Start firing again, damn it! We can down a few more before the beasts are out of range." The colonel paused. "Except you, Costigan."

"You don't want me to shoot, Colonel?" Costigan asked with a puzzled frown.

"No, I want you and that spyglass of yours up on one of the wagons. You're our lookout. Those heathens aren't going to sneak up on us and lift our hair."

Costigan felt like Bledsoe thought that was some sort of punishment for not agreeing with him. But whatever the colonel's motive, posting a lookout was actually a good idea, even though Costigan didn't think this particular bunch of Indians meant them any harm.

There might be other savages out here who did, and Costigan thought they had been putting entirely too much faith in the strength of their numbers.

He took the telescope and one of his rifles and climbed onto a wagon seat. The driver was sitting in the shade of the vehicle, so Costigan didn't have to worry about making conversation with the man.

Costigan was thankful for that. He got along all right with Dave McGinty, but small talk wasn't something he enjoyed. He turned his head frequently, scanning the vast, mostly flat landscape around them.

The stink that rose from the wagon bed was powerful, but he didn't let it bother him.

The smell of death had been in Costigan's nostrils for so long, he barely even noticed it anymore.

Chapter 7

When outlaws had attacked Redemption earlier in the summer, the town hadn't had much warning. Because of that, there hadn't really been time for panic to set in.

That wouldn't be the case with this threat of Indian attack, Bill knew.

Mayor Fleming asked him to spread the word that everyone in town should assemble in the street in front of the town hall as soon as possible. He headed first for the café owned by Gunnar and Helga Nilsson.

It was a little early for the lunch rush, but the Swedish couple dished up such good food, Bill wasn't surprised to see that the café was busy already.

"Marshal, good morning!" mustachioed Gunnar Nilsson greeted him. "Mama, a cup of coffee for the marshal."

Bill lifted a hand to stop Helga from pouring the coffee. "There's nothing I'd like better right now," he said, "but I'm sort of in a hurry. You mind if I say something to your customers?"

Gunnar frowned in obvious puzzlement, but he said, "Yah, sure, go ahead."

Bill lifted his voice. "Folks, if I could have your attention, please?" When the people sitting at the tables and the counter turned to look at him, he went on, "Mayor Fleming and the council have called an important town meeting. We need everybody to get together in front of the town hall as soon as you can. And I'd sure appreciate it if you'd pass the word to anybody you run into who's not headed in that direction already."

Phillip Ramsey, the editor and publisher of the Redemption *Star*, was one of the people eating an early lunch in the café. As soon as Bill finished with the announcement, Ramsey said, "What's this all about, Marshal? Something to do with that cavalry troop that came through earlier, I suspect."

Bill had figured when he saw the newspaperman that Ramsey would want to know what was going on. He said, "Sorry, Mr. Ramsey, you'll have to wait and hear what the mayor has to say along with everybody else."

"The people have a right to know, Marshal."

And newspapermen had a right to be damn nosy critters, Bill thought, but he said, "They'll know when the mayor tells 'em."

"You're as tight-lipped as those soldiers," Ramsey complained. "I couldn't get anything out of them, either."

Bill was a little surprised none of the troopers had said anything about their mission. He supposed Captain Stone had drummed it into them to keep their mouths shut.

Another man asked, "Is it all right if we finish our meals, Marshal?"

Bill shrugged. "I reckon that'd be fine. It's gonna take a while to round up everybody. Just don't dawdle." He lifted a hand in farewell to the owners as he turned toward the door. "I'll take that cup of coffee some other time, folks."

His next stop was Smoot's Saloon. At this time of day, it wouldn't be very busy, but Bill knew some people would already be there drinking and gambling.

Fred Smoot was at one of the tables entering figures into a ledger. He looked up when Bill pushed through the batwings and came into the saloon.

Putting his pen aside, Smoot grasped the wheels attached to the side of his chair and pushed himself backward, away from the table. With growing skill, he was able to turn himself so he could roll toward Bill.

A badman's bullet had wounded the saloon owner and cost him the use of his legs. Josiah Hartnett, who was handy at such things, had built him a wheelchair so Smoot could get around and continue to run his saloon once he had recuperated some.

Smoot still had the slick hair, the narrow mustache, and the fancy taste in clothes that he'd had when he was a professional gambler, before he had settled down in Redemption and opened the town's only saloon. He gave Bill a wary nod of greeting.

"Marshal," Smoot said. "What brings you here this morning? Official business, I suppose, since I hardly ever see you take a drink."

As a wild young cowboy, Bill had put away plenty of who-hit-John and had helped break up a few saloons in drunken brawls.

He was still young, but since pinning on the marshal's badge, he sort of thought he should set an example. A proper lawman didn't go around boozing it up all the time, at least not in his experience.

"Yeah, I'm afraid so, Mr. Smoot," he said. "I need to make an announcement."

Smoot waved a carefully manicured hand. "The floor is yours."

"Gents," Bill said, since there were no women in the saloon at the moment, "there's gonna be a meeting in front of the town hall in a little while. Mayor Fleming has something important to say, and I'm trying to let as many people know about it as I can."

One of the men at the bar grinned and said, "I never knew a politician to have anything to say that was really important to anybody except him. And Roy Fleming's more in love with the sound of his own voice than most of 'em."

Bill wouldn't disagree with that last part, but he wouldn't agree publicly with it, either. And he happened to know that this time, the mayor *did* have something important to say.

"I think y'all ought to be there anyway," Bill said. "And I'd be obliged if you'd help spread the word."

"You expect the town's businesses to close in the middle of the day?" Smoot asked with a frown.

"Just for a little while."

"I'm not sure that's a wise idea. Unless, of course, you're ordering us to do so in your position as city marshal."

Bill was tempted to do just that. However, he had a natural aversion to throwing his weight around, and he wasn't going to start issuing orders unless he absolutely had to.

"It's up to you," he told Smoot. "I'm just spreading the word, that's all. But for what it's worth, I really think y'all ought to be there."

Smoot looked at him for a second, then shrugged. "Of course. I've always cooperated with the local law, wherever I've been."

"Appreciate that," Bill said. He left the saloon and started up the street to Monroe Mercantile.

When he got there, he found the doors open but a big, hastily printed sign in the front window that read IMPORTANT TOWN MEETING. GATHER IN FRONT OF TOWN HALL RIGHT AWAY.

Some people were already doing that, he saw. About two dozen people were milling around in front of the town hall, talking and asking questions. Nobody had any answers yet, but they would soon.

Eden and her father came out of the store. Monroe pulled the doors closed behind them. "I told everybody about the meeting as soon as we got back here," he said.

"You didn't say what it was about, did you?" Bill asked.

Monroe nodded toward the knot of people in front of the town hall. "If I had, that bunch would be upset, not just puzzled."

"I'm going to go house to house and spread the word," Eden said.

"I'll handle the rest of the businesses," Bill said with a nod. He saw men leaving the saloon and heading for the town hall. "We ought to have a pretty good crowd in a little while."

"Roy's still over in the hall," Monroe said. "I'll go help him figure out what he's going to say. It won't be easy. We have to make people take this seriously and start getting ready for trouble, but we don't want them running around like a bunch of chickens with their heads cut off."

Bill could imagine that. Things in Redemption might get just that crazy if folks panicked. It wasn't called "losing their heads" for nothing.

For the next fifteen minutes, he went up and down the street, stopping at every business to make sure the owners and customers knew about the meeting. A lot of them had heard about it already and were full of questions that Bill didn't answer.

The crowd in front of the town hall continued to grow. Bill estimated there were a couple of hundred people in the street, and their curious murmuring created a constant buzz, like a swarm of hornets.

When he figured he had notified everybody he could, he headed for the town hall himself. His bad leg was starting to ache a little from all the hurrying around town he'd been doing for the past hour or so.

As he limped along the boardwalk toward the front doors of the hall, people in the street called questions to him, wanting to know what was going on and what the meeting was all about.

"The mayor will be out in a few minutes to talk to you," Bill told them.

"If there's trouble, we want to know about it now!" a man called.

"Yeah, go ahead and tell us, Marshal," another man urged.

"The people have a right to know!"

Bill's eyes narrowed. Phillip Ramsey might have thought he could get away with that because he was in the middle of a crowd, but Bill knew good and well the newspaperman had shouted out that last statement. He picked Ramsey out of the crowd and glared at him. Ramsey didn't look the least bit repentant.

A big man who looked like one of the bullwhackers who passed through town with freight wagons pushed his way to the front of the crowd.

For quite a while, Redemption had banned cowboys with the herds of Texas longhorns coming up to the railhead from even setting foot in the settlement, supposedly because of all the trouble they caused. No matter what the previous marshal's other failings had been, he had enforced that ban.

But the teamsters and bullwhackers were allowed free rein in the town, and as far as Bill was concerned, they caused just as much or even more trouble than any Texas cowhands ever had. For the most part, the freighters were tough, ornery, profane men, and they liked to drink and fight.

The ban on cowboys had been lifted earlier in the summer, but since then only a couple of herds had passed close enough to the town for some of the punchers with them to visit Redemption.

None of them had gotten too rambunctious, maybe because Bill knew the way they thought, having been one of them himself not that long before. He had been able to head off most trouble before it broke out.

Not so with the bullwhackers. He'd had to jail several of them for disturbing the peace.

But not this particular hombre, who Bill had never seen before as far as he recalled. The man had the look of a troublemaker on his beefy, sunburned face as he said in a loud, belligerent voice, "There's somethin' bad goin' on here! If there wasn't, they never would've called this meetin'. And now this damn tin star's afraid to tell us what it's all about!"

"Take it easy, mister," Bill snapped. "I told you, the

mayor'll be out here in a few minutes." He paused, then against his better judgment added, "Anyway, I'm not sure it's even any of your business. You don't live here in Redemption, do you?"

"I'm here now, and so are my men and my wagons. If there's somethin' wrong, I want to know about it!" The man looked around. "The last time I heard about somethin' like this, there was an outbreak of cholera! Wiped out damn near the whole town!"

"Oh, my Lord!" a woman said in a voice shrill with terror. "Has somebody come down with cholera, Marshal? Are we all going to get sick and die?"

"Blast it," Bill muttered under his breath. He raised his hands to try to get the crowd to pay attention to him. "Nobody's got cholera! Not that I know about, anyway. This doesn't have anything to do with anybody bein' sick."

"That's just what they'd tell you if they didn't want to start a panic," the bullwhacker insisted.

More people started to yell questions as the crowd continued to grow and pressed closer to the boardwalk. Bill motioned for quiet and raised his voice to call over the hubbub, "Settle down, folks! Everybody just settle down!"

The bullwhacker turned to face the crowd and bellowed, "I say we go in there and *make* that damn mayor tell us what's goin' on!"

Shouts of agreement filled the air. The crowd surged forward, only it wasn't just a crowd anymore, thought Bill.

These folks were well on their way to becoming a mob, and a lot of it was the fault of that blasted bullwhacker.

The man turned back toward the town hall and put a booted foot on the step up to the boardwalk.

"We're comin' in, Marshal," he said. "Better get the hell out of our way!"

Bill planted his feet and didn't move . . . except to wrap his hand around the walnut grips of the Colt holstered at his hip.

Chapter 8

He didn't want to shoot anybody. Yeah, the bullwhacker was acting like a jackass, but that was probably just because he was scared.

Fear was behind all the anger that now flowed from the crowd, Bill sensed. They didn't know what was happening, but their instincts told them it was something bad, something dangerous. And not knowing was always frightening.

But that didn't mean Bill was going to let them stampede into the town hall and start a riot. If it came to gunplay, he hoped a shot or two fired into the air would make them stop and think twice about trying to charge over him. If it didn't . . .

Well, a bullet in that bullwhacker's leg probably would. Bill just hoped it wouldn't come to that.

It didn't. Even as the bullwhacker scowled darkly and defiantly and started to come up onto the boardwalk, the doors behind Bill opened. He didn't take his eyes off the bullwhacker as he heard Mayor Roy Fleming's voice rolling out over the frightened crowd.

"Folks! Folks, please! There's no need for trouble!"

Fleming moved up beside Bill. The mayor's hands were

raised, motioning for calm and quiet just as Bill had a moment earlier, but in this case, the angry, upset townspeople paid attention.

"Please, just settle down and I'll tell you everything you want to know!" Fleming went on. He stood there and waited as the shouting gradually died down.

Bill finally felt it was safe enough to look away from the bullwhacker and glanced over his shoulder. All the town council members were there, lined up in a row behind Fleming. Behind them, peeking past her father's shoulder, was Eden.

"All right, everyone, listen to me," the mayor said when the street was quiet at last. The crowd looked up at him silently, expectantly. "As you may have guessed, the council and I called this meeting because of some news that Captain Stone delivered to us earlier today while he and his troops were in town. According to the captain, a sizable number of Pawnee Indians are on the warpath—"

That was as far as he got. A woman shrieked, "Oh, my God! The redskins are going to attack the town and scalp us all!"

That caused hell to break loose again. The racket was even worse than before as women screamed and cried and men shouted angry questions.

Bill's mouth tightened into a grim line as he watched and listened to all the carrying-on. There was a good chance that most of these people had never been through an Indian attack. Probably a lot of them had never even *seen* a hostile Indian.

But they had all heard stories about gruesome atrocities carried out in other places, and now they were afraid it was going to happen in Redemption.

And to be perfectly honest, Bill reminded himself, he had no reason to think it wouldn't. Those Pawnee warriors could show up at any time, looking for blood and scalps.

Phillip Ramsey fought his way close to the boardwalk and shouted, "Why didn't the cavalry stay here to protect us? Why did the troopers just ride away?"

"Their job is to warn all the settlements in this part of the state," Fleming said. "Captain Stone said they couldn't stay. It would be against his orders."

"To hell with his orders!" another man said. "It's the army's job to protect us! You've gotta get them back here, Mayor!"

Fleming shook his head and looked pained. "I can't," he said. "Don't you think I would if I could?"

The words flying back and forth caught the attention of some in the crowd and caused the shouting to die down a little. More and more people started to listen as Ramsey asked, "Well, then, what *are* we going to do?"

Bill was startled when Fleming's hand came down on his shoulder and the mayor said, "I'll let Marshal Harvey explain that. He's the law here in Redemption, after all."

Bill turned his head to give Fleming a wide-eyed look. The mayor leaned closer and urged quietly, "Go on, son. Just tell them how we're going to protect the town."

There was no way out of this. Bill took a deep breath and said, "First of all, folks, we're not gonna panic—"

"That's easy for you to say!" a man accused. "The jail's nice and sturdy! You'll be locked up in there when the savages come, I'll bet!"

"Now hold on! What I was about to say is that we don't even know for sure the Pawnee will show up here. The cavalry has patrols out lookin' for them now, and the last time anybody saw them, they were quite a ways off from here."

"They could be coming in this direction," a man in the front ranks of the crowd said.

Bill nodded. "Yeah, they could. That's why we have to be on our guard." His brain was working furiously. "We're going to post sentries on the highest buildings in town. That way we can keep a good watch in all four directions. We'll need volunteers for that. And we'll need volunteers to patrol outside of town, too."

"You mean out where the Injuns can get 'em?" a bearded old-timer asked. Bill had seen the man ride into town a week or so earlier but hadn't met him yet.

"The outriders won't get too far from town," Bill explained. He was putting together this plan on the fly, but so far the things he'd come up with seemed to make sense to him. "And nobody will go out alone. There'll always be two or three men together. At the first sign of any Indians, they'll hightail it back to town." Something else occurred to him. "Not only that, but we'll work out some sort of signals so the outriders and the men on the roofs can communicate with each other."

"That's all well and good," the old-timer said, "but I've fought Injuns before, and I'm here to tell you, there ain't no sneakier critters anywhere on the face o' the earth. I've seen 'em pop up where you would've sworn up and down there weren't no hidey-holes. It's like they come up from the ground itself, like worms outta the earth."

"Now, there's no need to exaggerate—" Fleming began.

"Exaggeratin', am I?" the old man interrupted. His beard seemed to bristle with anger at the mayor's suggestion. "How many Injun fights have you been in, mister?"

"Well, ah . . . none," Fleming admitted.

"I been in a whole heap, goin' all the way back to the Shinin' Times when the only white men west of the Mississipp' was fur trappers like me. More recent-like, 'fore I drifted over here to Kansas, I been in scraps with the Comanch' down in Texas and the 'Pache out yonder in Arizona. So I know what I'm talkin' about when it comes to fightin' Injuns." The old-timer snorted. "Know a lot more'n any of you folks, I'll bet."

"So you don't think we should send riders out of town?" Bill asked.

"Didn't say that. Just lettin' you know it could be mighty dangerous. I wouldn't send no married men with young'uns, if I was you."

Bill nodded. "All right, we'll keep that in mind. You have any other suggestions, Mister . . . ?"

"Flint. Mordecai Flint. And yeah, I got some suggestions, and the main one is to make sure ever' able-bodied man in town's got a gun and knows how to use it. Repeatin' rifles, if there's enough of 'em to go around."

Fleming turned to look at Perry Monroe. "What do you think, Perry? Can you and the owners of the other mercantiles supply some extra rifles if we need them?"

"I reckon we can," Monroe said with a nod. His forehead was creased on a frown, and Bill knew what caused it.

Monroe had to be aware that if there was a battle, some of those rifles would be damaged or lost. Monroe wasn't a skinflint by any means, but still, he had to be thinking about what he stood to lose by providing those extra weapons.

But if he didn't, he might stand to lose a lot more, starting with his daughter. Bill had no doubt that his father-in-law would do whatever was necessary to protect Eden.

So would he.

"Next thing you do is get some barrels and stack 'em up here and there around town," the old-timer called Mordecai Flint went on. "That'll give you some extra cover, and if the varmints manage to get in town without any warnin', folks in the street might be able to get behind a barrel quicker'n they could make it to a buildin'."

Fleming nodded. "That makes sense. We appreciate the advice, Mr. Flint. Is there anything else?"

"Get all your preachers prayin' double-time," Flint said. "If a bunch o' bloodthirsty Pawnee show up, you're gonna need all the help from the Almighty you can get."

A grim silence descended over the crowd after Flint said that. After several moments, a man in the rough work clothes of a farmer spoke up.

"My wife and kids are out at my farm," he said. "I just came into town this morning to pick up a new blade for my plow. All these precautions you folks in the settlement are taking aren't gonna help us one little bit."

"I'm sorry, friend," Fleming said. "We can only take care of the people here in town. Maybe you can go get your family and bring them back in. You can find a place to stay here until the crisis is over."

"And when's that gonna be?" the farmer wanted to know. "Those soldiers who were here didn't even know where the Indians are. You said so yourself, Mayor. They might not ever show up. I can't just abandon my farm! There are crops to be harvested and other work that has to be done."

Several other men who had farms nearby echoed that sentiment. The level of anger in the street began to rise again.

"I'm sorry," Fleming said over the commotion. "There's just so much we can do. We can't protect the town and all the countryside for miles around! You just can't expect us to do that. It's not possible."

Bill had an idea. He said, "There are . . . what? Fifteen or twenty farms hereabouts? Why don't you men go back to your homes and fetch your families in? Let your neighbors who aren't in town today know about what's going on, too. Then every day the whole passel of you can ride out and tend to the chores on two or three farms, maybe more, since there'll be quite a few of you. That way you can keep things going, but there'll be a big, well-armed bunch together in case of trouble."

A couple of the farmers still objected, but more of them nodded as they thought about Bill's proposal. "That could work," one of the men admitted. "It's not perfect, but it would keep our wives and kids safe, and taking care of our places wouldn't be as dangerous for us."

It didn't take long for those who saw the wisdom of the idea to win over the holdouts. Bill was starting to feel a little better about the situation. They had a plan of sorts for defending the town, and the outlying settlers would be safer, too, and not on their own if the Indians came.

And as soon as word came that the Pawnee had been rounded up and forced back onto the reservation, then everything could go back to normal.

The surly bullwhacker wasn't through muddying the waters, however. He spat disgustedly at the base of the boardwalk and said in a loud, abrasive voice, "You people are fools. What about the freighters?"

"You and your men are welcome to stay here in town as

long as you need to, mister," Fleming said. "We're not going to turn anybody away in this time of crisis."

"That's not what I'm talkin' about. I'm not goin' anywhere, sure enough, and neither are any of the wagons in my train. But you can bet every other teamster and bullwhacker in this part of the state feels the same way right now. There's no spur line from the railroad down here. The only way you can get supplies that don't grow on farms is by wagon. What's gonna happen when none of 'em have been rollin' for a month or six weeks? How long are the bullets gonna hold out while the Pawnee are on the rampage?" The man looked around with an arrogant sneer and shook his head. "Run out of ammunition and see how long you last then."

Chapter 9

Costigan didn't see any more signs of Indians that day. He stayed up on the wagon seat while the rest of the shooters finished killing enough buffalo to fill all the wagons with hides.

Bledsoe called a halt when they reached that goal. There was no point in wasting bullets killing beasts that would start to rot before the skinners could get the hides off them. Left overnight, the carcasses would bloat, damaging the hides and making them difficult and even more unpleasant to remove.

Dave McGinty cleaned his rifles and stowed them away in the sheaths strapped to his horse's saddle, then ambled over to the wagon where Costigan was still standing watch.

"Well, we made it through the day with our hair still on our heads," McGinty said with a grin.

Costigan nodded. "Yeah, but I can still feel 'em out there somewhere, Dave. The thing of it is . . . I don't know what they want. With the Rebs, I always knew. You could just feel it in the air that they wanted us all dead. Maybe all those Indians want is to be left alone."

"They've got a funny way of showing it if they do, what

with all the spyin' on us they've been up to. First that one last night, then the three this mornin' . . ."

"But when a big bunch showed up, they went around us," Costigan pointed out. "That doesn't sound like somebody who's looking for a fight."

McGinty's brawny shoulders rose and fell. "Who can figure out what a redskin's thinkin'? Not me, that's for sure."

The skinners finished their work by late afternoon, and the party of hunters headed back to the main camp. There the hides would be unloaded, spread out, and pegged down to dry, a process that took five to eight days. The hides would be turned over and pegged down again several times during that interval.

The hunt had been successful enough so far that a large swath of prairie around the camp was black with hides in various stages of drying. Every day, wagons came out from Dodge City to pick up bundles of the hides that were ready and take them back to the Rath & Wright warehouses in town, but fresh hides came in to take their place.

Bledsoe had a partner in Dodge who dealt with the hide buyers, Charles Rath and Bob Wright. The colonel himself, as he was fond of pointing out, preferred being out on the open plains. Sitting in an office was no way for a war hero to spend his days.

When they got back to the main camp, Costigan took his rifles and put them in his tent, then unsaddled his horse and picketed it along with the others.

The aroma of stew simmering drifted from the cook pots. Some of the skinners brought back fresh meat every day, although the hunting party could eat only a small fraction of what was available. The rest of it was left on the plains.

Costigan could understand why the Indians didn't like that. A warrior whose wives and children might be hungry had to be filled with rage every time he saw all those hundreds of dead buffalo going to waste.

A decade earlier it had seemed that the herds were so

vast as to be endless, but Costigan was already starting to see signs that someday, the buffalo might be gone.

If that happened, many of the Indians would be done for as well. They depended on the buffalo for so much, and some of them just weren't capable of becoming farmers the way Washington insisted they should. Costigan understood that, too.

After the war, he could have returned to the farm where he had grown up. That was what his brothers had done. They had married local girls, tilled the rich Ohio soil, and were raising families there along with their crops.

Costigan couldn't do that. If he had found a girl to marry, he always would have worried that she could smell the death on him. He couldn't get away from it himself. How could he expect some innocent girl to put up with that?

He couldn't. All it had taken to realize that was a few days back home. Then he had packed up what little gear he had and headed west . . .

Eleven years gone since then, he thought as he picked up a pot of coffee from the edge of one of the fires and filled his cup. Eleven years and still the stench clung to him.

Of course, it didn't help that he killed buffalo for a living, he told himself wryly. But he knew that even if he didn't, the smell would still be there.

From the first time he had seen a man's head explode from the impact of a ball fired from his rifle, it had been there.

Colonel Bledsoe came over to him and said, "You'll be on guard duty tonight, Costigan."

"All right," he nodded.

Bledsoe peered at him through narrowed eyes. "What's bothering you, son? Frightened of the Indians?"

Anger welled up inside Costigan. He didn't like the colonel's patronizing tone, and there wasn't enough difference in their ages for Bledsoe to be calling him "son." Besides, Costigan's father was still alive back in Ohio, as far as he knew.

"Nothing's bothering me, Colonel. And I'm not afraid of the Indians, just cautious, the way any man ought to be out here if he wants to stay alive."

"It's just that if trouble comes, I've got to be able to count on my men, each and every one of them."

"You think I'll run and hide if the Indians attack?"

"Now, I never said that—"

"Because I won't, Colonel," Costigan said. "If anybody tries to kill me—red, white, or hell, even blue!—I'll fight. You can count on that."

Bledsoe started to lift his arm, as if he intended to clap a hand on Costigan's shoulder, but something in the buffalo hunter's gaze must have stopped him.

Instead the colonel said, "Well, ah, that's good to hear. Mighty good to hear. Get you something to eat, Costigan. You'll stand first watch along with Tolbert and Stennis."

Costigan nodded. He didn't care about which watch he stood. He just wanted Bledsoe to go on and leave him alone.

The whole world could leave him alone as far as Costigan was concerned . . . but that wasn't likely to happen.

There were no thunderstorms that night, and no bad dreams for Costigan. His shift on guard duty was quiet. When it was finished, he crawled into his tent and slept like a dead man.

The next morning the hunters rode out again, trailing the herd and being trailed by the hide wagons. Costigan felt better, and he even summoned up a smile at some of McGinty's joshing.

For years now he had gone through bleak moods like the one that had gripped him the previous day. Some were worse than others, but he always shook them eventually.

It was hard to dwell too much on the bloody past on a beautiful day like this. A fresh, slightly cool breeze blew out of the west, carrying a few white puffballs of cloud through a magnificent, arching blue sky.

The hide wagons were behind the hunters, so Costigan couldn't smell the blood stink that had soaked into them over the months. Soon enough the musky smell of buffalo, the thick, cloying odor of their dung, and the sharp tang of powder smoke would fill the air, but for now Costigan breathed in the aromas of grass and earth and wildflowers.

The smell of life instead of death, he told himself. The thought brought another faint smile to his lips.

Costigan felt better about things, but that didn't mean he'd gotten careless. His pale gray eyes constantly scanned the landscape around him.

McGinty was just as watchful. "Think we'll see those redskins again today, Ward?" he asked.

"They're liable to be fifty miles away by now," Costigan replied.

McGinty chuckled. "That's not really the same as answerin' my question, now is it?"

"I hope we don't see them," Costigan said. "I hope we just kill some buffalo and don't run into any trouble."

"Amen to that," McGinty said. But the words had barely left his mouth when he said, "Uh-oh."

Costigan stiffened in the saddle. "What is it?"

"Dust to the south."

Costigan turned and looked. Sure enough, McGinty was right. A column of dust curled up to join the clouds in the sky.

It wasn't nearly as innocent as those clouds, though, Costigan thought. Riders were on the move, and if they kept coming, their path would soon intersect that of the hunting party.

"Ride back and tell the colonel," Costigan said to McGinty. "Might be a good idea to circle up the wagons."

"What are you gonna do?"

Costigan reached for the telescope in his saddlebags. "Thought I'd see if I can tell for sure what we're dealing with."

"Blast it, Ward, don't go riskin' your life—"

"I don't intend to," Costigan said. "Not any more than

any of the rest of us are. Don't worry, if I spot feathers and war paint, I'll hustle back to the wagons on the double."

"You'd better," McGinty said. He turned his horse and galloped toward the wagons.

Seeing that something was going on, the other shooters rode over to find out what it was. Costigan waved them away.

"Head for the wagons!" he called to them. "Might be Indians coming!"

A couple of the men hesitated, but not for long. None of them stayed around to argue. The biggest safety was in numbers, so they headed for the wagons.

In a matter of minutes, Costigan found himself alone, half a mile ahead of the others.

He found that oddly satisfying. He didn't like being responsible for anyone's safety except his own.

With a cluck of his tongue, he heeled his horse into a run that would take him closer to the oncoming riders.

Despite what he had told McGinty, a part of him felt the urge to charge those riders if they turned out to be a war party of Indians. That would mean certain death, of course. But Costigan had heard that the Indians had a saying about a day being a good one to die.

Nobody would ever find a more beautiful day to die, that was for sure. A man could do worse than to draw his last breath looking up at that Kansas sky.

He was getting ahead of himself. He didn't know who the men on horseback were. However, they were close enough now that he could see them as dark specks at the base of the dust cloud their horses were kicking up.

Costigan reined in, extended the telescope, and lifted it to his eye.

Blue uniforms leaped to vivid life. Costigan grunted in surprise as he saw them. The morning sunlight glinted off brass buttons and fittings. He even spotted a guidon fluttering in the breeze as the standard bearer rode a short distance behind the two men leading the group.

Costigan watched them for a few moments, then closed

the telescope and tucked it away. He turned his horse and sent it in a gallop toward the wagons.

Bledsoe had taken his advice, brought the caravan to a halt, and had the wagons drawn into a loose circle. There weren't enough of them to make a strong defensive formation, as wagon trains full of immigrants did when they were attacked by Indians, but it was still better than having them stretched out in a line.

As things had turned out, the maneuver wasn't necessary, but Costigan was glad to see that Bledsoe had done it anyway.

He might not care that much about his own life anymore, but he didn't want to see his friend Dave McGinty and the other men massacred. Not even the colonel.

The horses were milling around inside the circle of wagons. Men crouched behind each of the vehicles, rifles at the ready.

With their deadly aim and those long-range weapons, the hunters could hold off an attack for a long time even though they would be outnumbered, if it came to that. Whether they survived or not would depend largely on how stubborn the Indians were.

But not today, Costigan thought. Not now, anyway.

Colonel Bledsoe straightened up from his crouch and called, "Costigan! Costigan! Are they Indians?"

Costigan didn't answer until he reached the wagons. He saw every man in the party looking at him with faces taut from fear.

"Rest easy, Colonel," he said. "It looks like we're about to get a visit from the United States Cavalry."

Chapter 10

Bledsoe's eyes widened in surprise at that news. "The cavalry!" he repeated.

"That's right," Costigan said. He couldn't resist adding, "You know, Colonel, the sort of men you commanded a regiment of during the war."

It wasn't that he doubted Bledsoe's service. He had no reason to think the man hadn't commanded a cavalry regiment.

But something about the colonel never had seemed right to Costigan. His hunch was that Bledsoe never had seen as much action as he claimed in his stories.

Bledsoe must have sensed that Costigan felt that way, too, because his face flushed even more than usual. He said, "That's splendid. Perhaps if any of them were in the war, they might have served under my command."

"Maybe," Costigan said. "You want me to ride out and meet them?"

"An excellent idea. Take McGinty with you and guide them back to us."

Costigan didn't figure the troopers would need much guiding. Out here in this big, flat, mostly empty landscape, the wagons were pretty easy to spot. He was glad for the excuse to ride out again, though.

"Come on, Dave," he called. "You're with me."

All the men had heard Costigan report that the riders were soldiers, not Indians on the warpath. They stood up from where they had been kneeling and crouching behind the wagons and looked visibly relieved.

A big grin wreathed McGinty's bearded face as he led his horse out of the circle and mounted up to join Costigan in welcoming the troopers.

"You reckon those soldier boys are out on a routine patrol?" he asked as the two of them rode away from the wagons.

"Could be," Costigan said. "On the other hand, they're a long way from anywhere out here. Maybe they're looking for something in particular."

"Like an Indian war party?"

Costigan shrugged. "Could be. We ought to know pretty soon."

The soldiers were closer now. Costigan didn't need the telescope anymore to make out the blue uniforms and the flapping guidon.

He and McGinty rode on until they were about fifty yards from the troopers. Costigan reined in to wait for them, and McGinty followed suit.

The cavalrymen closed that gap to twenty yards before the officer in the lead held up a hand to signal a halt. The sergeant right behind him turned around and bellowed the order.

As the troopers pulled their mounts to a stop, the cloud of dust that had been following drifted over them, blurring them in Costigan's sight for a second. His brain leaped to an unaccustomed flight of fancy.

What if it was all an illusion, and the soldiers continued to shimmer and fade until they disappeared like one of those mirages he had read about in books?

Then the dust blew over Costigan and McGinty, too, and it stung Costigan's eyes and nose. He blinked away the grit.

The troopers were real, all right, and the officer in charge of them was walking his horse slowly toward the two buffalo hunters.

He reined in a short distance away and nodded to them. "Gentlemen," he said. "I presume you're with that hunting party I can see over there?"

The man's tone was crisp, the words bitten off curtly. He was an easterner, Costigan thought, and might not have been out here on the frontier for very long.

The sergeant appeared to be a grizzled veteran, though, and if this wet-behind-the-ears captain had any sense, he would rely heavily on the noncom's advice.

"That's right, Cap'n," Costigan said. "We saw your dust and didn't know but what you were hostiles."

"You've heard about the Pawnee, then."

Costigan and McGinty traded a surprised glance. Costigan told the officer, "No, sir, we've been out here for a while. I thought all the Pawnee were on the reservation down in Indian Territory since they were moved from their lands in Nebraska a while back."

"That's where they're supposed to be. However, a large number of braves led by Chief Spotted Dog slipped away from the reservation and have gone on the warpath."

"And you're looking for them?"

The captain drew in a sharp breath and didn't look pleased. "No, our orders are to warn the settlers in this area. We've been visiting the towns and farms and ranches and letting people know about the possible threat. I believe the hostiles to be a considerable distance west of here."

He didn't sound happy about that, either. The man was probably a glory hunter, thought Costigan.

He had seen plenty of officers like that during the war, ambitious men who had visions of fame and promotion dancing in their heads. Men who didn't care if they had to sacrifice some of their troops if it meant a good write-up in *Harper's Weekly*.

Costigan swallowed the bitter taste that came up in his

throat. He hated to tell this captain what they had seen the day before, but the man needed to be aware of it.

"There's no way of knowing if it's the same bunch you're talking about, Captain," Costigan said, "but we saw Indians a couple of different times yesterday."

The captain sat up straighter in his saddle. His narrow face grew animated.

"You did? How many?"

"Just three, the first time. They were sitting off on a bluff yesterday morning, watching my friend and I while we scouted for the herd our party's been following. Then later in the day we spotted a lot more of them in the distance."

"They didn't attack you?"

Costigan shook his head. "Nope. In fact, they were making a wide circle around us. It looked like they were doing their best to steer clear of us."

"That doesn't sound like the Pawnee war party," the captain said. A disappointed frown creased his forehead. "They've raided several ranches and attacked a train since they escaped from the reservation. And that's just what I'm aware of. They may have carried out other atrocities since we left the fort."

McGinty said, "Could be the same bunch, and they just didn't want to tangle with us. It's pert-near suicide to come after a group of buffalo hunters. We can shoot the whiskers off a gnat at a hundred yards, and we've got the rifles to do it, too."

"Yes, well, I'd like for you to show me where you saw these savages. I think they warrant investigation."

The tone of the captain's voice made it clear he was issuing an order, not asking a favor.

The sergeant cleared his throat and said, "Beggin' your pardon, Cap'n, but we weren't actually supposed to be huntin' those hostiles."

"But we have every right to engage them in defense of our own lives should we happen to encounter them, don't we, Sergeant?"

The middle-aged noncom shrugged. "I reckon we do."

"Very well." The captain turned back to Costigan and McGinty. "Show me."

Costigan kept a tight rein on his temper. There had been a time in his life when he had to take orders from stiff-necked jackasses like this officer, but that was more than a decade in the past.

"You'll need to talk to our boss first," he said. "He tells us what to do."

The captain didn't like that. He glared at Costigan and asked, "What's your employer's name?"

"Colonel William Bledsoe."

The rank seemed to take the captain by surprise. It didn't take him long to figure out, though, that it was probably honorary. A colonel on active duty wouldn't be bossing a bunch of buffalo hunters.

"I shall be sure to speak to Colonel Bledsoe about your attitude, sir," he said. "Now, if you'll take me to him . . ."

"Sure," Costigan said. "Come on."

He and McGinty turned their horses and rode toward the wagons. Behind them, the captain ordered, "Sergeant Hutton, bring the men forward but hold them a hundred yards away from those wagons."

The hunting party had come out of the circle and gathered in front of the wagons to wait for Costigan, McGinty, and the soldiers. Colonel Bledsoe strode forward to meet them, looking as dapper as usual in his suit and derby hat . . . or at least as dapper as any man could after spending nearly a week out on the prairie in a dusty buffalo camp.

Bledsoe stopped. "Colonel William J. Bledsoe, Fifth Pennsylvania Cavalry, retired," he announced himself.

If he was expecting the captain to salute him, he was going to have a long wait, thought Costigan. The officer dismounted and gave Bledsoe a curt nod.

"I'm Captain Timothy Stone, Mr. Bledsoe."

Costigan saw a flash of anger and hurt in Bledsoe's eyes, and in that moment he almost felt sorry for the man, even though he didn't like him in the slightest. Bledsoe set a lot of store by his former rank, and Captain Stone couldn't have offended him much more if he'd taken the derby off Bledsoe's head and relieved himself in it.

Mister. That had to hurt.

"As I was explaining to this rather insolent individual who works for you, there is a Pawnee war party at large, having escaped from the reservation in Indian Territory, and you should consider yourself duly warned that you and your men may find yourselves in danger from these hostiles."

"Pawnee," Bledsoe repeated. "Why, they haven't given any trouble in—"

"They're giving trouble now," Stone said. "And you should take all necessary precautions. I'm told you encountered the savages yesterday?"

"We saw some Indians. We don't know if it was the bunch you're looking for."

Costigan hadn't really expected Bledsoe to take the same reasonable stance he had. He'd assumed the colonel would jump to the conclusion that the Indians they had seen were the ones who had raided those ranches farther west.

"We'll determine that," Stone said. "I'd like for your man to show me where the Indians were yesterday, but he seems to think you need to approve that."

Bledsoe glared at Costigan. "What the hell? Do what the captain wants, Costigan. You don't argue with the cavalry."

"Fine, if that's what you want, Colonel."

"I'll go with you, Ward," McGinty said.

Bledsoe shook his head. "I can't afford to lose two shooters. You stay with us, McGinty. And you get back as soon as you can, Costigan."

Captain Stone had heard enough. He said, "Come along, Mr. Costigan," and swung back up into his saddle. "That *is* your name, correct?"

"Yeah." Costigan turned his horse and fell in alongside the officer as they rode back toward the rest of the cavalry patrol. "Ward Costigan."

He thought about adding *Corporal, Twelfth Ohio Infantry*, but he didn't want to sound like Bledsoe.

Anyway, it wasn't like he had spent all that much time with his regiment. Not after his commanding officers had found out what he could do with a rifle.

After that he was always posted up at the front lines, or even out ahead of the front lines, hidden in a tree or some brush or a bunch of rocks, his telescope trained on the enemy camps, waiting for some careless Confederate officer to step out where Costigan had a clear shot at him . . .

Costigan looked over his shoulder. The wagons were already rolling again. Bledsoe was eager to get to the herd and start the day's killing.

For the next hour, Costigan led Captain Stone, Sergeant Hutton, and the rest of the cavalrymen at an angle to the northwest, toward the area where he had seen the Indians the day before.

The only real landmarks he had to go by in this mostly featureless landscape were the two small hills between which the Indians had ridden out of sight. Costigan knew he could pick up the trail there, and Stone could follow it, backtrack the savages, or do whatever the hell he wanted to. What the cavalry did was none of Costigan's business, and he intended to keep it that way.

The hills were visible for a long time before the men got to them. Gradually, they seemed to grow larger as Costigan and the patrol approached. Finally, Costigan slowed his horse to a halt when the hills were only about half a mile away.

He pointed to them and said, "You'll find the trail right up there between those hills, Captain. The group of Indians we saw was large enough that you shouldn't have any trouble spotting the tracks their ponies left. There was no rain last night to wash them out, and there hasn't been much wind."

"You're supposed to *show* me where the Indians were, Costigan," Stone said.

"I am. I told you, they rode right through there."

"Take me to the tracks. Remember, Colonel Bledsoe ordered you to cooperate with me."

Costigan bit back the angry response that tried to spring to his lips. He supposed another half a mile didn't matter. He was about to nod and agree when he heard some very faint noises in the distance. They were coming from the south, Costigan thought . . . from the area about where that buffalo herd ought to be grazing today.

Sergeant Hutton heard the sounds, too. "Shots," he said. "That huntin' party must've found those buffs."

Costigan thought so at first, too, but then something twisted inside his guts as he realized the shots were *wrong*.

When all the hunters were set up and firing into a herd, they fell into a steady rhythm that Costigan knew as well as he knew the beating of his own heart.

These shots were coming faster, at a more ragged pace, and interspersed with the dull booms of the heavy-caliber buffalo guns were the sharper cracks of Henrys and Winchesters.

"They're not hunting," he said. "They're fighting."

McGinty, Colonel Bledsoe, and the others were under attack.

Chapter 11

The idea that they might run short of supplies didn't sit well with the citizens of Redemption, of course. After the bullwhacker gave voice to that potential danger, a lot of worried, angry complaining broke out among the crowd in the street.

Bill let the commotion run its course for a couple of minutes before he raised his voice and called, "Folks! Folks, settle down!"

They ignored him. He had to repeat that request several times, raising his voice even more, before the crowd got quiet enough for everybody to hear him.

"Nobody's gonna starve. We have a lot of supplies on hand here in town, and those farms can supply more if need be. But I don't think it's going to come to that, because it won't be long until the army runs those Pawnee to ground."

"You don't know that," a man said. "It could take them weeks to catch those savages, maybe even months!"

Shouts of agreement went up from the crowd.

"Hold on, hold on!" Perry Monroe said as he stepped forward and raised his hands for quiet. He was an impressive figure with his long white beard, and people quieted down a little faster for him, Bill noted.

Monroe continued, "Marshal Harvey is right. My shelves were stocked not that long ago, and I reckon the other mercantiles in town have plenty of supplies on hand, too. Plus there are all the goods on those wagons our friend here brought into town today."

Monroe swept a hand toward the bullwhacker.

"Now wait just a blasted minute!" the man protested. "Those goods have to be paid for."

"They already have been, or you wouldn't have brought them here to deliver."

"Yeah, but they're worth more now."

That brought angry howls from several members of the crowd. "You can't do that," Roy Fleming said. "You can't raise the prices simply because we need those supplies."

The bullwhacker folded his brawny arms across his chest and sneered. "I can do whatever I damned well please," he said. "Those goods are still on my wagons, and they're gonna stay there until I get the price I want for them."

"Maybe we'll just take them!" one of the townsmen shouted as he shook a fist at the bullwhacker.

"My teamsters are all armed, and we'll use our guns if we have to."

Bill said, "Hold on now, there's no need to start talking about guns—"

It was too late. One of the men in the crowd stepped up behind the bullwhacker, grabbed his shoulder, hauled him around, and slammed a fist into his face.

The man probably wouldn't have been able to do that if he hadn't taken the bullwhacker by surprise. The bullwhacker was too big and strong to be jerked around under normal circumstances.

As it was, the punch to the face seemed to have no effect on him except to rock his head back a little. He roared in anger, grabbed his attacker by the neck, and lifted him off the ground. The man kicked desperately as the bullwhacker's ham-like hands around his throat cut off his air.

Bill yelled, "Hey! Let him go!" but the bullwhacker ignored him. He was about to leap off the boardwalk and try to rescue the townsman, when one of the man's friends rushed up behind the bullwhacker and hit him across the back of the neck with a piece of two-by-four.

Bill didn't know where the man had gotten the board, probably out of a nearby alley, but it made an effective weapon. The bullwhacker staggered forward a couple of steps, let go of the man he was choking, and fell to his knees.

The townie wasn't the only one with friends. One of the teamsters from the wagon train shouted a curse and punched the man who had wielded the board. Someone leaped to his defense, and in a heartbeat, chaos erupted in the street as scared, angry people on both sides started trying to whale the tar out of each other.

Bill grabbed his father-in-law's arm and shoved Monroe toward the door of the town hall.

"Get Eden inside!" he said. "And both of you stay there!"

"These people have gone crazy!" Monroe said.

Bill couldn't argue with that. Fear had made the crowd as crazy as a bunch of longhorns that had gotten into the locoweed.

But it was up to him to stop this anyway. Somehow.

"Bill!" Eden cried. She tried to get around Monroe to reach his side.

"Go with your father!" he told her as Monroe caught hold of her. He couldn't look out for her safety and deal with this riot at the same time.

By now the tumult in the street was incredible. Everybody was yelling. Fists flew and thudded into flesh.

Bill wished he had one of the shotguns from the marshal's office. Nothing settled people down quite like the blast of a Greener.

All he had, though, was his Colt, and as worked up as those folks were, he wasn't sure they would pay any attention to it if he let off a few rounds at the sky.

For now he had to make sure the rest of the town council was safe. "Get inside!" he told them, waving an arm toward the doors.

"The hell with that!" Josiah Hartnett rumbled. The burly liveryman leaped down from the boardwalk, grabbed a couple of men by the neck, and banged their heads together. They collapsed limply.

Hartnett was big enough to take care of himself. Leo Kellogg and Charley Hobbs weren't. Wisely, they scurried into the building behind Monroe and Eden.

Roy Fleming clutched at the sleeve of Bill's shirt. "What are we going to do?" he wailed.

"Get inside," Bill said again as he pulled free and gave the mayor a hard shove toward the door.

That left Judge Dunaway. The justice of the peace stood at the edge of the boardwalk bellowing, "Order! Come to order, by God!"

This wasn't a courtroom, though, and nobody was paying attention to any judicial edicts. Somebody tackled the judge around the knees and toppled him off the boardwalk. Dunaway fell into the street, flailing his arms wildly as he went down.

Bill leaped after him. The judge might get trampled in that mad melee.

He wasn't the only one in danger of such a fate. There were women and kids in this mob, too, Bill knew. If any of them fell, they might be done for.

Right now he had to save Dunaway. A man aimed a kick at the judge's head, but Bill caught the collar of his shirt and jerked him back before the man's foot could land on Dunaway's skull.

The man yelled a curse and twisted in Bill's grip. Bill's other fist came up and landed with a solid thud on the man's jaw. A shove sent him reeling away to fall over a hitch rail.

Bill bent and grabbed the judge's arm. Dunaway was too heavy for Bill to lift him without the judge helping some, and Dunaway seemed stunned at the moment.

"Come on, Judge!" Bill urged. "We gotta get you out of here!"

With Bill bracing him, Dunaway finally heaved himself to his feet. "Madness!" he muttered. "Madness!"

"You got that right," Bill said. "Get in the town hall, Judge!"

Unsteadily, Dunaway clambered underneath a hitch rail and onto the boardwalk. He staggered upright again and made it to the entrance of the town hall. As he disappeared inside the building, he slammed the doors closed behind him.

That was a relief, Bill thought, but he didn't have time to enjoy it, because at that moment somebody leaped on his back from behind and started trying to choke the life out of him.

Bill stumbled forward under the unexpected weight. His bad leg threatened to give out under him, but he managed to catch himself.

His attacker had looped an arm around Bill's neck and now pressed down with it, threatening to crush his windpipe.

Bill braced his feet and reached up. Pulling hair was something a girl did in a fight . . . but when a man was about to strangle him, he didn't care about such things. Bill grabbed a couple handfuls of his attacker's hair and hauled on it as hard as he could, bending forward sharply at the waist at the same time.

The man let out a howl of pain and his grip on Bill's throat came loose. He slid over Bill's head and shoulders and went crashing to the ground, spilling a couple of other men as he rolled into their legs. They all tangled up into a thrashing mess.

Somebody bumped Bill's shoulders. He turned, fist cocked to throw another punch, but held off when he recognized Josiah Hartnett. Blood from a cut on the liveryman's forehead smeared his rugged face.

"We've got to stop this!" he shouted.

"How?" Bill replied.

The sudden boom of a shotgun answered him.

Bill had wished earlier for a Greener. Somebody must have gotten hold of one. He hoped that load of buckshot hadn't scythed through the struggling crowd. He didn't want any innocent blood spilled in Redemption.

The ominous blast did the trick. People stopped in their tracks and looked around to see who had fired the shotgun . . . and where it might be aimed next.

Bill was just as curious as anybody else. He didn't hear any screaming, so he thought maybe whoever had fired the shot had aimed into the air. He turned toward the town hall . . .

He wasn't prepared for what he saw. His wife stood there on the boardwalk, the scattergun clutched tightly in her delicate little hands that were stronger than they appeared. Smoke curled from the barrel she had fired.

Eden wore a fierce expression on her face and looked ready, willing, and able to cut down the next man who threw a punch.

"Son of a—"

Bill forced his way through the mob, shouldering people aside. As he reached the boardwalk, Eden cried, "Are you people insane? You're fighting each other when you should be getting ready to fight Indians!"

Bill stepped up onto the planks and reached for the Greener. She let him take it out of her hands. She was trembling, but whether it was from anger, fear, or both, he didn't know.

"Everybody settle down!" he roared as he turned back toward the street. "The next person who throws a punch is under arrest!"

"And you'll feel the full force of the law, I guarantee it!" Judge Dunaway put in from the doors of the town hall, which stood open again.

Perry Monroe stepped past the judge and said, "Sorry, Bill. She slipped out the back door and took off for the marshal's office before I knew what she was doing."

Bill had thought he recognized the shotgun.

Eden snorted at her father's words and said, "It's a good thing I did, or those idiots would still be trying to kill each other."

Quietly, Bill told her, "I appreciate what you did, Eden, but in the future—"

He stopped short at the look she gave him. He hadn't been married long, but he already knew when to hold his tongue.

He turned back to the crowd instead and went on, "Everybody just needs to calm down. Is anybody hurt bad?"

Other than some black eyes and bloody noses, everyone seemed to be all right. A lot of angry muttering was still going on, and Bill sensed that violence might erupt again at any moment, but for now the shotgun blast had quelled the riot.

Bill spotted the bullwhacker whose obstinance and greed had started the ruckus. "You," he said. "What's your name?"

"Gus Meade," the man answered with surly reluctance.

"All right, Mr. Meade, if you don't want to live up the terms of the bargain you made with the merchants here in town, I don't reckon you have to."

Meade started to sneer.

Bill went on, "So that means you don't have any reason to stay here. You can refund any money you were paid in advance, then take your wagons and go."

Meade's forehead creased in a frown. "Go?" he repeated. "Your mayor said we were welcome to stay! You can't go back on his word!"

"Reckon if you can go back on your word, we can go back on ours," Bill said. "You and your men and your wagons be out of town in half an hour."

Roy Fleming had emerged from the town hall. He said, "Now, Bill, I'm not sure—"

"You said I was in charge of law and order in Redemption, right, Mr. Mayor?" Bill asked.

"Well, yes, of course—"

"Which means I got a right to run troublemakers out of

town." Bill fixed a stony glare on Gus Meade. "More than a right. I've got a duty to do it."

"Hold on here," Meade blustered. "It's a long way back to Dodge City. If we start back across there with loaded wagons and those Pawnee spot us, they'll come after us, sure as hell!"

Bill nodded. "I expect they will. But maybe they won't see you. Maybe they're not anywhere around these parts."

"We ought to wait a few days, at least, to see if the army rounds up those renegades."

"Thirty minutes," Bill repeated. "Otherwise I lock up the whole bunch of you."

That was a mostly empty threat—he didn't have the room for all the freighters in Redemption's small jail, and he was unlikely to be able to arrest them, anyway—but Meade didn't have to know that. A steady gaze and an equally steady shotgun could be mighty convincing.

"Or you could go in the town hall and talk to the council about living up to your bargain," Bill went on after a tense moment. "How's that sound?"

"All right, damn it," Meade grumbled, obviously glad for the chance to save face and remain in town where he and his men would be safer from marauding Pawnee. He looked around in the street. "Where's my hat?"

Somebody handed him the broad-brimmed headgear, which had been trampled into something that barely resembled a hat. Disgustedly, Meade began trying to punch that hat back into shape as he climbed onto the boardwalk. He disappeared into the town hall with Roy Fleming.

While Bill had everyone's attention, he went on, "The rest of you go back to your homes and businesses. Men, get your guns and stay armed from now on. If you want to volunteer to be one of the guards or outriders, come to the marshal's office. We'll work out a schedule." He took a deep breath. "We're gonna come through this all right. You'll see. We just have to work together, that's all."

Why they would believe him when he wasn't much more than a kid, he didn't know, but he was gratified to see several people nodding in agreement. The crowd began to disperse.

He turned to Eden and said, "That was a mighty brave thing you did—"

She stopped him by coming into his arms and pressing her face against his chest as she put her arms around his waist. He felt a shudder go through her.

"Just hold me," she said, her voice muffled by his shirt.

Bill figured the best thing he could do right now was to oblige her.

Chapter 12

Bill had stood there on the boardwalk for a minute or so, comforting his wife, when he felt a tug on his sleeve.

Without letting go of Eden, he looked around, then looked down. The old frontiersman named Mordecai Flint, who was short and scrawny as well as bearded, stood there beside them.

"You ought to deputize me," Flint said. "I been to see the elephant, and I reckon I've forgot more about fightin' Injuns than anybody else in this town ever knowed."

Bill had a hunch the old-timer might be right about that. Still, he was sort of busy right now.

"Fine," he told Flint. "Go on down to the marshal's office. I'll see you there in a few minutes."

"How much you gonna pay me?"

"We'll talk about that later," Bill said.

"I don't come cheap, you know."

"Just go," Bill said through clenched teeth.

"All right, all right," Flint muttered as he walked off toward the marshal's office. "No need to get testy about it."

Bill continued to stand there holding Eden, and after a

few moments she took a deep breath that made her breasts lift against his chest.

This was hardly the time to be noticing such things, Bill told himself, but he was only human. A young, recently married, very-much-in-love-with-his-wife human, to boot.

So when Eden said, "I'm all right now," Bill was sort of grateful that he could rest his hands on her shoulders and put a little distance between them before his reaction got too unseemly.

"I think you and your pa need to go back over to the store and close it up for now," he told her.

"Close it? But people are going to be needing supplies."

"Yeah, but we don't know how long this whole thing is gonna last. We don't want everybody rushing in right at first and cleanin' out the shelves."

Eden was smart and grasped that right away. "You're right," she said. "I'll find Father. I just hope Benjy's not swamped already. I'm not sure he'd know what to do."

She caught hold of Bill's hand, squeezed it for a second, and smiled at him. She was so blasted pretty at that moment, he wanted to kiss her, but he didn't figure he ought to delay her. So he just squeezed back and then let her go into the town hall.

Even though the crowd had broken up, the street was still full of people hurrying here and there. A steady hum of frightened talk filled the air. Bill ignored the questions that were directed at him as he moved steadily toward the marshal's office.

When he reached the sturdy stone building that housed the office and jail, he found the front room already crowded. More than a dozen men had already responded to his call for volunteers.

He was glad to see that most of them were younger, unmarried men, although a few older citizens were there, too.

The oldest man in the room was Mordecai Flint, and Bill stopped short in surprise as he realized the old-timer was standing on top of his desk.

"Settle down, settle down," Flint called over the hubbub in the room. He waved his gnarled hands in the air. "I'm the deputy here, doggone it."

The tin star that had once been worn by the previous deputy was pinned to Flint's greasy old buckskin shirt. That badge had been put away in one of the desk drawers.

Bill felt a flash of anger. Flint had gone pawing through the desk, and he didn't have that right.

Bill raised his voice and said, "Quiet. Mr. Flint, get down from there."

"Just tryin' to get things under control, Marshal." Flint hopped down from the desk with a spryness that belied his obvious years.

The men in the office stepped aside to let Bill through. He went to the desk and pulled open the middle drawer. Taking out a pad of paper and a pencil, he set them on the desk and said, "You men who are volunteering, write your names here. Put down whether or not you already have a gun, and what kind if you do."

The men started to crowd up to the desk. Flint said, "Keep it orderly now."

The old-timer took to giving orders real well, Bill thought. Maybe too well. But he had to admit that under Flint's urging, the volunteers formed a rough line and stopped jabbering so much.

While the men were signing up, Flint turned to Bill and said, "We best figure out how many guns and rounds of ammunition we got on hand here."

"That's a good idea. You can do that later. You can count things up and write 'em down, can't you?"

Flint scowled and drew himself up to his full height, which was still a head shorter than Bill.

"Of course I can cipher! You reckon I'm uneducated or somethin', Marshal?"

"I wouldn't know. We never met before today, remember?"

"I'll have you know I went to school for two whole years when I was a younker back in Kaintuck. I can cipher, I can sign my name, and I can even read a mite."

"That's good," Bill said. "A lawman needs to be able to read a little sometimes. Speakin' of which . . . stay out of the desk from now on unless I tell you otherwise."

"You talkin' about this badge? I figured if I didn't have it, folks might not believe you really deputized me." Flint fingered the tin star. "I ain't been in town long. What happened to the last fella who wore this?"

"I killed him," Bill said.

Flint's eyes widened. After a couple of seconds of silence, he burst out, "Are you just gonna leave it at that?"

"Ask somebody else," Bill said. "I'd just as soon not hash it all out again."

The men had finished signing the list of volunteers. Bill turned the paper around, looked it over, and nodded in satisfaction. It looked like all the men owned at least one gun.

"If you know anybody else you think would like to help, talk to them and tell them to look me up," he told the men. "Right now, let's figure out who wants to climb up on the roofs to stand guard and who wants to ride the circuit around the settlement. You heard what Mr. Flint—"

The old-timer cleared his throat meaningfully.

Bill took a deep breath. "You heard what Deputy Flint said," he went on. "Being an outrider is a dangerous job, so keep that in mind. Any man who takes it on needs to have a good, dependable horse and a rifle. Probably be better if you've got a handgun as well."

He paused so they would understand the importance of what he said next.

"You'll be our first line of defense. You'll be taking the biggest risks, and we'll be depending on you the most. So be sure you're ready for that before you volunteer."

The men were quiet for a moment. Several of them exchanged glances.

Then a young man with a thatch of fair hair under a battered hat stepped forward and said, "I'll be an outrider. I've got a fast buckskin pony no Injun can catch, and I'm a fair hand with a rifle."

"What's your name?" Bill asked.

"Aaron Wetherby."

"You married, Aaron?"

Bill thought that was unlikely, since Wetherby was even younger than him, but he figured he needed to ask anyway.

"No, sir, Marshal." A cocky grin appeared on the young-ster's face. "I've still got a heap of wild oats to sow before I settle down."

"Let's hope you live to sow them," Bill said. That prob-ably wasn't the smartest comment in the world to make, but he wanted Wetherby to take this seriously. "Now, who else thinks they can handle the job?"

For the next fifteen minutes, Bill sorted out the tasks and got volunteers for all of them. He drew up a schedule of shifts and saw right away that they were going to be short-handed if nobody else came forward to help.

But this was a start, he told himself. If the Pawnee showed up now, they wouldn't find Redemption com-pletely unprepared. Even though he didn't have any experi-ence fighting Indians, Bill sensed how important that was.

As long as they weren't taken by surprise, they would have a fighting chance.

That was all most folks ever got out of life, anyway.

"I hate a damn cripple," Jacob Fraker said as he watched Fred Smoot roll across the floor of the saloon's main room. "He gives me the fantods."

Luther Macauley said, "The way I heard the story, it's not his fault he's stuck in that chair. Somebody shot him."

Fraker downed the shot of whiskey in his hand and thumped the empty glass back down on the table. "I don't care. A man who ain't whole shouldn't be out in public where people can see him. It's disgusting."

The third man at the table, whose name was Oscar Kipp, asked, "What if you was to lose an arm?"

"Same thing," Fraker said. "If something like that ever happened to me, I reckon I'd drink down a whole bottle of whiskey and then blow my own brains out."

"Seems a mite drastic to me," Macauley said.

Fraker snorted. "Yeah, well, you use words like 'drastic,' whatever the hell that means."

In addition to cripples, Fraker also hated the way Macauley sometimes acted like he was so much smarter than him or Kipp. It was true that Macauley had gone to college down in Louisiana or somewhere, but in the real world that didn't mean squat.

When it came time to figure out how to go about robbing a bank or holding up a train, all the book learning in the world wasn't any help.

That took a man with guts and cunning, and Jacob Fraker had both of those things in spades.

Macauley came in handy for other reasons, though. For example, he could kill a man without blinking, just like Fraker and Kipp. He'd proven that more than once.

Fraker was a lantern-jawed man with dark hair under his tipped-back black Stetson. The hat matched the black leather vest he wore over a faded red shirt and the black gun belt strapped around his lean hips.

In the thirty years Fraker had been on earth, he had killed eight men: two in face-to-face gunfights, six from ambush. He had cut a whore's throat, too, but that didn't count because she had tried to stab and rob him first.

Shocked the hell out of her when he took the knife away from her and carved her a new grin.

He had cleaned out seven banks, stopped and robbed three trains, and even held up a few stagecoaches—he didn't remember how many for sure.

He had been partnered up with Kipp, a big, sandy-haired man with a mustache that hung over his mouth, and Macauley, a skinny blond dandy who had been a tinhorn gambler before turning outlaw, for several years now.

Other hombres came and went sometimes, depending on what sort of job they were looking at, but those three were the core of the gang.

They were also the only ones in Redemption at the moment. They had ridden in a day earlier to take a look around, leaving the rest of the bunch camped in a canyon several miles northwest of the settlement.

And what did they find? A town all worked up over a possible Indian attack. That was just going to complicate things.

But if there was a way to turn the situation to their favor, Fraker thought, he would find it. He always did.

Earlier today they had stood on the edge of the crowd, listening to that kid marshal and those stuffed-shirt politicians on the town council talking about how the Pawnee might raid the town and how they had to get ready. With all the talk about hostiles, nobody had given the three hardbitten strangers a second glance.

Night had fallen now, and those guards the marshal had recruited were out there somewhere in the darkness trying to protect the town.

The possibility of an Indian attack was still all that the people in the saloon could talk about. Fraker listened to the buzz of conversation in the room and heard the fear in their voices.

Those yokels just don't know what they really ought to be scared of, Fraker told himself with a faint smile as he poured another drink from the bottle in the center of the table.

Sometimes the real threats came from within, where folks hardly ever thought to look.

Kipp leaned forward and said, "You reckon we ought to get out of town while the gettin's good, Jake? I'd sure hate to run into those Pawnee."

"Getting out of town's the last thing we need to do," Fraker snapped. "There's no proof those Indians are anywhere near here."

"Anyway, we're safer here than we would be elsewhere," Macauley pointed out. "It's the boys out at the canyon who really have something to worry about . . . and they probably don't even know it."

Fraker had thought about the rest of the men in the gang.

If that war party jumped them, they might not have a chance.

But life was full of risk, he reminded himself. There were no guarantees.

Except that no matter what the situation, he would find a way to make some money out of it.

"The boys can take care of themselves," Fraker said. "As for us, we're staying right here in Redemption." He lifted his glass and looked at the amber liquid in it. "And we're not leaving until we're rich men, Pawnee or no Pawnee."

Chapter 13

Costigan's pulse hammered wildly inside his head as he listened to the distant shots. There was no doubt in his mind what they meant.

"Come on!" he said to Captain Stone. "We've got to go help them!"

"Wait!" Stone said. "You said the Indians' trail is here."

Costigan yanked his horse into a tight circle and leveled an arm toward the south.

"But now they're *there*, you idiot! They're attacking the hunting party!"

"We don't know that. Perhaps your friends are firing at the buffalo herd."

Hutton said, "Beggin' your pardon, Cap'n, but Costigan's right. That ain't the sort of shootin' they'd be doin' if they were killin' buffalo. They're tryin' to *keep* from gettin' killed."

"The hell with all of you," Costigan said. He jammed his heels into his horse's flanks and sent the animal leaping into a gallop.

Behind him, he heard Stone shout, "Sergeant! Sergeant! Stop that man!"

No shots rang out. Either Hutton was being slow about
following the order . . . or he wasn't obeying it to start
with.

Costigan didn't care which it was. He leaned forward in
the saddle and raised his left hand to hold his hat on as the
wind threatened to pluck it from his head. His horse raced
southward, toward the sound of battle.

Not the first time, he thought. Not the first time he had
hurried toward death while it claimed those who were his
friends.

If he had been the sort of man to pray, he would have
sent a plea heavenward right about then, a prayer that Mc-
Ginty and the others would survive until he got there to
help them.

It had been years since he had believed that anybody
was up there to hear his prayers, though, so he concentrated
on keeping the horse from stepping in a prairie dog hole or
tripping on some other obstacle instead. That was the best
thing he could do right now.

After a few minutes, curiosity made him look back over
his shoulder. Dust boiled up in a cloud behind him. The
troopers were coming after him, whether to arrest him or
help him, Costigan didn't know. With the lead he had on
them, he didn't think they were going to catch him.

With his horse's hooves pounding the ground the way
they were, he couldn't hear the shots anymore. After he had
covered a couple of miles, he reined in for a moment after
checking to see that the cavalry patrol hadn't narrowed the
gap between them.

Breathing hard, Costigan sat there and listened. He
didn't hear any shots . . . because there weren't any to hear.

The prairie was silent except for the faint moaning of
the wind.

Or was it the moaning of dead spirits? Costigan asked
himself. Had the rest of the hunting party been wiped out?

"Hyaaah!" he said as he kicked his mount into a run
again. He knew he was asking a lot of the horse, but he
would ride it right into the ground if he had to.

I should have stayed with the others.

That thought echoed through his head. It didn't matter that Stone and Bledsoe both had ordered him to accompany the patrol.

Nor was it important that other than Dave McGinty, he didn't particularly like any of the other men in the hunting party. He had signed on to come out here with them. They were all partners, in a way, and if they had fallen into danger, he should have been there with them.

A dark mass bulked on the horizon. The buffalo herd, Costigan thought when he spotted it. The hunting party would be somewhere near the herd.

A couple of minutes later, he saw the wagons parked off to his right and veered in that direction. He fully expected that when he galloped up to the vehicles, he would find the bodies of McGinty, Bledsoe, and all the others littered on the ground around the wagons, bristling with arrows and probably scalped and mutilated.

He wasn't prepared for what he found instead.

A lot of shots had been fired here. The air still carried the acrid tang of burned powder. Men holding rifles stood around the wagons. They weren't dead after all, Costigan thought as his heart slugged. They had survived.

But there were bodies on the ground anyway. More than a dozen of them in buckskin leggings and breechcloths. Their coppery bodies were bloody and torn apart where they had been riddled with lead.

Costigan slowed his horse to a halt and sat there looking around at the carnage. None of the members of the hunting party paid any attention to him at first. They seemed as stunned as Costigan was.

Then Dave McGinty turned his head and looked at Costigan with haunted eyes. His voice was hoarse with strain when he spoke.

"We didn't know, Ward. I swear we didn't know."

Costigan knew what McGinty was talking about.

All the Indians appeared to be no more than fourteen or fifteen years old.

McGinty's words seemed to snap Bledsoe out of his reverie. The colonel looked at Costigan and said, "They're all savages, by God! We have nothing to apologize for. They're savages!"

Costigan swung down from his saddle and stepped over to McGinty. A glance to the north told him that the cavalry patrol was still headed in this direction. The column of dust steadily drew closer.

"Tell me what happened, Dave," Costigan said.

Bledsoe stomped over, his face a mottled red.

"I'll tell you what happened!" he said before McGinty could respond. "We acted in self-defense to save ourselves from those bloodthirsty Pawnee!"

Costigan lost his temper. His hands shot out, grabbed the lapels of Bledsoe's suit coat, and shoved the colonel against one of the hide wagons.

"Shut up! I want to know what really happened, and I want to know fast, before Stone and the rest of those troopers get here."

"What does it matter?" Bledsoe asked with a sneer. "We didn't do anything wrong. Not one damned thing."

Behind his bravado, though, his eyes were filled with fear. Costigan saw that plain as day.

McGinty wiped the back of his hand across his mouth and said, "We came up on the herd, just like we expected to. But there was a bunch of redskins already goin' after those buffs. When they saw us, they charged us, whoopin' and yellin' and wavin' their bows in the air. We couldn't tell they were just kids, Ward. I swear we couldn't."

Costigan walked over to one of the corpses and looked down at it. The Indian youngster's face was twisted from his death agonies.

But it didn't bear even a trace of paint.

"They aren't painted for war," Costigan said. "Not one of them. You couldn't see that?"

Tolbert and Browne came up, cradling their buffalo rifles in their arms. Browne said, "What are you accusin' us of, Costigan? Are you sayin' we murdered these savages?"

"They came at us first," Tolbert added.

Costigan took his hat off and wearily rubbed his other hand over his face.

"They were scared of you," he said in a voice so quiet it was almost a whisper. "They were hunting, like their fathers and their fathers before that hunted, and then all of you came up, and they were scared. So they tried to run you off, because they were just kids and they weren't thinking straight." He looked around. "Did they have any rifles?"

"No," McGinty said. "Just the bows and arrows."

"They couldn't have hurt you. At worst, you could have shot the ponies out from under them."

"You weren't here, by God!" Bledsoe said. "Don't you judge us, you son of a bitch! You weren't here."

"No, but I am now. And so's the cavalry."

Costigan turned his back on the corpse-littered plains and walked over to one of the wagons. He didn't even notice the stink coming from it as he lowered the tailgate and sat on it, suddenly too tired to stand up anymore.

They came through the wheat field, the Stars and Bars waving in the sun, a piper somewhere in their midst piping "Dixie," an officer in front carrying his sword above his head as he led his troops into battle. The sun was bright and warm, and a breeze ruffled the stalks of wheat.

In the trees, Costigan lifted his spyglass to his eye. It was his job to kill that officer, and as soon as his shot rang out, all the other troops in the trees would fire, too. The battle would be joined.

Costigan peered through the lens and settled the glass on the commanding officer. His breath hissed through his teeth as he saw that the man had to be seventy-five years old, at least. He swung the glass to the soldiers in the front rank of the Confederate troops advancing through the field.

Children. Boys as young as ten, none older than fourteen or fifteen.

But they had muskets in their hands, muskets that could kill no matter how old the fingers that pulled the triggers.

A hand fell on Costigan's shoulder. "Corporal, kill that officer!" a major ordered. "What are you waiting for?"

Costigan lowered the telescope and turned his head. "They're children," he said. "An old man and children."

"What?" The major snatched away the glass and looked through it. He handed it back a moment later and said, "I don't care. They're still Rebs. Now you kill that old bastard, or I'll have you in front of a firing squad."

Costigan swallowed hard. Then he lifted the sharpshooter's rifle to his shoulder, settled the sights on his target . . .

And pulled the trigger.

The rattle of hoofbeats washed away the memories. He looked up and saw that Captain Stone, Sergeant Hutton, and the rest of the patrol had arrived on the scene of the massacre.

Stone signaled a halt. As the riders came to a stop and the dust began to settle, Sergeant Hutton looked at the bodies and muttered, "Good Lord."

Without dismounting, Stone said, "I must admit, I'm surprised to see that you and your men are still alive, Mr. Bledsoe. It appears that you gave a good account of yourselves when the savages attacked."

Costigan stood up from the tailgate and turned toward Stone. "A good account?" he repeated before Bledsoe could say anything. "Those are just kids!"

"And what do you think those *kids* would have done if they caught a white man alone out here?" Stone demanded.

Costigan's mouth tightened. Much as he hated to admit it, the captain had a point. Chances were, in a situation like that, the hunting party would have taken a lone traveler prisoner, then tortured and killed him.

But that wasn't what had happened. In this case, the young Pawnee hadn't had a chance.

"They charged us," Bledsoe said. "We acted in self-defense, Captain. Sure, it looks bad now, but we couldn't tell at first that they weren't full-grown warriors."

Costigan glanced at McGinty. The shamed expression

on the man's bearded face told Costigan that Bledsoe was lying.

Maybe when the first shots rang out, the hunters really hadn't realized how old the Indians were. But they had figured it out pretty quickly and kept firing anyway. On edge already because of the way the Indians had been hanging around the area for the past couple of days, once the men started pulling the triggers, they hadn't been able to stop.

Costigan understood what had happened and why it had happened. He wanted to think that if he'd been here, things would have been different.

But remembering that day in the wheat field, in the closing weeks of the war when the Confederacy was down to old men and boys to fight its battles, he couldn't be sure he would have stopped this massacre. He just couldn't.

"What are you going to do about this, Captain?" Bledsoe went on.

Stone shook his head. "There doesn't appear to be anything to do. You've already handled the situation." He paused. "To be honest, I'm surprised that a band such as this caused so much of an uproar from one end of the state to the other. How in the world did they ever manage to stop a train?"

The sergeant scratched his grizzled jaw and said, "Maybe this ain't them, Cap'n."

Stone turned to him with a frown. "What do you mean, Sergeant?"

"Maybe this is just part of the bunch," Hutton said. "That chief, Spotted Dog, could've sent these boys out to do a little huntin'. The rest of the renegades could be somewhere else around here."

The same thought had occurred to Costigan. The group of riders he had seen in the distance the day before had been considerably larger than this little hunting party.

"Do you think so?" Stone asked with sudden eagerness. "Then perhaps we could follow their trail and locate the other hostiles that way."

Bledsoe spoke up again, saying, "The one who took off left a good trail, that's for sure."

Costigan's head jerked toward the man. "What do you mean, Colonel, by 'the one who took off'?"

"The savage that got away, of course," Bledsoe said. "I think he was wounded, but he managed to stay on his pony. He turned the animal around and galloped off when it became obvious we were about to wipe out the rest of his fellows."

Costigan and Hutton looked at each other. Costigan could tell by the look in the sergeant's eyes that Hutton understood how bad this was.

"Colonel," Costigan said, "you'd better turn these wagons around and hightail it out of here."

"What? But the wagons are empty and the buffalo are right there!"

"I don't care. Unless I miss my guess, all hell's about to come rainin' down on you."

"Sergeant, what's this man talking about?" Stone asked.

"Well, Cap'n . . . that wounded boy who got away, he's gonna head back to the rest of the bunch and tell Spotted Dog what happened here," Hutton explained. "And then Spotted Dog and the rest of his warriors . . . they're gonna come lookin' for blood."

Chapter 14

Hutton's words of warning just seemed to excite Stone more.

"Then we won't have to search as hard for the hostiles," he said. "They'll be coming to us."

"Cap'n—"

"This is actually a stroke of luck," Stone went on, ignoring the sergeant. He turned to Bledsoe. "Show me which way the surviving Indian fled."

Bledsoe at least had the good sense to look worried as he pointed and said, "The redskin took off almost due west."

"Then that's the way we'll go. Under the circumstances, it's unlikely he tried to leave any sort of false trail. Wounded as he was, the savage no doubt took the most direct path back to the remainder of the war party."

Costigan was starting to have some doubts, even if Stone wasn't. What sort of war party took along a bunch of boys like this? Did they have women with them as well as children?

Maybe Spotted Dog hadn't set out to make war at all. Maybe he just wanted to lead his people off the reservation in a last attempt to live the way they always had before the white men came.

Costigan didn't know, and it didn't really matter, he told himself. Once Spotted Dog heard about the slaughter that had happened here, he and his warriors would be painting themselves for war.

The blood of those young men would cry out for vengeance.

As the cavalry patrol was preparing to move out again, Bledsoe turned to his drivers and ordered, "Get those wagons turned around. We'll go back to the main camp for now, until the threat's over."

"That's not going to do you any good," Costigan said. "If the Pawnee come after us, we're liable to be outnumbered two or three to one, maybe more. The camp's out in the open and can't be defended against odds like that. They'll overrun us for sure."

"Well, then, what do you want us to do, Costigan?" Tolbert asked harshly. "Just sit here and wait for the damned savages to wipe us out?"

Costigan shook his head. "We need a place to hole up for a while. A settlement, maybe."

Browne said, "Dodge City's a long way off, and we can't move all that fast with those wagons."

"Maybe we ought to leave the wagons," McGinty suggested. "We could unhitch the teams, and the drivers and skinners could ride those horses."

Bledsoe shook his head. "I'm not leaving my wagons. They cost too much for that. And by God, there's a small fortune in hides at the main camp! Are you saying we should just abandon them, Costigan?"

"The Indians won't care about those hides," Costigan said. "We can go back and get them later."

"Some other hunting party could come along and steal them!"

Costigan shrugged. "What's more important to you, Colonel? The hides or your life?"

Bledsoe didn't answer immediately. He had to think about the question first.

Captain Stone had ordered his men to dismount and take a few minutes to rest their horses before they moved out again. That respite was over now. As Sergeant Hutton bellowed orders, the troopers began to swing back up into their saddles.

Bledsoe said, "I suppose it wouldn't hurt to head for somewhere safer for a few days. It won't take long for Captain Stone and his men to deal with this threat."

Costigan agreed with the first part of that statement but not the second. The cavalry patrol, like the hunting party, numbered a couple of dozen men.

They might have superior firepower, but that probably wouldn't be enough to offset the odds against them.

Hutton knew that, too. Costigan saw the fatalistic look in the sergeant's eyes. Stone was bound and determined to lead them right into trouble, and there was nothing Hutton could do to change his mind.

Glory hunters, Costigan thought. Most of the time, all they did was get good men killed.

Raising dust again, the patrol galloped off to the west. As the soldiers dwindled from sight, Bledsoe's drivers turned the wagons around so they pointed east. The colonel stubbornly refused to leave them behind, even though they would slow the party down.

While they were doing that, Bledsoe delved into the saddlebags on his mount and pulled out a folded piece of paper.

"What's that?" Costigan asked.

"A map. I commanded a regiment, you know. I believe in being prepared."

Now that he was doing something, some of Bledsoe's natural arrogance came back to him. It was easier to push aside the fear when you were busy, Costigan supposed.

Bledsoe spread the map out on the lowered tailgate where Costigan had been sitting earlier. He leaned over it and frowned as he studied it. Several of the hunters crowded around him.

"Where do you reckon we should go, Colonel?" Tolbert asked.

Bledsoe pointed to a spot on the map. "As near as I can figure, this is about where we are now." He traced a line to the east. "That's our main camp." His finger moved off to the northeast. "And Dodge is that way."

"Then there's not really anything closer than Dodge," Browne said.

Costigan leaned in to look at the map. He said, "Yes, there is. It's not much closer, but half a day might make a difference."

"What are you talking about?" Bledsoe asked.

"When we get to the main camp, if we keep going due east instead of angling to the north, we can make it to that little settlement right there"—Costigan's finger rested on a dot on the map—"faster than we can get to Dodge City."

Bledsoe grunted. "I think you're right, Costigan. I never heard of the place, but its name sounds promising . . . Redemption."

The night had passed quietly, and Bill was grateful for that. He hadn't slept much, but despite his weariness he was able to return the smiles and nods the townspeople gave him as he walked toward the marshal's office.

Folks were making an effort to go on about their business normally, but when Bill looked close, he saw the fear in their eyes. He saw the worried glances they cast over their shoulders at every little sound.

Everybody was keyed up, waiting for warning shots from the guards, or worse yet, war whoops from a band of bloodthirsty painted savages.

As Bill stepped into the office, he smelled coffee. That was one of the advantages of having a deputy, he thought. Mordecai Flint must have put the pot on to boil.

The office was unlocked and empty. Bill didn't know where Flint was. Out looking around town, more than likely.

The old-timer had volunteered to stay in the office overnight, and Bill had accepted the offer. He wanted to be with Eden as much as he could during this time of trouble, although he wouldn't neglect his duties to do so.

The coffee smelled like it was ready, so he got one of the tin cups and filled it. The first sip of the hot brew made his eyes open wider. Flint had made the coffee strong enough to get up and walk around on its own two feet.

A step in the doorway made Bill look around. Aaron Wetherby stood there looking tired.

"The next shift of outriders just took over, Marshal," the young man reported. "I'm gonna go get some shut-eye."

"Thanks, Aaron. Any problems?"

Aaron shook his head. "It was mighty quiet and peaceful out there last night. Marshal . . . what if that cavalry captain had it wrong? What if there *aren't* any Pawnee on the warpath?"

"I reckon I'd rather get ready for trouble and not have it show up than the other way around." Bill nodded toward the potbellied stove in the corner. "Want some coffee?"

"No, thanks. Like I said, I'm gonna go get some sleep. I'll be ready to take my turn again tonight."

"Obliged," Bill said with a nod.

He needed to round up some more volunteers today, he thought after Aaron left. Otherwise the men he had assigned to guard duty were going to get mighty tired. And a worn-out man wasn't nearly as alert as one who had gotten enough rest.

He ought to take his own advice, he thought as he sat down at the desk. He had tossed and turned most of the night, not only keeping himself awake but Eden, too.

Flint came in a few minutes later. Despite being up all night, the old-timer appeared to be wide-awake.

"I done mornin' rounds for you, Marshal," he said. "This place is plumb peaceful. If it wasn't for worryin' about Injuns, there wouldn't be a damned thing goin' on."

Bill smiled. "That's the way I like it."

"Not me. I like a town with some hoopla, like Abilene in the old days, or San Francisco."

"Those Pawnee show up, you'll get your hoopla."

Flint headed for the coffee. "Yeah, that makes it kinda hard to know what to hope for, don't it?"

"If you want to get some breakfast and then turn in for a while, that'll be fine. The Nilssons' café has the best food in town."

"Naw, I'm fine," Flint said. "I'll catch a catnap later. I never sleep more'n a couple hours a day. When you get old, you start to realize you only got so many hours left, and I never was one to waste 'em sleepin'."

Bill sipped his coffee and thought about that. Flint might be right that people became more aware of the sand running through the hourglass when they got older . . . but it was falling all the time, right from the moment a fella drew his first breath.

One day closer to the grave. That's what the sun coming up every morning really meant.

He shoved those dark musings out of his head. There were more pressing concerns at the moment. He stood up and said, "If you don't mind staying here for a while longer, Mr. Flint, I'll go see if I can find some more volunteers for guard duty."

"Sure, I'm fine. And you can call me Mordecai."

Bill shook his head. "I was raised to respect my elders. And I reckon you're old enough to be my grandpaw." He smiled as he headed for the door. "Maybe my great-grandpaw."

"At least I ain't a wet-behind-the-ears kid!" Flint called after him as he left the office.

Bill walked over to the mercantile. Eden, her father, and Benjy Cobb were all there already. Eden and Perry Monroe were helping customers while Cobb unloaded airtights from a crate and stacked the canned peaches and tomatoes on a shelf.

Half a dozen customers were lined up at the counter.

Bill had expected to see even more people stocking up on supplies. He supposed the townspeople had listened to what he said the day before about not starting a rush for the goods on the shelves of Redemption's stores.

There would be enough of everything to go around and to last until the trouble was over . . . if they were lucky.

"Busy morning?" Bill asked his father-in-law between customers several minutes later.

Monroe grunted. "Steady, real steady. If it keeps up, you may have to put on an apron again, Bill."

"Not hardly," Bill replied with a grin. During his recuperation after the injury to his leg, he had helped out in the store as soon as he was on his feet again, as a way to pay back Eden and her father for what they had done for him, but that was enough clerking to last him the rest of his life. "I've got another job now."

"I was just joshing," Monroe said. "Anything I can help you with today?"

"I need some more volunteers to stand guard. Don't reckon you have any on the shelves."

Monroe shook his head. "No, but if I talk to anybody who might be interested, I'll send 'em your way."

"That's what I was thinking. Much obliged."

He stepped over to Eden and was about to hug her and give her a quick kiss on the cheek, but she was waiting on a customer and the glance she sent his way told him to back off and not bother her while she was working.

Discretion being the better part of valor, according to the old saying, Bill just smiled and said, "I'll see you later."

Eden flashed him a smile in return. That would do for now, Bill thought as he left the mercantile.

His next stop was the livery stable, where Josiah Hartnett greeted him and said, "Sign me up for guard duty tonight, Bill. I'm too heavy to make much of a fast rider, but I've got good eyes and ears and I can sit on a rooftop."

"Thanks," Bill said. "I was hopin' more folks would step up today. Would you rather take the first or second shift?"

"First, I think. That'll let me sleep a little before I have to keep the stable open again tomorrow."

Bill nodded. "Come on over to the marshal's office after supper. I'll have it figured out by then where we need you."

Leo Kellogg and Charley Hobbs made the same offer when Bill stopped by their places later, and he wondered if the members of the council had gotten together and decided it would be good for the town's morale if they volunteered.

Or maybe they had come to that decision on their own. Bill didn't know and it didn't really matter. He was just glad for the extra help.

During the day, several more men came by the marshal's office or stopped him on the street to tell him they wanted to help. Bill thanked them all and promised that their efforts would be put to good use.

Given enough time, most people would do the right thing, he told himself. Sometimes they just had to talk themselves into it.

That evening, he and Mordecai Flint stood on the boardwalk in front of the marshal's office, each of them sipping coffee from a tin cup.

Fresh volunteers were on the roofs of several buildings in town, and a new crop of outriders patrolled a large circle around the settlement. Bill looked along the street at the barrels that had been stacked up here and there, as Flint had suggested, and he was comfortable with the thought that he had done all he could to get ready for trouble, at least for now.

That comfort didn't last long, because Flint sighed and said, "I got a bad feelin' in my bones."

"Rheumatism, maybe?"

Flint snorted. "You know danged well what I mean, Marshal. Somethin' bad's out there, and it's headed this way. My bones ain't never wrong."

Even though Bill had known Mordecai Flint for only a day and a half, his instincts told him to trust the old man.

He said, "Do those bones tell you when it's gonna get here?"

"No, and that's the problem. But it's like the same feelin' I get before it rains. Just a damned annoyin' ache that tells me somethin's wrong."

"Maybe it's just another thunderstorm on the way."

Flint shook his head. "I wish it was, Marshal. I surely do."

Chapter 15

Sergeant Jasper Hutton had been in the army nigh on to thirty years and had lived through the Mexican War and the War between the States.

He had smelled more powder smoke and felt the hot breath of more musket balls and rifle bullets passing close to his head than any man ought to have to.

But in all those times, he had never felt closer to death than he did right now.

When Captain Stone called a halt to rest the patrol's horses, Hutton approached the commanding officer and said, "Beggin' your pardon, Cap'n, but are you sure—"

Stone didn't let him finish. "Have you ever noticed, Sergeant, how many of your comments are prefaced by the words, 'Begging your pardon, Captain?' It's as if you know you shouldn't be making them."

Hutton tightened his jaw against the anger that threatened to boil up inside him.

"It's my job to take care of these men, sir. That's why I speak up."

"Well, you're certainly incorrect about that. Your job is to follow my orders." Stone fixed him with a hard stare.

"That's your *only* job, Sergeant. And as for whether or not I'm sure about whatever you were going to ask me, the answer is yes. I'm sure. Otherwise I wouldn't be doing it. And *that* is all you need to know."

Stone turned away, making it clear that the conversation was over.

Hutton sighed and went back to the men, who had dismounted and stood holding their horses' reins. One of them, a young trooper named Watson, said, "The captain's gonna get us in trouble, isn't he, Sarge?"

"Keep your voice down," Hutton said. "In this man's army, enlisted men don't go around questionin' officers. They know what they're doin'."

"But if they don't, they're liable to get us killed."

Hutton glared at Watson. "What'd you think signin' up for the army meant, boy? That you'd just sit around smellin' rosewater and pickin' daisies all day?"

"I never said that, Sarge. But what if there's a whole mess of Indians out there waitin' for us?"

"Then we'll engage the hostiles at Captain Stone's command."

Hutton's flat tone made it clear there wasn't going to be any argument.

A few minutes later, the troopers mounted up again and rode west after Stone lifted his right hand above his head and waved it forward in a dramatic gesture.

Sergeant Hutton's gaze roamed constantly over the mostly flat landscape around them. At least if they met the Pawnee, they ought to have some warning, he thought. A man could see for a long way out here.

But Hutton was experienced enough to know how skilled Indians were at concealing themselves. Because of that, he stayed alert.

Not that it would do any good, he thought. If the Pawnee wanted them, the painted devils would find a way to get to them.

The cavalry rode for several hours, putting the site of the massacre far behind them. As Hutton's horse plodded along a short distance behind the captain's mount, Stone turned his head and said over his shoulder, "I don't think there are any hostiles out here."

He sounded both disappointed and disgusted.

"Might not be a good idea to say somethin' like that, Cap'n," Hutton replied.

"Why? Because it's tempting fate?"

"Well . . . that's sort of what I had in mind, sir."

Stone snorted and said, "I don't believe in fate, Sergeant. I believe in preparation and strategy. Those are the things that win the day, not blind luck, which is what most people mean when they talk about fate."

"Every man has a destiny, Cap'n."

"Nonsense. Each man *makes* his own destiny."

Hutton didn't believe that for a second, but he didn't see any point in continuing to argue with the captain, either. No noncom ever won an argument with an officer.

And if that wasn't destiny, he didn't know what was.

At least Stone didn't seem to have brought down any bad luck on them by speculating that there weren't any Indians out here. The patrol rode on without seeing anything more threatening than a prairie dog.

Hutton couldn't relax, though. He kept looking around, searching the landscape for any sign of trouble.

Despite the sergeant's vigilance, it was Captain Stone who had the first inkling that something was wrong. "What's that?" he said abruptly.

Hutton was checking their back trail when the captain spoke. His head jerked around and he looked ahead of them again.

A lone rider had popped up on the prairie about two hundred yards ahead of them, seemingly out of nowhere. Hutton had looked up there just a few seconds earlier, and no one had been in sight then.

"Cap'n, better hold it," he warned.

"There's no reason to be afraid, Sergeant. It's only one man on horseback."

But even as Stone spoke, another rider appeared next to

the first one, then another. From the way they climbed into view, Hutton knew the ground had to drop off up there, even though they couldn't see it from here. Might be a little gully, or more likely a wider arroyo, maybe even an actual valley.

Whatever it was, it was big enough to hide quite a few riders, because now a steady stream of mounted figures was appearing in front of the patrol. A dozen men were in sight already, with more showing up every second.

"Halt!" Hutton bellowed. "Halt!"

Stone reined in and whirled his horse. "Sergeant Hutton!" his voice lashed out. "How dare you give an order without me telling you to?"

"Cap'n," Hutton said, and his voice sounded strained and hollow in his ears, "you better take a closer look up yonder."

Stone watched the riders appear for a moment. They numbered more than two dozen now.

"All right, so there are slightly more of them than there are of us," Stone admitted. "We're better armed, and we're the United States Cavalry, for God's sake! You don't honestly believe that we're not a match for a bunch of ragtag savages straight off the reservation, do you, Sergeant?"

Hutton heard the frightened muttering from the troopers behind them. He snapped his head around and yelled, "Quiet back there!"

"Oh, dear," Stone said.

At least fifty Indians were in sight now, forming a line across the prairie in front of the patrol. They continued to appear. The breeze that blew across the plains made the feathers stuck in their hair move back and forth. Hutton thought their faces were painted, but he couldn't be sure about that.

At least he couldn't confirm that with his eyes.

He knew in his heart that the Pawnee were painted for war.

"Sergeant, what should we do?" Stone asked.

Now he wants my advice, Hutton thought.

"Should we attempt a retreat?"

"Wouldn't do any good," Hutton said. "Their ponies are probably fresher. We can't outrun them. They'd just pick us off one by one." He looked back at the men. "Dismount and form firing lines."

"But there are too many of them!" Stone said, his voice breaking with panic now. Close to a hundred Pawnee warriors sat waiting for the signal to attack. "We can't hope to defeat them."

A faint smile touched Hutton's lips as he said, "Then I guess that's our destiny, isn't it, Cap'n? And I reckon you're right after all. We made it ourselves."

The hunting party made steady progress across the plains and reached the main camp at midafternoon. Colonel Bledsoe told the men who had been left there to guard the hides to gather their gear and get ready to ride.

Bledsoe sighed in regret as he looked out over the prairie that was dark with drying buffalo hides.

"I'd bet you anything they won't be there when we get back," he said to Costigan in a bitter voice.

"I think they will be," Costigan said. "And even if they're not, you'll be alive to hunt more buffalo, Colonel. Isn't that more important?"

Bledsoe nodded. "Of course it is. But I can't really afford to lose that much money, either. Damn those Indians!"

The colonel was directing his curse the wrong way, Costigan thought. They wouldn't be in any danger if the hunters hadn't gotten trigger-happy.

But it wouldn't do any good to point that out, so he didn't.

When the other men were ready to go, the group moved out again, wagon wheels creaking as they rolled across the ground. The party now numbered thirty men, a good-sized force.

As tough and well-armed as they were, anybody would think twice about tackling them.

But Costigan knew they wouldn't be any match for a

large band of Pawnee warriors. He wished he had gotten a better look at those riders he had seen the day before. If they had been closer, he might have been able to estimate how many there were.

As it was, the possibility that there could be fifty, sixty, maybe even a hundred of the hostiles out there looking for them gnawed at Costigan's guts. Even with the young men dead, the hunting party could still be vastly outnumbered.

As far as he could remember, Captain Stone hadn't ever mentioned how many of the Indians had slipped off the reservation with Spotted Dog. And there was no guarantee that they hadn't joined up with other renegades since then.

Costigan wondered where Stone and the rest of the cavalrymen were now. He hoped for the best for them—even though Stone was a stiff-necked jackass—but he had a hunch they were heading straight into trouble . . . if they hadn't found it already.

"Ward, you look like somebody just kissed your wife and kicked your dog."

Costigan hadn't noticed McGinty riding beside him. He looked over, summoned up a smile, and said, "I don't have either one of those things, Dave. Had a dog when I was a boy, but no woman's ever been foolish enough to marry me."

"I was married once, you know."

McGinty kept looking behind him as he spoke, and Costigan knew the man was trying to distract himself from worrying about the Pawnee.

"No, I didn't know that."

"Yeah." McGinty scowled. "She up and ran off with another fella. A telegrapher, of all things. Hell, he wasn't even a gambler or a gunfighter or anything like that. He was more borin' than I was!"

Obviously not to Mrs. McGinty, Costigan thought. He was too fond of the bearded man to say that.

"I'm just glad we didn't have any kids," McGinty went on. "I was able to pick up and head west. That helped me to forget all about her. Only I ain't. Forgotten about her, that is."

"It's hard to forget the things that make us what we are."

"Ain't that the damned, disgustin' truth." McGinty looked back again. "We're gonna die, aren't we, Ward?"

"Hard to say."

McGinty cleared his throat and said, "I can't tell you how sorry I am about those redskins. I shot at 'em, too, you know. Everybody did. Once the guns started goin' off . . . I just couldn't stop myself from pullin' the trigger. I know it ain't no excuse . . . but I never got a good look at 'em and saw how young they were until . . . until it was all over."

Costigan didn't look over at his friend. He thought tears might be glistening on McGinty's weathered, bearded cheeks, and if that was true, he didn't want to see them.

"Everybody makes mistakes," he said. "I joined the army thinking I was gonna go off and do something good. But most of the time it was just killing. Both sides stood there and shot each other like they were buffalo instead of boys in blue and gray."

Before Costigan could dwell any more on the past, he heard a shout from somewhere in the group behind him. He and McGinty reined up and turned in their saddles to look.

"It's the Injuns!" Tolbert bellowed. "By God, the redskins are back there!"

The wagon drivers yelled and lashed at the teams with their whips. Riders slashed their mounts with their reins. The animals lunged ahead and broke into gallops. Riders held their hats on while the drivers struggled to control the rattling, bouncing wagons.

Costigan and McGinty were swept along with the flood. Costigan tried to look back to see what they were fleeing from, but it was hopeless. Dust and terror clogged the air and made it impossible to see anything.

After a few minutes at a dead run, the horses had to slow down. Costigan pulled his mount back to a walk, then a stop.

"Ward, what're you doin'?" McGinty called as Costigan

swung down from the saddle with his Henry rifle in his hands.

"I don't feel like running today," Costigan said. His eyes narrowed as he squinted back in the direction the hunting party had come from.

McGinty had stopped as well. The others were pulling away from them.

"Ward, come on," McGinty urged. "We can't take on the Pawnee by ourselves!"

"I don't see any Pawnee." Costigan swept a hand toward the western horizon. "Do you?"

Now that the others had moved on, the dust began to clear. As McGinty peered to the west, he saw what Costigan did . . . nothing but empty plains.

"There's nobody chasin' us," McGinty said.

"Not right now, anyway."

"But then what was all the yellin' and runnin' about?"

"Fear," Costigan said. "But a man can't outrun that."

He mounted again, and he and McGinty rode after the others and spread the word that the Pawnee weren't behind them after all.

When the group stopped a short time later to rest the horses, Bledsoe gave them all a disgusted look and said, "I don't know who let out the first yell, but next time make sure there's something to be alarmed about before you open your mouth. We can't afford to run these animals into the ground."

The colonel was right about that. When they pushed on again, it was at a more deliberate pace.

When the sun went down, there was no discussion of stopping because it would soon be dark. Everyone wanted to push on and put as much distance between them and the vengeful Pawnee as they could.

"You can steer by the stars, can't you, Costigan?" Bledsoe asked as the pinpricks of light began to appear in the blue black heavens above the Kansas plains.

"Yeah, pretty well. I can keep us going east."

"You do that, then," Bledsoe said. "You'll take the

lead. Eventually we'll have to stop for a few hours to let the horses rest for longer, but right now I want to keep moving."

Costigan knew everyone in the group felt the same way. He nodded and heeled his horse into a trot that carried them out in front of the hunting party.

McGinty didn't accompany him this time, and Costigan was glad. He was a loner by nature, and even a semblance of solitude was welcome right now.

He could still hear the men coming along a short distance behind him, though, and the night breezes were out of the west as well, carrying not only the thud of hoofbeats, the squeal of wagon wheels on axles, and the clink of bit chains, but also the stink from the wagons.

There was no peace to be had. Not tonight, and probably not anytime soon.

Maybe when they reached that town called Redemption, Costigan thought.

Chapter 16

Bill slept better the next two nights. A fella can only stay keyed up and on edge for so long a time, he thought. Then his body takes over and makes him rest.

It wasn't just that. Nothing had happened. Redemption was as peaceful as ever.

More peaceful than it had been when he first came here, he told himself. People weren't getting shot in the back now.

But despite the outward calm, the citizens were still worried, even fearful. Bill heard it in their voices when he talked to them. They still thought something was going to happen.

He stopped in at the marshal's office on the evening of the third day, after making rounds. Mordecai Flint was there, dozing on the sofa. The old-timer's eyes snapped open as Bill came in.

Flint sat up and said, "I wasn't asleep. I was just restin' my eyes."

"There's nothing wrong with getting a little shut-eye when you can, Mr. Flint," Bill told him. "You've been staying up all night, every night, and most of the day, too. You must be worn out by now."

"Not a bit," Flint insisted. "I'm fine as frog hair. Told you, I don't need much sleep."

Bill hung his hat on the nail beside the door. "Whatever you say."

"Darn right whatever I say," Flint responded with a snort. "Anything goin' on out there?"

Bill shook his head. "Not a blessed thing."

Flint rubbed his left shoulder with his right hand and shook his head. "I don't understand it. My bones are still pitchin' a holy fit. Somethin's gonna happen, I tell you."

"I think everybody in town feels the same way. I know I do."

"Yeah, but you ain't got bones like I do. I ever tell you about the time a bunch of trappers I was with got jumped by a passel o' Blackfeet up in Montana?"

"I don't think so," Bill said as he sat down behind the desk. "We've only known each other less than a week. I reckon you've got a lot of stories I haven't heard yet."

"Oh, a whole heap of 'em," Flint agreed. "But if you keep me on as deputy, I'll get around to all of 'em."

"You want the job permanent-like?"

That surprised Bill. He had figured that a fiddle-footed old pelican like Flint would move on as soon as the threat from the Pawnee was over.

Instead Flint scratched his bearded jaw and said, "I been givin' it some thought. You might not know it to look at me, but I ain't as young as I used to be. Fella gets to be my age, he starts to think about settlin' down instead of driftin' around like I been doin' for so many years."

"I'd have to talk to Mayor Fleming and the town council," Bill said. "I knew with all this Indian problem goin' on, nobody would mind me deputizing you, but they'd have to agree if I was to hire you permanent. They're the ones that would be paying your wages."

"I don't care that much about the wages. I'd just like to

have a roof over my head and some grub. That Scandahoovian woman over to the café is a mighty fine cook. Ain't been but a few days, but I've already gotten fond of the grub she and her husband dish up."

"I'll talk to the mayor and the council when this is all over," Bill promised.

"If I'm still alive, you mean. If I ain't, then it don't really matter, does it?"

"You'll be alive," Bill said. "We still don't know if the Pawnee are anywhere within two hundred miles of here."

Flint rubbed his shoulder again. "Somethin' is," he said. "Somethin' bad."

Starting out, Alvera Stanley had run Miss Alvera's Academy for Young Ladies in Wichita. That was her first house after toiling in one as a soiled dove for almost a decade, a hell of a long run for a whore. Wiser than some, she had steered clear of whiskey and laudanum and maintained her looks.

Because of that, she had been popular with the customers, and she had squirreled away her share of the money she made. She had a nice little nest egg when it came time to go out on her own and establish her own house.

It had been successful, too, but Alvera found herself restless. She moved on to Abilene, and most of the girls who worked for her had accompanied her because she treated them well.

From Abilene she had gone to Dodge City and done well there, as well. Dodge was still a booming place. She could have stayed and continued to make good money there.

But then one of her regular customers had died, and a lawyer came to call on her with the shocking news that the man had left her a house he owned in a small town to the southwest called Redemption.

Alvera knew a little about Redemption from talking to the man, who was a widower. There was no house of ill repute in the settlement, which was why he had to come to Dodge to take care of his needs along that line.

He'd had other needs, too, such as sitting and drinking brandy and talking with an attractive redheaded woman who still had some of the bloom on the rose. Friendship, if you would, and Alvera had been glad to provide that, free of charge . . . as long as he paid for the other things he did in the house, of course.

She hadn't been angling for a damned thing, and no one was more surprised than she was when the lawyer showed up and told her about her inheritance.

But when she stopped and thought about moving to Redemption to claim her legacy, the idea had a definite appeal. The owner of the town's lone saloon had a few girls working for him, but they were hardly of the same class as the ones Alvera could provide. It would be a smaller operation, so she would take only the cream of the crop with her, the best whores she had.

She probably wouldn't have to pay off the local law, either, she had thought.

She'd been wrong about that—really wrong—but those days were over now. That young cowboy from Texas wore the marshal's badge now, and he seemed as honest and upright as the day is long.

Good-looking, too, with that rugged but handsome face and long brown hair. Alvera had overheard some of her girls talking about how they wished the marshal would come and visit them from time to time.

That seemed pretty unlikely, though, considering that Bill Harvey was still newly married to the Monroe girl. There might come a time when he would stray, but not anytime soon.

And quite possibly not at all, Alvera sensed. She had a good feel for that sort of thing, and the marshal didn't strike her as the kind of man who would step out on his wife.

Mainly it was peaceful in Redemption . . . or at least it had been lately, until the threat of being massacred by savages cropped up. Like everybody else in town these days,

Alvera kept loaded weapons close at hand, including a rifle and a shotgun.

She knew how to use them, too. Any hostile who tried to bust in here would get a load of buckshot in his painted face.

Meanwhile, life went on, and that meant customers visiting the house on the edge of town, including the three who were coming down the stairs from the second floor now.

Tonight was their first visit, and Alvera hadn't liked the looks of them as soon as she saw them.

The first man, the one who seemed like their nominal leader, was a gunman. You could tell that by looking at him. Not bad-looking, with that dark hair under his tipped-back Stetson, but he had a cruel mouth and even meaner eyes.

The other two might be trouble as well. The big, hulking one had the look of a man who liked to hurt women, and the fancy-dressed one reminded Alvera of a fox, the kind of man you wouldn't turn your back on because he was so cunning and untrustworthy.

But she hadn't had any excuse to turn them away. It wasn't like she was shut down for the duration of the Indian threat. She had taken their money, they had picked out their girls, and as far as she knew everything had gone just fine upstairs. There hadn't been any ruckus.

Now they were finished, and Alvera greeted them with a smile and said, "Would you gentlemen care for a glass of brandy before you go?"

The dark-haired gunman returned the smile. "Don't mind if I do, Miss Alvera."

It didn't surprise her that he knew her name. Most people in Redemption did, although some of them wouldn't have admitted it. She didn't ask for his name, and he didn't offer it.

None of the three men did, which was another reason she thought they might be trouble. Maybe they were wanted by the law. That wouldn't surprise her a bit.

As long as they behaved themselves here, though, that was all she cared about. She poured four glasses of brandy, put them on a silver tray, and carried them over to the sofa where the big man and the dandy sat. The gunman had settled down in an armchair.

"To your health, gentlemen," she said when all of them had drinks in their hands, including her.

"And to yours, ma'am," the gunman said.

They drank.

"And to the Indians staying far away from Redemption," the man went on. "Are you as worried about them as everyone else in town, Miss Alvera?"

"I'm worried," she admitted. "Aren't you?"

The man shrugged. "My friends and I haven't had any run-ins with the Pawnee. They don't have anything against us."

"I don't think they're going to care about that," Alvera said. "If they raid the town, they won't be in any mood to talk. The fact that you're white is all they'll care about."

"Maybe we should leave now, while we still can."

"That's up to you. It's nearly a day's ride to Dodge. *I* wouldn't start out to make a trip like that with a Pawnee war party on the loose."

"Well, I said maybe." The man drank the rest of his brandy. "Chances are, we'll stay right here. After all, the townspeople seem ready to defend themselves, and you've got a good marshal, don't you?"

"Bill Harvey's a nice young fella, and he did all right when outlaws raided the town a while back, but from what I hear he's never fought Indians before."

The blond dandy asked, "What about the deputy?"

"That old man?" Alvera shook her head. "I don't know a thing about him. He's new in town, hadn't been here long at all when Bill deputized him. He claims to have a lot of experience, but who knows? He might be just an old windbag."

The gunman stood up and handed Alvera his empty glass.

"Finish your drinks, boys," he said. "We'd better be going." He grinned, but it didn't make his mouth any less cruel, Alvera noted. "There are guards all over town at night. Wouldn't want to make any of them think we're redskins and get them all trigger-happy."

"I won't let out no war whoops," the big man said with a bit of unexpected humor.

A minute later the three men were gone. Alvera went upstairs to talk to the girls who had been with them, just to make sure there hadn't been any problems she didn't know about. The girls didn't report anything out of the ordinary.

Despite that, Alvera couldn't shake the feeling that something was wrong. She knew men—hell, that was about all she did know!—and those three still struck her as trouble.

But with the possibility of a bunch of bloodthirsty savages about to attack the town at any minute, it was probably foolish to worry about something that might be just an unfounded hunch.

"All right, Jake, how long are we going to stay here?" Luther Macauley asked as they walked away from the whorehouse.

"Why don't we just go ahead and hit the bank?" Oscar Kipp suggested. "In a little place like this, the safe probably ain't any stronger than a crackerbox."

Fraker said, "You really think it would be a good idea to rob the bank when everybody in town is walking around with a gun, just achin' to shoot at something?" He shook his head. "We'd never make it out alive."

"So what do we do?" Macauley said. "We've been here for three days. We need to get back to the rest of the boys and move on, if we're not going to pull a job here."

"I didn't say we weren't going to pull a job," Fraker snapped. "What's going to happen if the Indians show up?"

"All hell's gonna break loose, that's what's gonna happen," Kipp rumbled.

"Exactly. Which means that everybody will be too busy to pay any attention to what might be happening at the bank. The townspeople and the Pawnee will be so caught up with killing each other, they'll never see what's going on."

Macauley chuckled. "Now I get it. But won't we be running the risk of the Indians killing *us*, too, Jake?"

"We'll just have to make sure that doesn't happen," Fraker said.

"So for now—"

"We wait and hope the redskins show up," Fraker said. "They're going to help make us rich men."

Chapter 17

Bill woke up to the sound of someone pounding on the front door of the Monroe house. It was a warm night, and he had thrown the sheet off and lay there in the bottoms of his long underwear.

As he sat up, he looked over at Eden lying next to him. Her nightgown was hiked up almost to her hips, and under other circumstances her bare legs would've been mighty tempting.

But Bill reached for the gun on the nightstand instead of his wife's warm flesh. It was a hell of a thing, being marshal.

The knocking woke Eden, too. She sat up with a gasp and said, "Bill . . . ?"

He was already on his feet beside the bed, his Colt gripped in his right hand. "I'm right here," he told her.

"What is that?"

"Somebody knocking on the door."

"At this time of night? Who in the world—Oh, my God. Do you think the Indians are coming?"

"Don't know, but I'm gonna find out."

He hurried across the room and stepped out into the second-floor hallway.

Perry Monroe's sleep had been disturbed, too. He emerged from his room in a long nightshirt, carrying a shotgun.

"Bill?"

"Here, Mr. Monroe," Bill told him. "Don't shoot."

"You think it's the Indians?" Monroe asked, just like Eden had.

"People say they don't attack at night." From the looks of the thick darkness outside, the hour was after midnight. "I never put much stock in that myself."

The two of them went downstairs, Bill taking the lead. As he approached the front door, he tightened his grip on the Colt and called through the panel, "Who's there?"

"It's me, Bill," Josiah Hartnett's voice came back.

Hartnett was on guard duty tonight, Bill recalled. In fact, he was supposed to be on top of the newspaper office right now. Something must have happened to make him abandon his post.

Bill jerked the door open and asked, "What is it?"

The liveryman's bulky form loomed on the porch. "One of the outriders came in," he reported. "He heard hoofbeats. Sounds like a big bunch of riders approaching town from the west."

Bill bit back a curse. "Did he get a look at them? Is he sure it's the Pawnee war party?"

Hartnett shook his head. "No, he lit out as soon as he heard them coming. But who else could it be?"

"The cavalry coming back, maybe," Monroe suggested.

But they couldn't count on that. Bill thought hard about what they should do next.

"Gather up all the volunteers," he told Hartnett. "I want most of 'em behind the barrel barricades at the western end of town. Not all of them, though. If it's the Pawnee coming, they could try to trick us and circle around, hit us from a direction we're not expectin'. Have the rest of the men spread out around town."

Hartnett nodded. "I'll do it. Should I ring the fire bell to roust out everybody in town?"

"Good idea," Bill said. "I'll be there as soon as I can get boots and pants on."

"So will I," Monroe said.

The two of them turned away from the door as Hartnett started running back toward Main Street. Eden waited at the bottom of the stairs, wearing a robe now and holding it tightly closed at her neck.

"I heard what Josiah said. The Indians are here."

"We don't know that," Bill told her, "but I sure don't see what else it could be." He turned to his father-in-law. "Mr. Monroe, I want you to stay here with Eden. If there's trouble, I need to know that you're lookin' out for her."

Eden didn't give her father time to respond. She said, "I'm coming downtown with you, Bill."

"I don't think—"

"Have you forgotten how I helped out in that last trouble? I can take care of myself, and you know it."

Bill had to admit she could handle a rifle, and it might be better if he kept her close by so he would know she was safe.

Or at least as safe as anyone in Redemption could be tonight with that galloping danger heading toward them.

"All right," he said with a curt nod. "We'll all get dressed as quick as we can."

They hurried upstairs. It didn't take long to throw on some clothes, but even that few minutes made Bill's nerves stretch tighter. He found himself listening for the gunfire and shouting that would mean the town was under attack.

Instead, all he heard was the clangor of the fire bell as Josiah Hartnett rang it. That would bring everybody out of their homes and businesses.

Eden pulled a simple gray dress over her head, slipped on some shoes, and took a Winchester and a box of shells out of the closet while Bill strapped on his Colt. He started to take the rifle from her, but she shook her head.

"There's another one downstairs," she said. "I'm taking this one."

Even under these nerve-wracking circumstances, her grit and determination brought a smile to Bill's face.

"All right," he said. "Let's go."

Perry Monroe had dressed even faster and was waiting for them in the foyer. Bill paused just long enough to pick up the Winchester he had leaned in the corner a couple of days earlier.

Then the three of them headed downtown to see what was going to happen.

Jacob Fraker, Luther Macauley, and Oscar Kipp had returned to Smoot's Saloon after their visit to the whorehouse on the edge of town.

Fred Smoot rented out rooms upstairs, not just to men who wanted to dally with the girls who worked for him, but to hombres who needed a place to stay, as well. The three outlaws had taken rooms there, and it was a good thing they had.

Redemption was crowded right now because all the teamsters and bullwhackers who worked for Gus Meade's freight line were still in town, too, along with their boss. All the rooms in the one hotel and the three boardinghouses were occupied.

Fraker heard the swift rataplan of galloping hoofbeats in the street, but the other two didn't seem to notice. They had drunk quite a bit this evening and were still otherwise sated from their visit to the soiled doves.

Fraker wondered who was in such a big hurry. It couldn't be because of anything good, he thought . . . although it might work to the advantage of him and his partners.

A few minutes later when the fire bell that hung in front of the town hall began to clang, Fraker knew something momentous was about to happen.

Macauley and Kipp couldn't miss that racket. They jerked their heads up, and Kipp nearly knocked over the half-empty mug of beer that sat on the table in front of him.

"Indians!" Macauley said. "It has to be!"

"This is it," Kipp said. "We gonna head for the bank, Jake?"

Fraker said, "Take it easy, you two. We need to find out exactly what's goin' on first."

The other men in the saloon were already heading for the door. The first one to get there slapped the batwings aside and ran out into the night, followed closely by the others.

Several of the men had drawn their guns already, and Fraker wouldn't be surprised if they started shooting at shadows.

"Ed, get my shotgun!" Smoot told the bartender. The aproned man reached under the bar and bought out a sawed-off Greener. It would be a fearsome weapon at close range but not much good otherwise.

Smoot probably didn't plan on fighting any long-range duels in that wheelchair, though.

The bartender handed the scattergun to Smoot, then pushed his boss toward the door where the batwings were still flapping. Before they got there, Smoot said sharply, "Hold it."

He turned to look at Fraker, Macauley, and Kipp.

"Aren't you three men coming along?" Smoot asked. "That signal means the town may be under attack by Indians at any minute."

Fraker had a hunch Smoot didn't want to leave them here in the saloon unattended. They were strangers, after all. They might raid the till.

As if they didn't have much bigger plans than that, thought Fraker.

"We're coming," he said as he pushed himself to his feet. Best to play along for now. "Let's go, boys."

Satisfied, Smoot nodded to the bartender, who pushed him outside onto the boardwalk. Fraker, Macauley, and Kipp were right behind them.

The street was full of people. Maybe there was some purpose and order to what they were doing, but to Fraker it looked like they were running around aimlessly and yelling. An air of hysteria gripped the settlement.

This could be it, all right. All it would take was a single

shot. Just one panicky townsman pulling the trigger, and then everybody would start shooting at everything that moved.

That would be their cue to duck down the alley beside the saloon and head for the back of the bank. Fraker knew how to get there, having planned out the route during the time they had spent in Redemption.

Breaking through the bank's back door wouldn't be a problem. Then Macauley could use his talented fingers and ears to open the door on the safe while Fraker and Kipp stood guard. There weren't many safes that Macauley couldn't crack.

Before they could do that, though, they had to be sure the townspeople were going to be occupied fighting the Indians.

"Hang on," Fraker told his tense partners. "Let's wait and see what happens."

"These people are loco," Kipp said. "They're ready to blow the lid right off this town."

That was true. But then a loud, commanding voice rang out, cutting through the clamor.

"Settle down! Everybody settle down! Get to your places! Josiah, where are you?"

Fraker looked along the street and saw a tall young man hurrying toward the west end of town, limping a little but not letting it slow him down. He was hatless, with his long brown hair hanging to his shoulders, and he carried a Winchester.

Fraker recognized the man as the kid marshal, only at this moment he didn't really look like a kid. His face was calm but determined, and he seemed more a battle-hardened veteran.

He was followed by an old man with a white beard and a young blond woman, both of them carrying rifles, and as the light from a window fell across the woman's face, Fraker was struck by how pretty she was.

That was the marshal's wife, he recalled. The lawman was a lucky bastard.

He wouldn't be if he got in Jake Fraker's way, though.

It took the marshal several minutes of yelling before everybody heard him and he was able to restore order. Once he did, he started getting people in position to defend the town.

Most of them gathered at the western end of the street, inside buildings or behind barrels that had been stacked up to form barricades. Others were on the roofs.

The marshal didn't stop at that. He placed men with rifles and shotguns here and there all along the street. Women and children had answered the call of the fire bell, too, and they were herded into several sturdy buildings that could be defended against an attack.

Fraker almost groaned in dismay when he saw that one of those buildings was the bank, which was made out of bricks.

Macauley and Kipp saw that, too. Kipp let out a curse and said, "Look at that, Jake. We can't get in there now without them seein' us."

Fraker thought furiously. "Looks like there are only a couple of men guarding the bank right now," he said. "Reckon the others plan to fall back there if they have to. What we'll have to do is make our move before that happens. You and I will take care of the guards, Oscar, and then we can keep the women and kids under control until Luther gets the safe open."

"Yeah, but there's more chance for something to go wrong," Macauley said.

"Damn it! Nobody ever said robbin' banks was gonna be easy, did they?"

The other two shut up in the face of Fraker's anger.

And a moment later, Fraker had something else to distract him.

He realized the marshal was striding straight toward them.

Chapter 18

"You three men," Bill called as he approached the strangers standing on the boardwalk just outside the entrance to Smoot's Saloon. "You need to find some cover in case there's any shooting."

"You mean if the Indians attack?" the tall, dark-haired, lantern-jawed one asked.

Bill ignored the flash of irritation he felt. He vaguely remembered seeing these three around town the past couple of days, but he hadn't talked to them and didn't know who they were.

They had to know what was going on, though. He wasn't sure why they were standing around asking dumb questions.

"That's right," he said. "We can use some more men behind the barricades."

The big sandy-haired one said, "This ain't our fight, Marshal."

This time Bill didn't bother to suppress his anger. "It's everybody's fight who wants to live through it," he snapped. "Now get out of the open, anyway. I don't want to have to worry about those Pawnee turning you into pin-cushions."

"Take it easy, Marshal," the first man said. "We'll be glad to help out. Come on, fellas."

The other two looked a little reluctant, but they followed the man as he trotted toward a pile of barrels about midway along Main Street, where they joined a group of defenders that included Charley Hobbs and Phillip Ramsey.

Bill looked around. The street was mostly clear, with only a few men left scurrying into position. He glanced toward the mercantile. Eden and her father were over there, behind the building's sturdy walls with half a dozen other men to help them if the fighting got that far.

Bill hoped they could turn the Pawnee back without the hostiles ever getting into the town itself, but they might not be able to accomplish that. The battle could wind up going from building to building.

And the Pawnee should have been here by now, he thought as he dragged in a deep breath.

Maybe the stories were right. Maybe the Indians had stopped out there, a mile or so from town, to wait for dawn before they attacked. It could be they didn't like to fight at night after all.

But that thought had no sooner gone through his head than someone called to him quietly.

"Marshal! They're comin'!"

Holding his rifle slanted across his chest, Bill hurried to the barrel barricade that was farther west than any of the others, just past the point where the buildings ended on Main Street. Mordecai Flint was there, along with Josiah Hartnett and a couple of other men.

The bottom row of barrels had been filled with sand, so they would probably stop bullets. They would definitely stop arrows and lances. The barrels on top were empty, so they provided cover only against the more primitive weapons. Bullets would punch right through them.

Bill crouched next to Flint and asked the deputy, "Can you see them yet?"

"Nope, but I can hear 'em," Flint replied. "But there's somethin' mighty odd. Listen."

Bill cocked his head and listened intently. In the silence that gripped the night, he heard the slow, steady sound of hoofbeats coming closer.

"They're not charging," he said in amazement. "They're takin' their time."

"That ain't all. I swear I hear wagon wheels creakin', too."

Bill caught his breath as he realized the old-timer was right. The strange sound mixed in with the hoofbeats came from at least one wagon, probably more.

"I never heard of a Pawnee war party traveling with wagons," Hartnett said. "Of course, I've never fought Indians before."

"I have," Flint said, "and you're right. That ain't Injuns. If it is, they ain't like any I've ever seen before."

Relief flooded through Bill. He didn't know who was out there in the darkness, coming closer to Redemption, but clearly it wasn't the war party they had been expecting.

Hartnett gave voice to the same question that occurred to Bill. "Who the hell is it, then?"

Bill leaned forward and peered past the barrels, his eyes straining to pierce the shadows. He saw some dark shapes moving around out there, gradually getting bigger.

"There's one good way to find out," he said. "I'm gonna go ask 'em."

Before Flint or Hartnett could stop him, he stepped around the barrels and strode toward the mysterious riders.

Bill's pulse boomed like thunder inside his head. He had managed to put up a good front while he was arranging the town's defenders, but he was scared, and even more so now that he was out in the open.

He heard Flint and Hartnett calling softly to him from behind the barrels, but he ignored them and kept going. If the riders approaching the town weren't Indians, the only other possibility he could think of was the army. A group of soldiers might have wagons with them.

He could make out men on horseback now, followed by

several wagons. The riders suddenly reined in and stopped short. Bill figured they had spotted him. He stopped, too, and raised his voice to call to them.

"Hold it right there, gents! Who are you, and what's your business here?"

He worked the Winchester's lever and threw a cartridge into the chamber. He figured the strangers would hear that metallic *clack-clack* and know that he was armed.

One man had been riding slightly ahead of the others. He started forward again, walking his horse slowly.

"Hold your fire," he said. "If you're from the town up there, we're friendly. Not looking for trouble at all. This is Redemption, isn't it?"

Bill swallowed. The voice obviously belonged to a white man, but that didn't mean it was telling the truth. He lifted the rifle to his shoulder.

"Mister, I said hold it and I meant it! Come any closer and I'll drill you. Now tell me who you are and what you're doing here."

The man stopped. Bill couldn't be sure, but he thought he heard a grim chuckle come from him.

"You sound a mite young, son," the stranger said.

"Old enough to pull a trigger," Bill snapped. "And old enough to be the marshal of Redemption."

"So that *is* where we are. I thought so. I'm sorry, Marshal. Didn't mean to get on your bad side. We're looking for help. We've got trouble behind us."

"Indian trouble?" Bill asked.

"Indian trouble," the stranger confirmed. "My name's Ward Costigan. This is Colonel William Bledsoe's party of buffalo hunters, out of Dodge City. If you'll allow us to come on into town, I can tell you all about it."

Bill hesitated. The man who said his name was Costigan sounded like he was telling the truth, but it was hard to be sure about such things.

"How many of you are there, Costigan?"

"Thirty men," the buffalo hunter replied.

"Well, there are more than a hundred guns pointed at

you right now, including mine," Bill told him. "So come on in, but if you try any tricks, you'll be mighty sorry you did."

Bill wanted to keep the newcomers covered until he was absolutely certain they didn't represent a threat, but that turned out to be impossible. Once the townspeople saw that the men weren't Pawnee warriors, they crowded around to ask questions.

The man he had spoken to, Ward Costigan, was a tall, rawboned man with shaggy brown hair and a mustache. Costigan wore a battered felt hat and a homespun shirt over corduroy trousers and high-topped boots. He didn't carry a revolver, but he had a Henry rifle tucked under his arm and a pair of Sharps Big Fifties strapped to his horse.

The weapons told Bill that Costigan was one of the men who did the actual hunting. Others would be drivers and skinners. A few buffalo hunters had passed through Redemption while he'd been here, so he knew a little about such outfits.

The riders and wagons moved past the barricades and stopped in the middle of Main Street as the citizens crowded around them. Bill waited until Costigan had dismounted and then strode up to him and held out his hand.

"Costigan, I'm Marshal Bill Harvey."

The buffalo hunter gripped Bill's hand. "Pleased to meet you, Marshal. Maybe more than you know."

"I doubt it," Bill said. "You and your friends came hustlin' into town because of that Pawnee war party that's on the loose, didn't you?"

"You could say that," Costigan replied. "Fact of the matter is—"

Another man bustled up and interrupted him. "The fact of the matter is, that's exactly what we did, Marshal," this man said as he held out his hand. "I'm Colonel William J. Bledsoe, the leader of this hunting expedition."

"Colonel," Bill said with a nod as he shook the man's

hand. Bledsoe might have been a dandy under other circumstances, with his suit, tie, and derby hat, but right now he just looked tired, dirty, and unshaven.

"We ran into a cavalry patrol that warned us about the savages," Bledsoe went on, "so we thought we'd better hightail for civilization." He looked around at the barricades and all the armed citizens. "Obviously you already know about the Pawnee being on the warpath."

"The cavalry was here, too. Captain name of Stone was in command."

Bledsoe's eyebrows rose in surprise. "Really! We met the same bunch."

"Captain Stone didn't say anything about coming back this way, did he?"

"No, not at all."

"I hoped maybe we'd have more help on hand if the Indians do show up here."

"You do have more help." Bledsoe waved a hand at his party. "Thirty good men and true. With your permission, Marshal, we'll be staying here until we hear word that the Pawnee threat is over."

"The town's pretty full up," Bill said with a frown. "I don't think there are any empty rooms."

"We're buffalo hunters! We're accustomed to roughing it. We'll simply camp here if that's agreeable."

Bill looked over and saw that Roy Fleming had come up during the conversation. He said, "What do you think, Mayor?"

"I think that Colonel Bledsoe and his men are more than welcome," Fleming said. He shook hands with Bledsoe and introduced himself. "Mayor Roy Fleming, Colonel. Welcome to Redemption."

"We're glad to be here, Mayor, I assure you."

"What about supplies?" Bill asked. "We're sort of limited in that area."

"We have supplies of our own," Bledsoe assured him. "Enough to last for a while, anyway."

"Well, then, if it's all right with the mayor, it's all right with me." Bill glanced at Ward Costigan, who stood there stony-faced with the Henry under his arm. "If there's trouble, we can use the extra guns, that's for sure."

"We'll do everything we can to help, Marshal," Bledsoe said. "Don't hesitate to call on us."

Costigan turned away to tend to his horse. Bill had chores of his own to deal with. He sought out Hartnett and said, "We need to get all the guards back in place, Josiah, and the outriders, too."

"The fellas who volunteered to be outriders are a mite more nervous now," Hartnett said. "They've seen that something could actually happen, so some of 'em aren't sure they want to go back out there."

"Blast it," Bill said in exasperation. "Didn't they know the job was dangerous when they took it?"

"Sure, but they were all hoping the Indians wouldn't really show up."

"The Indians *haven't* shown up," Bill pointed out.

Hartnett shrugged. "I'm just tellin' you the talk I've heard, Bill. That Wetherby boy says he's going back out there, but I don't know if anybody else is."

Bill clamped his mouth shut against the frustrated curse that tried to come out. After a moment he said, "All right. Reckon you can go back to the stable and saddle my horse, Josiah?"

"Wait a minute. *You're* gonna ride patrol around the town?"

"Somebody needs to besides Aaron Wetherby."

"But you're the marshal. You're in charge here. Folks look to you to take over whenever there's trouble."

"This needs doing," Bill said. "If there's nobody else to do it, the job falls to me." He sighed. "Wish we had at least one more man to help out, though."

A voice behind him said, "I'll do it."

Bill recognized the deep, powerful tone. He turned to see Costigan standing there, holding his horse's reins. Clearly, the buffalo hunter had heard enough of the conversation to know what was going on.

"You just got here, Mr. Costigan," Bill said. "If you've already been ridin' all night, nobody expects you to go back out and stand guard."

"I don't mind. I'm not much for sleeping these days, anyway."

Bill didn't ask the man why that was. It was none of his business. Instead he said, "If you're sure about this, I'm not in any position to turn down volunteers."

"We're agreed, then. I *could* use a fresh horse, though."

Hartnett said, "I can provide that. I'm Josiah Hartnett. Own the local livery stable."

The two men shook hands. Bill said, "Take Mr. Costigan on down to the stable, Josiah, so he can put his rig on another mount. I'll be there in a few minutes. There's something else I have to do first."

"What's that?"

Bill laughed and shook his head. "I have to tell my wife what I'm about to do. And I'm not sure but what I'd rather face those dang Pawnee."

Chapter 19

"I say we give up and light a shuck out of here right now," Oscar Kipp declared in his rumbling voice. "We got fast horses. We can pick up the rest of the gang and be back in Dodge City in a few days. There ain't nothin' for us here, Jake. Nothin'."

It was unusual for Kipp to speak that many words at one time, Fraker thought. And there was a reason for that.

Kipp was dumb. He had just proved it.

"I told you, we're hitting the bank."

"When?"

"When the time is right, damn it." Fraker leaned forward over the table. "Are you questionin' my judgment, Oscar? Is that really what you want to do, after all the successful jobs I've planned?"

"Nobody's questioning your judgment, Jake," Macauley put in. "Oscar just got excited because he thought tonight was the night. He's disappointed things didn't work out. That's natural."

"Yeah," Kipp said, not meeting Fraker's eyes now. "I'm just a mite disappointed, that's all."

Fraker sat back in his chair as the killing tension that

had gripped him at being challenged eased. "All right," he said. "I reckon I can understand that."

"I just hope when the time comes, it's worth it."

Kipp hadn't been able to resist getting in that last word. Fraker decided to be generous and let him have it.

Sure they were getting nervous and tired of hanging around this backwater town. So was he. But a man had to be patient if he was going to clean out a bank.

Their bottle and glasses had still been on the table when they got back to the saloon after that party of buffalo hunters arrived in town. They had just about finished off the whiskey since then.

The saloon was doing a booming business now. The bar was crowded with men in greasy clothes that stunk of blood and death. Those were the skinners. The hunters had taken tables. The divide between the two sorts was clear. They would drink in the same place, but they wouldn't sit together.

Macauley said quietly, "Isn't it just going to make things trickier, having more men in town?"

"And what if the cavalry shows up again?" Kipp asked.

"None of that will matter if they're all busy fighting the Pawnee," Fraker said. His eyes narrowed as an idea occurred to him. "We need to make everybody even more nervous, and I think I know a way to do that."

He leaned forward again and clasped his hands together on the table as Macauley and Kipp listened.

"I heard the marshal talking about havin' outriders patrolling around the town. What would happen if one of those outriders got his throat cut, like a redskin had snuck up on him and done it?"

"Who could do a thing like that?" Kipp asked.

"I know somebody who's good at cuttin' throats," Fraker said, remembering what had happened to that whore.

Macauley said, "You'd be taking a big chance, Jake. Slipping out of town without anybody seeing you wouldn't be easy."

"No, but think how worked up people will get if I can pull it off. This town's already a powder keg . . ." Fraker grinned. "And that would burn a few more inches off the fuse."

"Why you, Bill?" Eden asked. "Isn't there anybody else?"

"Now, honey, I can't very well ask somebody else to do a job I won't do. Anyway, accordin' to Josiah everybody except Aaron Wetherby is too spooked tonight to go back out there. So I don't have much choice. One of the buffalo hunters, a man called Costigan, volunteered, too, so that'll be three of us." He put his hands on her shoulders. "Don't worry, I'll be careful."

"You'd better be," she said, trying to sound stern. Bill heard the faint tremble that fear put in her voice, though.

"You and your pa go on back to the house. I'll see you later."

He kissed her forehead and left her standing there in the mercantile's doorway. That had gone better than he expected it would.

He hadn't been looking forward to arguing with a woman who had a Winchester in her hands.

When he reached the stable, Hartnett had his horse saddled and ready. Costigan had switched horses, moving his saddle to a leggy chestnut gelding that was the liveryman's personal mount.

"Take care of this big fella," Hartnett told Costigan as he patted the horse's shoulder. "He's the steadiest animal I've got, and probably the fastest, too."

Costigan nodded. "I'll do my best to bring him back safe, Mr. Hartnett."

Aaron Wetherby rode up to the front of the barn. His fair hair shone in the lantern light.

"Are you gents ready to go?" he asked. Bill heard the eagerness in Aaron's voice and asked himself if he had ever been that young. He supposed he had, but it was getting harder all the time to remember those days.

Bill and Costigan swung up into their saddles and joined Aaron. Side by side, the three of them rode toward the western end of town. Once they got there, they would split up and go their separate ways to start their patrols.

"Remember, if you see anything that looks like trouble, don't try to handle it by yourself," Bill told the other two. "Just light a shuck for town as fast as you can. When you get close enough, start hollering so the guards on the roofs will know it's you comin' in. Otherwise they might start shootin'."

"How far out are we going?" Costigan asked.

"Half a mile, maybe a little more. Whatever you feel comfortable with. But if those Pawnee show up, the more warning the town has, the better."

Costigan nodded. "I understand."

Still eager, Aaron asked, "Have you ever fought Injuns before, Mr. Costigan?"

"No," Costigan said. He was silent for a couple of seconds, then said, "But I've seen my share of combat."

"You were in the war?" Bill said.

"That's right." Costigan glanced over at him. "Is that a Texas drawl I hear, Marshal?"

"Yeah, but if you're worried because you were on the other side, don't be. I was too young to enlist."

"So was I," Aaron said, sounding disappointed.

"Count yourselves lucky, both of you." Costigan's voice was hard and flat. "I saw too many boys like the two of you—"

He stopped short and didn't say anything else. Bill didn't figure it would be a good idea to press him on it. Anyway, they had left the settlement behind and were riding across open prairie now. It was time for them to split up.

He sent Costigan north and Aaron south. "I'll ride out a little farther and then start circling. You don't have to ride any particular route, just keep movin' and keep your eyes open."

Costigan lifted a hand in farewell and turned his horse.

Aaron said, "See you later, Marshal," and urged his mount into a trot that carried him away into the night. Costigan, moving slower, faded from sight in the other direction a few moments later.

Bill was left alone on the prairie.

Costigan was a little surprised Dave McGinty hadn't volunteered to ride patrol around the town, too.

McGinty had been avoiding him more and more over the past few days, though, so Costigan supposed that was the reason. McGinty was ashamed of the part he had played in the massacre, and the journey to Redemption had given him plenty of time to brood about what had happened.

Colonel Bledsoe wasn't ashamed, that was for sure. Bledsoe had stepped in to prevent Costigan from telling Marshal Harvey about the killings because he didn't want any blame from them coming back on him. By now Bledsoe would have talked himself into believing that none of it was his fault, that he and the other men hadn't had any choice but to shoot those Indian boys.

If that was the way Bledsoe wanted to think, then so be it. Costigan didn't care anymore. When this was over—assuming that he came through it alive—Costigan intended to ride away and give up buffalo hunting. Bledsoe owed him wages and a share in the profits, but he didn't really care about those, either.

He wasn't sure what he would do, but as long as it didn't involve killing, it would be fine. He'd had enough of spilling blood, whether human or buffalo. Maybe if he gave it up, he could start sleeping better again.

Of course, in the meantime he might be forced to kill some more. If the Pawnee followed them to Redemption, Costigan knew he wouldn't be able to stand aside and do nothing. He would do his best to help fight off any raid.

He didn't know much about the citizens of the town, but that young marshal seemed like a good man—

Costigan reined in abruptly as movement caught his

eye. He sat up straighter in the saddle and narrowed his gaze. His hands tightened on the Henry.

Then he grunted and relaxed as the prairie dog he had seen ducked back down into its hole. Nothing to worry about there.

Unless something had spooked the prairie dog by skulking around. Or someone . . .

Costigan kept Josiah Hartnett's horse motionless as he slowly turned his head and scanned the landscape around him. A quarter moon hung in the sky, along with millions of stars, and the silvery light from them was enough for Costigan to make out his surroundings.

Nothing was moving. After a few moments, Costigan lifted the reins and nudged the horse into motion again.

If he was seeing things that weren't there, he supposed he was lucky that at least he hadn't imagined seeing that old colonel and those boys marching across the plains tonight. He didn't need to relive that. Not tonight. He had found out later that they were from a military academy. By that time in the war, the Confederacy was down to using "troops" like that in a futile effort to slow the advance of the Union army.

They had known what they were getting into. Costigan had told himself that a thousand times, and he was convinced that he was right.

But that didn't make the memories any easier to bear.

He shoved those memories away. If he didn't concentrate on the real reason he was out here, he might wind up with a Pawnee arrow sticking all the way through him.

Haunted he might be, but he wasn't ready to die just yet. As he rode through the night, he moved his fingers a little on the smooth wooden stock of the Henry rifle.

Getting out of town was easier than Fraker thought it would be. He told Macauley and Kipp that he was going to take a leak, just in case anybody was listening, and headed for the alley beside the saloon after pushing through the batwings.

Once he was in the shadows, he stayed there, working his way along the alleys and lanes until he reached the edge of the settlement. His clothes were dark and helped him blend in, and he kept his head down so the brim of his hat shielded his face.

As Fraker slipped through the darkness, he kept waiting for a yell of alarm from one of the rooftop guards, but obviously none of them spotted him. When he reached the north edge of town, he took a deep breath and dashed across the twenty yards or so of open ground between him and the little cottonwood-lined creek that meandered along that side of the settlement.

He didn't breathe again until he was in the shadows of those cottonwoods. Sticking to them, he followed the stream as it curved to the northwest. The banks were shallow, only a few feet, but between them and the trees, nobody could see him. Not easily, anyway.

Fraker had heard how the outriders were making circuits all the way around the town. When he was about half a mile away from the settlement, he stopped.

He didn't have to find one of the outriders. If he waited here, sooner or later one of the men would come to him.

That would be their bad luck.

Fraker hunkered on his heels under the trees. He reached into his pocket and slid out the straight razor he always carried. It was honed to a keen edge, but he had never used it to kill anyone before, only to shave.

The best tools served more than one function, though, he thought with a grim smile.

Life as an outlaw and killer had taught Jake Fraker how to wait patiently for what he wanted. Time passed, but he wasn't really aware of it. All his attention was focused on the sounds of the night around him.

That was why he didn't know how long he had been waiting when he heard the steady hoofbeats of a horse.

Fraker tilted his head and listened. The rider was off to his north, coming toward him from the east. He came up out of his crouch and ran noiselessly along the creek.

If the rider crossed the stream and continued on his way before Fraker could get there to intercept him, it wouldn't be a total loss. At least Fraker would know where to wait for the man to come around again.

But if he could reach the right spot in time, he could carry out his mission now and be done with it. For that reason, Fraker hurried.

He paused to listen again. The hoofbeats were closer, and now they sounded like they were right across the creek. Fraker pressed his back against the trunk of a cottonwood and opened the razor.

The rider, a looming figure on horseback, came out of the darkness and splashed across the creek only a few yards from the tree where Fraker waited, holding his breath.

As soon as the man was past, Fraker made his move. Still moving as quietly as he could, he dashed out of his cover and lunged at the outrider from behind. The man's horse must have sensed him, because the animal suddenly spooked and danced skittishly to the side.

That bit of bad luck made Fraker's first leap miss. The rider twisted in the saddle and said, "Hey! What the hell—"

Then fortune turned in Fraker's favor. The horse reared up. Taken by surprise, the rider yelled and grabbed for the saddle horn, but his fingers slipped off of it and he toppled out of the saddle.

Fraker was on him in a flash, driving his knee into the man's back and pinning him to the ground. His left arm went around the man's neck and jerked his head back, pulling his throat taut.

Easy as pie. Even though Fraker had never killed anyone like this, he swept the razor across the man's throat like he had done it a hundred times before, feeling the blade slice deep through flesh. Blood spurted hotly across the back of Fraker's hand. The dying man spasmed underneath him but couldn't shake him off.

It didn't matter. The son of a bitch was dead already, even though he was still moving.

Fraker held the man until he stopped twitching. He let

go, pushed himself to his feet, and stepped back. Even in the starlight, he could see the black pool around the head of the sprawled figure.

Fraker leaned over and wiped the razor on the back of the dead man's shirt. He wiped his hand as well, and after he had put the razor away, he scooped up water and sand from the stream bed and scrubbed the back of his hand to remove any lingering traces of blood.

Not that it was likely anybody would suspect him, he thought. As soon as the body was found, everybody in the settlement would jump to the conclusion that the Indians were responsible for the killing. That would make them even more likely to panic when the Pawnee showed up for real.

Satisfied with his night's efforts, Fraker turned and started back toward Redemption.

Chapter 20

Bill had gotten a little sleep earlier that night, before Josiah Hartnett's pounding on his door woke him, but even so it didn't take long for weariness to catch up to him as he began riding circuits around the settlement.

Like most cowboys, he had perfected the art of sleeping in the saddle. Head drooping, eyes closed, he could doze off and let the horse do all the work.

Not tonight, though. Tonight he had to remain alert.

In order to do that, he thought about Eden. That was sort of a mistake, because those musings quickly turned into a distraction.

Shaking his head in an attempt to banish the tempting images that came to mind, he approached the little creek that wandered down from the northwest, skirted the settlement, and then turned south. If the stream had a name, Bill had never heard it in the time he'd been in Redemption. Folks just called it the creek.

He had just forded the shallow stream when he heard a horse nicker somewhere nearby.

Bill reined in and lifted the Winchester. His finger

curled around the trigger as he wondered if that had been an Indian pony he'd just heard. His muscles tensed in anticipation of an arrow whistling out of the night and striking him.

Nothing happened except the strange horse nickered again.

Bill relaxed slightly. If that had been an Indian pony, surely its Pawnee master would have clamped his hand over the animal's nose to keep it quiet.

Unless the Pawnee was trying to trick him. That thought made Bill stiffen again in alarm.

He knew he should turn his mount and gallop as hard as he could for town right now, and he would have done that except just then he spotted the horse walking slowly along the creek bank toward him.

No one was on the horse's back, but as it came closer, Bill was able to make out the empty saddle cinched onto it. That was no Indian pony.

But his heart suddenly slugged hard anyway as he realized what that empty saddle could mean.

Don't get ahead of yourself, he thought. Maybe something had spooked the horse and caused it to buck off its rider. Bill knew he had to try to find out.

He rode closer. The horse came to meet him, obviously eager for the guiding hand of another human. Bill recognized the animal now.

It was the horse Aaron Wetherby had been riding.

Bill let out a quiet, dismayed, "Oh, hell," as he reached over to take hold of the dangling reins.

"Where'd you come from, horse? Where's Aaron?"

The horse couldn't answer him, of course. But Bill knew the circle he had been making around Redemption was larger than the course Aaron had been riding. And the loose horse was between him and town.

Which meant that Aaron ought to be between him and town, too.

Leading the riderless mount, Bill urged his horse along

the creek. His eyes never stopped moving, and he held the rifle where he could bring it into action instantly if he needed to.

He had ridden maybe five hundred yards when he spotted something lying motionless on the ground up ahead. He breathed another curse as he saw moonlight and starlight shining on fair hair.

Bill kicked his horse into a run. It took only seconds to reach the body. Bill dropped the reins and flung himself out of the saddle, dropping to a knee beside Aaron.

The dark stain on the ground around the youngster's head told Bill there wasn't much hope, but he placed the Winchester on the ground, grasped Aaron's shoulders, and rolled him onto his back anyway.

The sight of the gaping wound in the young man's neck, curving up and around like a ghastly second smile, made Bill grimace and look away. He didn't bother checking to see if Aaron's heart was beating. No one could survive having his throat cut open like that.

Bill snatched up the rifle and pushed himself to his feet. He took a quick step back, leveled the Winchester at hip level, and turned from side to side as his eyes searched the darkness along the creek.

Whoever had killed Aaron Wetherby might still be somewhere close by. The body could have been left there on the ground as bait in a trap to lure in another of the outriders.

The night was quiet, though, except for soft snuffling sounds that came from the two horses.

Bill forced himself to take a deep breath, thinking that might slow his racing heartbeat. The thick, coppery smell that rose from that pool of blood just made things worse. With his face set in grim lines, he backed away from the corpse.

The Pawnee had done this, he thought. One or two members of the war party had snuck up and jumped Aaron as he rode his circuit.

More of them might be out there right now, stalking him

and Costigan, aiming to get rid of all the outriders so they could creep up on the settlement and be in Redemption, ready to kill, before anybody knew they were there.

He needed to get back to town and sound the warning, but at the same time a part of him rebelled at the thought of leaving Aaron's body out here.

After a moment, Bill went to his horse and slid the Winchester into the saddle boot. He caught hold of the other horse's reins and tied them around the trunk of one of the cottonwoods to keep it from bolting.

Then he got his hands under Aaron's arms and with a grunt of effort lifted the dead youngster. When he dragged the body over to the horse, sure enough, the smell of blood made the animal try to spook.

Bill had tied the reins securely, though, so the horse couldn't go anywhere. Bill lifted Aaron's limp form and draped it over the saddle. He didn't have any way to tie it down, so he would have to just take things slow, even though the urge to hurry was strong inside him.

He swung up onto his own mount, rode close to the tree, and untied the reins of Aaron's horse. Leading it, he started along the creek toward the settlement.

He hadn't gone very far when he heard more hoofbeats approaching.

Bill reined in and drew the Winchester. The hoofbeats sounded like they came from just one horse, so he risked calling softly, "Costigan?"

The steady thuds stopped abruptly, followed by a few seconds of silence before the buffalo hunter asked, "Is that you, Marshal?"

"Yeah. Are you alone?"

"That's right. Have you seen young Wetherby? I thought he and I would have crossed trails again by now."

"I've got him here with me," Bill said. "He's dead."

A couple of seconds of stunned silence went by. Then Costigan muttered, "Damn it. Indians?"

"Looks like it. His throat's been cut."

"Has he still got his scalp?"

"Yeah," Bill said, and for the first time that struck him as odd. Aaron had a fine head of hair, just the sort of trophy some bloodthirsty savage might want.

Of course, it was possible something had happened to spook the Indian before he had a chance to lift Aaron's scalp.

They could puzzle that out later. For now, Bill went on, "Costigan, head on back to town as fast as you can and tell folks what happened. That war party could be sneaking up on the settlement right now, so be careful."

"What about you?"

"I'm taking Aaron's body in."

Costigan had brought his horse closer. Bill could see him now in the faint light from the moon and stars.

"We'll stay together," the buffalo hunter said. "Just in case there's trouble between here and there."

"Blast it, I said—"

"No offense, Marshal, but I don't work for you."

Anger welled up inside Bill. He forced it back down. Arguing was just wasting more time.

"All right," he said. "Let's go."

Aaron's horse trailed behind them with its grisly burden as the two men rode side by side toward the settlement. The yellow glow of lamplight was visible in quite a few windows, even though the hour was long after midnight, so they had that to steer by.

Both men rode with their rifles drawn and ready, but no one tried to bother them. As they approached Redemption, a guard called from the roof of one of the buildings, "Who's there?"

"Marshal Harvey," Bill answered. "We're coming in."

Josiah Hartnett was waiting for them when they reached Main Street. The liveryman cursed when he saw the body lying across the saddle.

"Is that—"

He stopped, evidently unwilling to go on.

"Aaron Wetherby," Bill finished for him. "Yeah. Somebody cut the boy's throat."

Hartnett cursed. "Had to be the Pawnee. Did you see any of them?"

Bill dismounted and looped the reins of both horses around a hitch rail.

"No, I never saw anything except Aaron's body. Might not have found it this soon if his horse hadn't wandered up to me, loose and confused."

"They've got to be around here, though, trying to sneak into town."

"That's what I thought."

Costigan said, "I'm not so sure."

"Because he's still got his hair?" Bill asked.

"That and the fact that nothing happened to you and me. If they were trying to get rid of us, why didn't didn't they send a man or two after each of us?"

"Maybe they did," Hartnett said. "Maybe you and the marshal were just lucky and they didn't find you in time."

"I suppose that could be," Costigan said.

"Let's go get Mordecai," Bill suggested. "He's fought a lot more Indians than any of us have."

"You won't have to look for me," the deputy's voice said as he walked up out of the darkness. "I was takin' a turn around town when I seen you fellas standin' here. What'n blazes is goin' on?"

Flint's breath hissed between his teeth as he looked at the body draped over the horse's back.

"Is that the Wetherby boy?"

"Yeah," Bill said. "His throat's cut."

"Get him down. Lemme look at him."

Costigan and Hartnett lifted the corpse from the saddle and placed it carefully on the boardwalk. Flint knelt beside the body and dug a lucifer from the pocket of his old buckskin shirt. He snapped the match to life with his thumbnail, putting the stink of sulphur in the air.

The glare from the lucifer washed over Aaron's face. His features were surprisingly calm and untroubled, Bill thought. They weren't twisted in pain at all. Instead he bore a puzzled expression, as if he had died not knowing what was going on.

Flint flicked the match into the street, where it guttered out in the dirt. "Injuns didn't do this," he said.

"How can you tell that?" Hartnett wanted to know.

"This boy died fast, and as dyin' goes, it wasn't that hard. Might've hurt for a second or two, but by then he would've lost so much blood he wouldn't really be feelin' it no more." Flint lifted his head to look at Bill, Hartnett, and Costigan. "Injun would've made sure he died slow and painful-like. Then he would've taken the boy's hair."

"That seems pretty shaky to me," Hartnett said.

Flint snorted. "Don't care how it seems to you, mister. That's what happened. A white man did this, and all he cared about was gettin' it done and leavin' a body behind."

"You mean somebody from here in town?" Bill asked as he struggled to understand what Flint was talking about.

"Wouldn't know about that. All I'm sayin' is that it weren't the Pawnee who killed the boy."

That didn't make sense. Who else would have any reason to cut Aaron Wetherby's throat? Bill didn't really know Aaron, but it seemed unlikely that such a friendly young man would have such a deadly enemy.

"We got to do somethin' about this," Flint went on, breaking into Bill's confusion.

"I suppose we should carry the body down to the undertaker's," Hartnett said.

Flint shook his head. "That ain't what I mean."

"We can't let anybody know about this," Bill said, suddenly grasping what his deputy meant.

"That's right," Flint said. "We can all talk until we're blue in the face, but if folks find out somebody jumped this boy and killed him while he was ridin' patrol around the town, they'll all blame the Injuns. And that'll just make things worse."

Costigan added, "The old-timer's right. I just got here,

but even I can tell the lid's ready to blow right off this town."

"We still have to handle this properly," Hartnett insisted. "The boy deserves a decent burial."

"We can give him one, the four of us," Bill said.

The other three men turned to look at him.

"There's time to dig a grave in the cemetery and cover it back up again before morning," Bill went on.

"People will see it and want to know who's buried there," Hartnett said.

"Maybe not if we put it over at the side of the graveyard, and . . . I dunno . . . park a wagon on top of it or somethin'," Flint said.

Costigan asked, "Does the boy have family here? Somebody to miss him?"

Bill looked at Hartnett, who shook his head. "Don't ask me," the liveryman said. "I don't know."

"Neither do I." Bill took off a hat and wearily rubbed his other hand over his face. "If we're gonna do this, we'd better get busy."

"It's not fittin'," Hartnett said. "He should have a coffin, and the preacher should say words over him—"

"Dig him up later and do all that," Flint snapped. "Unless you want panic worse'n what you seen so far."

"We're doing this, Josiah," Bill said, his voice firm. "If you don't want to go along with it, that's fine. Same goes for you, Mr. Costigan."

The buffalo hunter shrugged and said, "I'll give you a hand. I don't think it's a good idea for the town to go crazy, either."

Hartnett sighed. "I've got a wagon and a nice thick horse blanket. We can wrap him in that, I suppose. We'll need a shovel."

"I've got a key to the mercantile," Bill said. "Mr. Monroe wouldn't mind if we were to borrow a shovel, as long as it was for a good cause."

"I wish I knew if it really was," Hartnett muttered.

So did Bill, but right now, he didn't see any other choice.

As they split up to gather what they needed for this grim chore, a thought forced itself into his mind, and it was as unwelcome as any Pawnee war party would be.

From the looks of what had happened tonight, there was a good chance another cold-blooded murderer was lurking somewhere in Redemption.

Chapter 21

Because Bill and Costigan were busy putting Aaron Wetherby in the ground, there were no outriders patrolling the area around Redemption the rest of that night. Luckily, the hours before dawn passed quietly.

With help from Mordecai Flint and Josiah Hartnett, they got the unfortunate young man buried. Hartnett stretched a tarp over the grave, then parked one of his wagons on top of it.

Come morning, they would have to let Jeffrey McKenna, the minister of the Methodist Church, know why there was a fresh burial site in the graveyard behind the whitewashed sanctuary. That way, if anyone noticed the tarp and the wagon, McKenna could pass it off as some sort of work going on.

The preacher probably wouldn't like lying, Bill thought, but under the circumstances it was necessary.

The sun wasn't quite up when Bill finally made it back to the Monroe house. As he hung up his hat and then stretched his back, making it pop, he heard somebody moving around in the kitchen.

Eden must have heard him come in. She stepped out of the kitchen and came up the hall toward him. She wore her robe, and her hair was still tousled from sleep.

He held out his arms and she came into them. With a sigh of relief, she rested her head against his chest.

"Thank God you're back. I barely closed my eyes last night from worrying about you."

"I'm fine," he told her as he lifted a hand and stroked her hair. "Nothing happened."

The words threatened to catch in his throat. He didn't like lying, either, especially to his wife. Sooner or later, the truth was bound to come out, and when it did he would catch holy ned from Eden. He knew that. It was just a price he had to pay to try to keep the citizens of Redemption from going loco with fear.

"I just put the coffee on to boil," she told him. "Why don't you sit down and rest a few minutes while I fix breakfast?"

Bill smiled. "That sounds mighty good." He kissed her on the forehead, then went into the parlor and sank down in an armchair.

Not surprisingly, he was sound asleep less than a minute later.

When he woke up, he didn't know how much time had passed, but judging by how tired he still was, he didn't think he had slept for very long.

Eden knelt beside the chair. "I'm sorry," she said. "I hated to wake you, but I was afraid you might sleep for a long time, and I knew you wouldn't want that."

"You're right," Bill told her. "I got to get back downtown and make sure there are still guards on duty."

"Coffee and something to eat first." Eden stood and held out her hand. "No arguments."

Bill smiled and took her hand. "Nope, not a one."

Flapjacks, eggs, and bacon, washed down with three cups of strong coffee, made him feel almost human again. He wasn't groggy and his step was steady when he reached the marshal's office a short time later.

Mordecai Flint was dozing in the chair behind the desk. When Bill came in, he started to get up, but Bill waved the old-timer back into the chair and propped a hip on a corner of the desk instead.

"Appears the town's pretty quiet this morning," he commented.

Flint nodded. "Yeah, so far. Folks are tired after gettin' rousted outta bed last night when them buffalo hunters come in." The deputy paused and added, "It wouldn't be near so peaceful if they knew what really happened last night."

"You haven't heard any more about that, have you? Nobody saw us when we brought in Aaron's body?"

"Nope. If they did, they ain't talkin'."

"Where are Josiah and Costigan?"

"Hartnett headed back to his place to get some sleep. The buffalo hunter went back out to ride patrol again, just a little while ago."

Bill frowned. "Costigan was up all night."

"Yeah, I know, but he claimed he was fine. Even said he'd get some other fellas from his bunch to help him. I didn't figure we was in any shape to turn down the help," Flint added.

"No, not hardly," Bill said. "I'll talk to him later, let him know how much I appreciate what he's doin'."

"In the meantime, you might start thinkin' about what you'll tell folks if they ask about the Wetherby boy. Somebody's liable to notice that he ain't around no more."

Bill's mouth tightened. "I've already thought about that. I'll tell them that he decided to make a run for Dodge City. Nobody will be able to prove that he didn't."

"Yeah, I reckon that might work," Flint said. "I talked to the boy some. Don't recall him ever sayin' anything about bein' particularly close to anybody here in town. Think he said his folks lived on a farm over around Wichita somewhere, and I got the feelin' he didn't want to be stuck on the place the rest of his life."

"He wasn't," Bill said.

The night before, the drivers had pulled the wagons into an open area at the eastern edge of the settlement, then unhitched the teams and picketed the horses.

The men who had tents gathered around the supply wagon to take them out and pitched them near the wagons. Some of the men simply spread their blankets underneath the vehicles and crawled into them to sleep on the ground.

Colonel Bledsoe had picked a couple of men to stand guard. They had done so, muttering objections all the while.

Now most of the men were awake and moving around as Costigan approached the camp, leading his own horse. He had stopped by Hartnett's on the way here to return the liveryman's horse and put his saddle back on his own mount.

Dave McGinty hunkered on his heels next to a campfire, sipping on a cup of coffee. He looked up at Costigan and grunted a greeting.

Costigan started to ask his friend how he'd slept, then decided that would be unnecessarily cruel. He knew from the haunted look in McGinty's deep-set eyes that sleep had not been peaceful.

"Morning, Dave. Spare a cup of that coffee?"

"Sure," McGinty said without looking up at him. "Help yourself."

Costigan took his tin cup from his saddlebags and filled it. "I could use your help," he said as he put the pot back in the embers at the edge of the fire.

That made McGinty glance at him. "Help doin' what?"

"The marshal needs volunteers to ride patrols around the town and watch for the Pawnee."

"Ain't that what you did last night?"

"Yeah, but I thought I'd take another shift," Costigan said with a shrug. He added dryly, "This place appears to be a mite short of folks willing to step up and do what needs to be done."

"Then why should we help 'em?" McGinty asked in a surly tone.

Because we're the biggest reason they're in danger right now, Costigan thought. *Or rather, you and the rest of the bunch are.*

But that wasn't fair, he told himself. It was pure chance he had been with Captain Stone and the rest of the cavalry-men when the hunting party encountered those Pawnee youngsters. He could never be absolutely certain what he would have done if he had been there, too. He might think that he knew . . . but he couldn't be sure.

"They're letting us stay here," Costigan said instead. "They could have turned us away. I reckon we owe them some help for that."

"They wanted us here. We're thirty more guns to help them if there's trouble. Ain't that enough?"

Costigan shrugged again. "Suit yourself," he said as he turned away.

McGinty muttered a curse, then said, "Wait a minute, wait a minute. I never said I *wouldn't* pitch in. Lemme finish my coffee, and then I'll saddle my horse."

"Thanks, Dave," Costigan said. "I'm going to see if I can round up another couple of boys to help."

While he was walking through the camp, he spotted Bledsoe coming toward him. The colonel looked weary and harried, as he had for the past several days, and Costi-gan thought again that Bledsoe probably hadn't really had all the combat experience during the war that he claimed.

Bledsoe took hold of Costigan's arm and said in a low, urgent voice, "I've got to talk to you."

Costigan looked down at Bledsoe's sausage-fingered hand clutching his arm, then raised his cold gaze to the man's face.

"Speak your piece, Colonel."

"Not here." Bledsoe let go of Costigan. "Let's go over by the wagons."

Costigan started to tell Bledsoe that he was too busy for this, but he decided he had better hear the colonel out. If Bledsoe was thinking about doing something crazy, it would be better to know about it.

"All right," he said, "but make it fast."

They walked along the line of wagons until they reached a spot where no one was close by. When they stopped,

Bledsoe took off his derby and ran his hand over his bald dome. He looked scared.

"Did you say anything to that marshal about . . . what happened out there?"

"You mean those youngsters you massacred?" Costigan didn't care enough about Bledsoe to worry about hurting his feelings.

The colonel stiffened. "Damn it, man, I say again that you have no right—"

"I didn't tell anybody about it, Colonel," Costigan broke in, not wanting to listen to the man's false bravado. "Anyway, some small-town marshal doesn't have any jurisdiction over what happened a long way west of here."

"Maybe not, but he could tell tell somebody else. He could send a wire to the army."

Costigan shook his head. "No telegraph here. I already looked for lines coming into town."

"That doesn't mean he can't write a letter or take a ride to Dodge or send word some other way."

Bledsoe had a point. Costigan had seen enough of Bill Harvey to know that the marshal was the sort who tried to do the right thing, to do his duty as a lawman. He might have a little trouble figuring out exactly what the right course of action was, since he was still a young man, but he would do his best.

"If that's all you're worried about, Colonel, you might as well rest easy. I don't intend to say anything to the marshal or anybody else. It wouldn't change what's already been done, would it?"

"No. No, it wouldn't," Bledsoe said quickly. "Not at all."

"But you can make it easier for me to keep quiet," Costigan went on, smiling faintly.

Suspicion instantly leaped to life in Bledsoe's eyes. "What do you want?" he asked.

"We're going to do everything we can to help these people," Costigan said, and the firm strength of his voice, despite his exhaustion, made it clear that he wasn't going to put up with any argument. It no longer mattered that Colonel Bledsoe was his employer. "We're going to pitch in to defend Redemption any way we can, and right now I need some men to volunteer as outriders."

"Fine. You want me to pick out a couple?"

"They might take it better coming from you than me. McGinty's going to help, but he's my friend."

Bledsoe rubbed his jaw in thought for a second. "You can take Stennis and Rawley. How's that?"

They were both sharp-eyed men and good shots. Costigan nodded.

"That'll do."

"I'll go tell them to get their horses saddled." Bledsoe started toward the men, then stopped and looked back. "I know you blame me for all this, Costigan. But sometimes things happen that aren't anybody's fault. They're just bad luck, all the way around."

"Sure, Colonel," Costigan said.

If the man wanted to try to make himself believe that, it was none of Costigan's business.

But the stain of innocent blood would always be there, whether Bledsoe wanted to admit it or not. The colonel would see it every time he looked at his hands.

Costigan knew that from experience. He had tried to wash it off his own hands often enough . . . and always failed.

Men like Jacob Fraker, Luther Macauley, and Oscar Kipp seldom saw the morning sun when they were in a settlement. Drinking, gambling, and whoring were best done at night, so they usually didn't get up until midday, sometimes even later.

This time Fraker was awake by midmorning, however. His nerves wouldn't let him sleep any longer.

He had taken one of Smoot's girls upstairs with him when he got back to the saloon. Killing that boy and then sneaking back into the settlement had him all keyed up, and he'd needed something to take the edge off.

The soiled dove hadn't done a very good job of that. She was a little long in the tooth and probably hadn't had much real enthusiasm for her work since the boys came marching back from the war.

But Fraker's time with her had relieved enough of his tension that he was able to drop off to sleep.

Now he pushed himself up on an elbow as sunlight slanted in through the gauzy curtain over the room's single window. The woman still lay beside him with her gray-streaked hair spread out on the dingy pillow. She snored and wheezed.

Fraker found his hand clenching into a fist. He wanted to wallop the woman a couple of times and chase her out of the room.

He forced his hand to unclench and settled for giving her a sharp slap on the rump through the sheet. The blow made her jerk away and exclaim, "Oh! What the hell?"

"Get out," Fraker told her.

The angry look on her face went away and was replaced by a coy expression. She slid closer to him.

"Aw, now, honey, that ain't no way to wake up. There's no hurry. I can show you some things—"

"Nothing I want to see right now." Fraker's voice was flat and hard. "Go on. Out."

She sniffed, rolled out of bed, and tried to give him a haughty look. That was pretty much impossible to pull off since her hair was tangled like one of those Medusas Fraker had seen in a book sometime and other things were sagging every which way. He put his back to her and ignored her, not getting out of bed until she slammed the door behind her on her way out of the room.

Macauley and Kipp were sharing the next room. That offended the fastidious Macauley's sensitivities, but Fraker didn't give a damn. He pounded on the wall to wake them, then pulled his clothes on.

Macauley was up and dressed by the time Fraker knocked on the door, but Kipp was still in bed, moaning.

"What's the matter with him?"

"What do you think?" Macauley asked. "He guzzled down too much rotgut whiskey last night. I had to listen to him puke into the thunder mug a while ago."

Fraker sniffed the air and could smell the vomit. "Yeah. Come on."

"Gladly," Macauley said.

The two of them went downstairs. Fraker expected to find a commotion going on. Saloons usually weren't very busy at this time of day, but he thought more men might be drinking this morning since everyone in town would be up-set about the "Indians" killing that outrider.

Instead, the tables were empty except for one where Fred Smoot sat in his wheelchair, drinking coffee and look-ing at an old newspaper. No one was at the bar. The place was as dead as it could be.

Smoot looked up at Fraker and Macauley and frowned. "Lorrie's not happy with you," he said to Fraker. "She says you slapped her."

"I gave her a swat on that butt of hers, which has got enough meat on it I'm surprised she even felt it," Fraker said. "Did she tell you that?"

Smoot shrugged.

"I told her to get out, and she was too slow about it. That's not my fault."

"Just forget it," Smoot said.

Macauley put his hands in his pockets, rocked forward and back on his toes, and said, "Quiet morning."

"Yeah." Smoot went back to his coffee and paper.

"No trouble last night after those buffalo hunters showed up?" Fraker asked.

"Not that I'm aware of."

Fraker and Macauley glanced at each other. Fraker had told his partners about his successful mission. Now it ap-peared that it hadn't been so successful after all.

But that kid had to be dead, Fraker thought. There was no doubt about that in his mind. Maybe the body just hadn't been found yet, although that seemed unlikely to him. One of the other outriders should have come across it by now.

"Seen the marshal this morning?"

Smoot didn't look up this time. "Nope. You need him?"

Fraker shook his head. "No, just wondering, that's all. And still no sign of the Pawnee?"

"No, and I'm starting to think they're not going to show up." Smoot took a sip of his coffee. "A man can hope, anyway."

Fraker scratched his jaw. "Yeah. A man can hope."

And he could wonder what the hell had gone wrong, too.

Chapter 22

Costigan was gone already by the time Bill reached the buffalo hunters' camp, but Colonel Bledsoe, the leader of the party, informed him that Costigan and three other men had left to ride wide circuits around Redemption.

"I'm mighty obliged to you and your men for the help, Colonel."

"Glad to do it, glad to do it," Bledsoe had said. "We're, uh, all in this together, aren't we, Marshal?"

"I reckon so. We're all here in Redemption, anyway."

Something about Bledsoe's attitude struck Bill as odd. The man was nervous, of course, but so was everybody else in town. It was more than that.

Bill didn't have time to ponder the question, nor was he really inclined to. He spent the next couple of hours going around town, talking to everyone, trying to reassure the really frightened ones, and making sure sentries were in place on the rooftops.

From the sound of it, Costigan and some of the other buffalo hunters had the outrider jobs covered for now.

By the late morning, though, Bill found himself wanting

to make sure of that, so he went to the livery stable to get his horse.

Josiah Hartnett greeted him by asking, "Did you get any sleep, Marshal?"

Bill smiled. "I dozed off for a while, waiting for Eden to fix breakfast."

"You can't keep pushing yourself like you have been. You've got to have some rest."

"I'm young," Bill said. "And remember, I was a cowboy. I'm used to stayin' in the saddle for a long time. Speakin' of which, I'm gonna ride out and see how Mr. Costigan and those other buffalo hunters are doing."

"Yeah, I heard they were handling the outrider chores. Why don't you sit down in the office? I'll go throw your saddle on your horse."

"I can do it," Bill said, but Hartnett pointed sternly at the door leading into the small office built onto the side of the livery barn. "I think you're forgettin' who's the marshal here."

"You still ought to respect your elders," Hartnett said with a grin.

Bill gave up, shook his head, and went into the office.

Hartnett found him there a few minutes later, asleep in the chair.

"Hate to disturb you, Bill," he said, "but I've got your horse ready to go."

Bill's head jerked up. "What?" He looked around for a second as if he didn't know where he was or what he was doing here. His surroundings soaked in on him and brought with them memories of what was going on. He rubbed a hand over his face. "Yeah. Thanks, Josiah."

"I've got a cot in the tack room, if you want to stretch out," Hartnett offered.

Bill stood up and shook his head. "Thanks, but I've got things to do."

He climbed into the saddle and rode out of the livery barn with a wave of farewell for Hartnett.

Despite the fact that it was the middle of the day, Redemption's Main Street wasn't very busy. A few people were going in and out of the stores, but not many. Men holding rifles or shotguns stood here and there, watching. Bill glanced up and saw more armed men on the roofs.

The air of tension that had gripped the town for days was just as strong as ever. But the guards were at their posts, and Bill felt a little better for knowing that he had done what he could to get the citizens ready for trouble.

He waved to some of the men on the rooftops as he rode out of the settlement. He headed west, thinking that he would be likely to intercept at least one of the outriders that way.

A mile west of town, a grassy knob rose from the plains around it. The knob wasn't very high, but out here on these flats, it didn't take much height to let a man see a long way.

Bill rode to the top of the knob and reined in. He turned his head and shifted in the saddle as well, trying to see as much around him as he could. When he looked back over his shoulder at the town, he could see the roofs of the buildings and the steeple on top of the Methodist Church.

From this distance, Redemption looked like a peaceful little place, the sort of community where a fella could settle down and raise a family, and be content with the knowledge that he was making the world a better place.

It didn't look like a town plagued by murder and gun battles, and yet that was exactly what recent months had brought.

Now Redemption was facing danger again, Bill thought. And it was up to him to do what he could to head it off.

A moment later he spotted a rider heading in his direction from the north. Bill waited until the man was closer, then took off his hat and waved it over his head to get the rider's attention. The man turned his horse a little, angling directly toward the knob as Bill rode down the slope to meet him.

The rider wasn't Ward Costigan. He was a shorter, stockier man with dark hair and a close-cropped beard.

As he and Bill reined in, he gave the young lawman a curt nod.

"Howdy, Marshal," he said. "Come out to check on us?"

"That's right. We haven't met. I'm Bill Harvey."

"Dave McGinty."

"I'm pleased to meet you, Mr. McGinty. Wish it was under better circumstances."

McGinty grunted. "You and me both, Marshal."

"So, have you seen anything out of the ordinary?"

"Not a thing," McGinty replied. "Haven't seen anything at all besides a few prairie chickens and a snake."

Bill turned his head again and let his gaze sweep over the western horizon.

"Do you think they're out there, Mr. McGinty? The Pawnee, I mean."

For a moment, McGinty didn't answer. When he did, his voice had a harsh edge to it.

"I know damn well they are. I can feel 'em, same way as I could always feel where a herd of buffalo was."

"I'm sorry to hear that," Bill said. "I was hopin' maybe the hostiles would pass us by."

"I wouldn't count on it," McGinty said. "I'd better get movin', Marshal."

Bill nodded. "I won't keep you. Thanks for your help. I was mighty glad to see you and the rest of your party last night."

McGinty just grunted again. Bill didn't know what provoked that reaction or why the man seemed so surly, but he didn't say anything else, just lifted his hand in farewell as McGinty rode off.

The buffalo hunter didn't return the wave.

Bill didn't wait to see if any of the other outriders showed up. If they had run into bad trouble, shots would have been fired, and the way sound traveled out here on the plains, the other outriders probably would have heard the gunfire. Even the people in town might have heard it.

Instead Bill rode back to the settlement, confident that the outrider duties were in good hands for the moment. He thought he would get some lunch, and then maybe . . . just maybe . . . he could catch a few winks.

Shame it didn't work out that way.

When Oscar Kipp stumbled down the stairs in the saloon not long after noon, Fraker knew there was going to be trouble.

Kipp wasn't really a mean drunk, but he was a bear when he was hungover, as he was now. Pausing at the bottom of the stairs and hanging on to the banister as if he were still dizzy, the big man glared around the room.

Looking for a fight, Fraker thought. Kipp wanted to hit somebody, and the more damage he could deal out, the better.

"Uh-oh," Macauley said from the chair where he sat at a table with Fraker.

"You see it, too, eh?"

"We should get him out of here. Maybe take him back down to that whorehouse."

"So he can start a ruckus there?" Fraker shook his head. "We'll stay here. If we can get some more rotgut in him, maybe that'll calm him down enough to keep him from raising hell. Go get him."

"Me? Why don't you go get him?"

"He's less likely to throw a punch at you."

"I don't know how you figure that," Macauley said. "He doesn't like me any more than he does you."

"Well, one of us had better—" Fraker sat up straighter. "Oh, hell!"

The soiled dove he had slapped on the rump and kicked out of his room earlier that morning—Lorrie, that was what Smoot had called her—was on her way over to Kipp. She had put on a dress and combed her hair, but she still looked like what she was: a worn-out whore in a squalid frontier saloon.

Fraker came to his feet, but he couldn't get there in time to stop her from rubbing a hand up and down Kipp's arm and saying, "Hello, big fella. How'd you like a little eye-opener this morning, if you know what I mean?"

Kipp's lumbering reaction reminded Fraker even more of a bear. The man's shaggy head swung slowly toward Lorrie.

"Get away from me," he said, adding a vile name that made Lorrie flinch even though surely she had heard it before.

"You got no call to talk to me like that," she said, her voice going up shrilly.

Fraker was only a few feet away now. He held out a hand and said, "Oscar, why don't we—"

Kipp didn't let Fraker finish. Instead his arm came up, and even though he was sick and dizzy, he moved with surprising speed. The back of his hand smashed across Lorrie's face. She didn't even have time to cry out in shock and pain before she sailed backward and fell across one of the empty tables.

The saloon was busier now than it had been earlier when Fraker and Macauley first came down from upstairs. Several men stood at the bar, and a couple of the tables were occupied besides the one where Fraker and Macauley had been sitting.

When Kipp hauled off and hit Lorrie, one of the men at the bar thumped his beer mug down and said, "Hey, you son of a bitch! You can't treat a woman like that!"

Fraker reached for Kipp, saying, "Oscar, no!"

But Kipp lowered his head and charged toward the man at the bar, barreling past Fraker like a runaway bull. Fraker stood just about as much chance of stopping him as he would have of stopping a bull, too.

The man got his fists up and swung a punch at Kipp's head, but the blow missed and Kipp plowed into him, driving him against the bar. The man yelled in pain.

One of the other men at the bar grabbed a bottle and swung it at the back of Kipp's head. The big man hunched his shoulders and took the blow on them. The bottle shattered, spraying him with whiskey, but didn't do any real damage.

Kipp lashed out. His arm struck the man who had just

broken the bottle on his shoulders and drove the man off his feet.

Continuing the move, Kipp turned and grabbed the shirtfront of another man. With a bellow of rage, Kipp lifted the man and slung him all the way over the bar. The man's legs hit bottles lined up along the back bar and broke them with a crash of glass.

Fred Smoot wheeled himself toward the melee and shouted, "Stop it, you idiots, stop it!" He cast a desperate look at Fraker and Macauley. "Do something!"

Fraker knew it was too late for that. If Smoot thought he and Macauley could control Kipp when the big man went on a tear like this, the saloon owner was sadly mistaken.

The only thing they might be able to do was get close enough to Kipp to bend a gun barrel over his head and knock him out, and even that was doubtful.

Considering their plans, though, drawing attention to themselves wasn't a good idea, so Fraker slipped his gun from its holster and moved in. He had to draw back when Kipp grabbed one of the other men and used the yelling hombre like a battering ram to clear a space around him.

The bartender came up behind Kipp on the other side of the hardwood and tried to use a bungstarter on him. Some instinct must have warned Kipp, because he twisted around and flung up an arm to block the blow.

His other fist shot out and crashed into the bartender's face. As the blow drove the bartender backward, he let go of the bungstarter. It dropped to the bar with a thud.

"Stop it!" Fred Smoot screeched from the sidelines of the brawl as he clenched his fists and beat them against his useless legs. "You bastard!"

At that moment, Fraker didn't know if Smoot was talking to Kipp . . . or cursing himself for not being able to get up and stop the fight.

There was no time to think about that. Kipp grabbed the bungstarter from the bar. He flailed around him with it, and the men who'd been trying to throw punches at him had no choice but to dive out of the way.

With that much force behind it, the bungstarter could crush a skull like an eggshell if it landed against somebody's head.

Even in Kipp's addled, hungover state, he had something specific in mind, though. He fixed his fierce gaze on Smoot and shouted, "You cripple! I hate a damn cripple!"

Fraker's jaw clenched. He had made the same comment a few days earlier, and Kipp must have remembered it. The state he was in, though, he had recalled it incorrectly and thought *he* was the one who had expressed that sentiment.

He was in the mood to take action on it, too. He lifted the bungstarter over his head and charged at Smoot, who paled in sudden fear and grabbed the wheels on the sides of his chair to try to push himself out of the way.

He didn't have a chance. Kipp swung the bungstarter but missed, hitting the back of the chair instead. His momentum made him crash into Smoot anyway. The chair went over with a splintering of wood, and Smoot spilled out onto the sawdust-littered floor.

"Should we shoot him?" Macauley asked Fraker in a tense voice.

Fraker had considered that idea, too. As loco as Kipp was now, plugging him might be the only way to stop him.

Kipp was still important to his plans, though, and any time you took a shot at a man, you risked killing him, even if you were just shooting to wound and subdue him. All it took was a bullet nicking a vein, and a fella could bleed to death in a hurry.

Kipp scrambled after Smoot on hands and knees, still holding the bungstarter. Smoot tried to pull himself along with his hands as his legs trailed limply behind him, but he had no chance to get away.

Kipp loomed over him, the bungstarter raised high. When it fell, it would shatter the saloon owner's head and splatter his brains all over the floor.

Chapter 23

Bill had just swung down from the saddle and looped the reins over the hitch rail in front of the marshal's office when he heard someone shout, "Marshal! Marshal Harvey!"

That sounded like trouble. He turned quickly, his hand going to the Colt on his hip.

A man was running across the street toward him. Bill recognized the man and knew he lived here in Redemption, but he couldn't recall the fella's name.

"What is it?" he asked as the townie came up to him, panting and out of breath.

"Big fight . . . down at Smoot's," the man said. He bent over and put his hands on his knees, looking a little green around the gills as he did so. "Fella's actin' like . . . he's gonna kill somebody."

"Who is it?"

The man shook his head. "Don't know. One of the strangers in town."

That didn't narrow it down much, Bill thought. In addition to the full-time citizens of Redemption, currently the town was populated by the teamsters and bullwhackers from Gus Meade's train of freight wagons, Colonel Bled-

soe's buffalo hunters, and the usual assortment of folks
who drifted in and out of town all the time . . . gamblers,
wandering cowboys, immigrants, and the like.

Of course, it didn't really matter. Whoever was causing
trouble, it was Bill's job to stop it.

"Thanks," he told the man who'd reported the fight. "I'll
go on down there. Can you see if Deputy Flint is in the office, and if he is, send him to Smoot's, too?"

He didn't think he'd have any trouble subduing one
troublemaker, but you never could tell.

The man nodded and said, "Sure, Marshal, but you'd
better hurry. That big varmint is hell on wheels."

That didn't sound like anybody Bill knew. He started toward the saloon, moving as quickly as his bad leg would
allow.

He heard yelling before he got there. Men were crowded
around the entrance, peering over the batwings as they tried
to see what was going on.

Bill called in a commanding voice, "Step aside, there!
Step aside!"

The knot of men around the door parted. Bill put his
hand on the butt of his gun but didn't draw the weapon yet.
He didn't want to shoot anybody unless he had to. He had
seen some trigger-happy lawmen down in Texas, and he
didn't ever want anybody accusing him of that.

Bill shouldered through the batwings and stepped into
the saloon. The first thing he saw was a big man on one
knee next to Fred Smoot, who had fallen or gotten
knocked out of his chair somehow and was sprawled on
the floor.

The big man had a bungstarter in his hand, and clearly
he was about to brain Smoot with it. Bill slid his Colt out of
its holster as he yelled, "Hey!"

The bungstarter didn't fall. The man's head jerked
around toward Bill. Rage contorted his features as he stood
up, let out an incoherent yell, and charged, waving the
bungstarter.

Bill's eyes widened. Clearly, this hombre was loco and

intended to kill him. A man had to be crazy to charge right into the barrel of a gun.

Bill dropped his aim and pulled the trigger.

The Colt roared and bucked in his hand. The slug tore through the big man's right thigh and knocked that leg out from under him. Bellowing like an angry bull, the man tumbled off his feet. The bungstarter flew out of his hand and clattered across the floor.

The wounded man clutched his leg and rolled back and forth. Blood welled between his fingers.

But somehow he pushed himself to his feet. From the look on his face, he intended to tear Bill apart with his bare hands, even if he had to drag his bloody leg behind him to get there.

Bill wondered if he was going to have to kill the man to make him stay down.

Before things got to that point, another man stepped up behind the stranger and chopped down with the butt of the gun he had reversed in his hand. The blow landed with a solid thud on the back of the big man's head.

The big man dropped to his knees and toppled forward like a falling tree. He didn't even put out his hands to catch himself. His face hit the floor. He didn't move.

The man who had hit him from behind slipped his revolver back in its holster and said, "Thanks for not killin' him, Marshal."

Bill's heart was still pounding hard in his chest, but he managed to keep his voice calm and steady as he asked, "Friend of yours, mister?" He recognized the men from outside the saloon a few days earlier.

"That's right."

"What in blazes is wrong with him? Is he touched in the head?"

The man laughed, but it wasn't a happy sound. "No, just hungover. He gets like this sometimes, when he's had too much to drink."

Bill took a fresh cartridge from one of the loops on his shell belt and replaced the round he had fired. Doing that routine chore gave him the chance to get his pulse and breathing under control even more.

"If he's your friend, maybe you should try to see that he doesn't drink that much."

"That's probably a good idea," the man said with a shrug, "but it's not always easy to do."

Bill supposed that was true. Grown men had a habit of doing what they wanted to.

"Is there a doctor in this town?" the man asked. "That bullet hole in his leg needs to be patched up before he bleeds to death."

"No doctor." Bill remembered how Eden had taken care of him when he was gored by that steer, and later when he was shot. "My wife's pretty good at taking care of wounded men, though." He looked around and his gaze stopped on one of the townies. "Run across to the mercantile and fetch Mrs. Harvey if she's there, would you, Jimmy?"

"Sure, Marshal." The townsman hurried out of the saloon.

Bill went over to Fred Smoot, who still looked dazed despite having pushed himself up into a sitting position.

"Somebody set up that wheelchair and give me a hand with Fred," Bill ordered.

"Won't do any good, Marshal," a man said. "The chair's busted."

Bill looked closer and saw that one of the wheels had broken off.

"Go get Josiah Hartnett. Maybe he can fix it." Bill hunkered on his heels next to Smoot. "Are you hurt, Fred?"

Smoot passed a shaking hand over his face. "No . . . no, I reckon not. Just shaken up. That monster was going to kill me, and I don't even know why! I didn't do anything to set him off. Nobody did, except—" The saloonkeeper looked around. "Where's Lorrie? Is she all right?"

One of the soiled doves who worked for Smoot came over. She had a bruise starting to come out on her face, but other than that she didn't seem to be injured.

"I'll be fine, Fred," she told him. "It's sweet of you to

worry about me, though. Maybe some of the boys should carry you up to my room and put you to bed."

Smoot shook his head. "No, I'm all right. If somebody will just help me into a chair . . ."

The bartender and a couple of the saloon's patrons did that while Bill checked on the other men who had been injured in the brawl. Some of them were still groggy, and there were plenty of bumps, bruises, and scrapes, but no one was hurt seriously.

Eden hurried into the saloon, followed by the man who had gone to fetch her. Relief lit up her eyes when she saw that Bill was on his feet and apparently unhurt.

"Thanks for coming, Eden," he told her. He motioned toward the unconscious man. "You think you can wrap up that leg and stop the bleeding?"

"I can certainly try," she said. "Some of you men shove a couple of tables together and lift him onto them so I can work on him."

Bill smiled at the way she took charge. While she was taking care of that, he went over to the man who had knocked out the loco varmint and said, "I'm much obliged to you for your help."

The man shrugged. "I understand why you had to shoot Oscar, Marshal, but I didn't want you to kill him."

"That's his name? Oscar?"

"Oscar Kipp. I'm Jake Fraker." He inclined his head toward a dapper man who had come up beside him. "This is Luther Macauley."

"The three of you are partners?"

"That's right. We've been riding together for a while."

"You know your friend's gonna have to go to jail once he's patched up?" Bill said.

Fraker nodded. "I figured as much. There'll be damages to pay, and probably a fine."

"Judge Dunaway will have to sort out all of that."

"Whatever it comes to, we'll pay it."

"Fair enough." Bill looked over at the tables where Eden had cut away Oscar Kipp's trouser leg to reveal the bullet holes in his leg. It appeared that the slug had gone clean through.

"His leg doesn't seem to be broken," Eden said as if reading Bill's mind. "So the bullet missed the bone. He should be all right once it heals up, as long as I can get this bleeding stopped. I need some clean rags for bandages."

The bartender handed her several rags. She stuffed one in each bullet hole, then used Kipp's own belt to tie them in place. Red stains spread on the rags, then slowed and stopped.

"You can get him over to the jail now," Eden told Bill.

"He's your friend," Bill said to Fraker and Macauley. "How about lending a hand?"

Macauley didn't look very happy about that, but Fraker said, "Sure, Marshal."

A couple of other men pitched in, too. Together they carried the still-unconscious Oscar Kipp toward the jail. Bill and Eden trailed behind.

On the way they met Mordecai Flint. "I just heard about what was goin' on," the deputy said. "You all right, Marshal?"

"Fine," Bill said with a nod. "We're gonna lock this fella up. He raised a ruckus in the saloon, tried to kill Fred Smoot, and came at me with a bungstarter like he had the same thing in mind."

"He's lucky you didn't blow a hole through his innards, instead of just wingin' him."

Bill nodded. "I thought about it. A saloon brawl didn't seem worth killin' a man over, though."

Once the men had Kipp on the bunk in one of the cells, Eden sent a man over to the mercantile for some actual bandages. She asked Bill to go back to the saloon to get a bottle of whiskey so she could use it to clean the wounds, but Flint cleared his throat, opened a drawer in the desk, and took out a bottle.

"Figured this might come in handy for, uh, medicinal purposes," the old-timer said. "And it looks like I was right."

Bill tried not to grin as he took the bottle and carried it into the cell to hand to Eden.

Kipp began to come around as Eden used the fiery liquor to swab blood away from the bullet holes. Bill stood nearby with his hand on his gun.

"Take it easy, mister," he warned as Kipp's eyelids fluttered open. "You're in jail, you're under arrest, and you're not goin' anywhere. Now let the lady take care of that wounded leg for you."

Fraker and Macauley were standing outside the cell, along with Flint. Fraker said, "Oscar, it's me, Jake. Do you hear me?"

"Jake . . . ?" Kipp muttered.

"That's right. You went on a rampage in the saloon because you were hungover. You remember that? That's all that happened, so you just lay there and let the lady tend to you. You've caused enough trouble already."

Something about the urgency in Fraker's voice struck Bill as a little odd. It was like the man was really trying to get through to Kipp and make him understand the situation.

But Bill supposed that was because Fraker didn't want Kipp trying to fight again. That made sense.

"Jail," Kipp said as his head dropped back on the bunk.

"Don't worry," Fraker said from the other side of the bars. "Luther and I will see to it that you're all right. We've got enough money to cover the damages and pay for the fine. You'll be outta there before you know it."

"The judge will determine that," Bill said.

"Yeah, but surely he won't lock our pard up for too long over a simple bar fight. A night or two to cool off, maybe."

"We'll see," Bill said, a curt edge in his voice now. He wasn't going to make any promises.

He could see Fraker's point, though. As things turned out, Kipp had been hurt worse than anybody else. And besides, everybody in Redemption had more to worry about right now than some saloon brawl. The threat of the Pawnee war party still loomed.

The man got back from the mercantile with a roll of

bandages. After a few more minutes of work, Eden had the bullet holes cleaned and bandaged.

"Those dressings will need to be checked and changed every day," she said, "but I think he'll be all right."

Fraker said, "We're sure obliged to you, ma'am. That was some fine doctorin'." He smiled. "Maybe you should hang out your shingle."

Eden frowned. "You mean be a doctor?" She shook her head. "I don't think so. I have to patch up enough wounds just being a marshal's wife."

They stepped out of the cell. Bill clanged the door closed and told Fraker and Macauley, "You fellas can go on now. We'll take care of your friend."

Something stirred in Fraker's dark eyes. Anger at Kipp being locked up, maybe.

But he nodded and said, "Thanks again for not killing him, Marshal. I can promise you, there won't be any more trouble."

"Not with him behind bars, I reckon."

"Yeah, but when he's out, we'll be leaving Redemption and movin' on. Assuming, of course, that the threat of those savages is over by then."

"That's a big assumption," Bill said as he ushered the two men out of the cell block and into the marshal's office. Eden and Flint followed them, and the deputy closed the heavy wooden door between the office and the cell block.

Fraker said, "The army's bound to round up those Indians sooner or later. Didn't I hear that a patrol's out looking for them?"

"Several patrols," Bill said. "And the one that came through here to warn us is out there somewhere, too. They could've run into the war party, I suppose."

"I reckon we'll get word any day now that it's all over," Fraker said.

"Can't be too soon to suit me," Bill said.

Chapter 24

"What the hell are we going to do now?" Macauley demanded, low-voiced, as he glared across the table at Fraker.

They were back in the saloon. The tables and chairs that had been overturned were upright again. The broken glass and other debris left over from the fight had been swept up and thrown in the trash, and the bartender had mopped up all the spilled booze. The smell of raw liquor still hung in the air. Fred Smoot must have gone upstairs after all, because he wasn't in the barroom.

"Don't worry," Fraker told his partner. "Everything is still all right."

"All right, hell!" Macauley snapped. "You've been saying that for days, Jake, and we're no closer to the money in that bank than when we rode in here."

"Keep your voice down. We're going to get that money. The right time—"

"The right time is never going to come," Macauley said. "We've been waiting on those damned redskins, and you said it yourself . . . there's no guarantee they'll *ever* show up. Your plan to stir up the town even more didn't accomplish a blasted thing—"

"I killed that boy just like I said I did. Are you callin' me a liar, Luther?"

Macauley held up a hand. "You know I'm not. But you've got to admit, whatever happened, it didn't work out like you planned."

Fraker shrugged and said, "I don't understand it. That should've worked."

"Now Oscar's in jail, and with bullet holes in his leg, to boot! He's not going to be any good to us if we need him, Jake."

"That *is* a shame," Fraker said.

"You should've plugged that marshal before he could shoot Oscar."

"Oh, and gunning down the town's lawman wouldn't have ruined our plans?" Fraker snorted in disgust. "We'd have had to shoot our way out of town, otherwise these people probably would've strung us up. I tried to knock Oscar out before things got that far, but I couldn't get close enough to him until then. At least I kept the marshal from killing him."

With a grudging nod, Macauley said, "That's true, I suppose. But it still doesn't change the fact that everything's gone wrong since we got here."

"We can still empty the safe in that bank, just you and me," Fraker insisted. "If the Indians cooperate, we can do like we planned, only without Oscar."

"And then we bust him out of jail while the rest of the town is busy fighting the Pawnee?"

"If we can," Fraker said. "If we can't . . . that'll be Oscar's bad luck."

"You'd leave him here?"

"You think he wouldn't run out on us if things were the other way around?"

Macauley looked uncomfortable with the idea, but after a moment he said, "Well, yeah, he might. But you're forgetting, Jake . . . if we leave him behind, he can tell the law who we are."

"The marshal already knows who we are."

"Only because you told him."

"There aren't any reward posters with our names on them," Fraker said. "And you and the rest of the boys have me to thank for that. All the jobs I've planned have gone off so well nobody knows who pulled them."

"Until now," Macauley insisted.

Fraker shook his head. "There'll be so much confusion in town that no one will be sure who robbed the bank. They may have their suspicions, but they won't be able to prove it." He tossed back the shot of whiskey he had poured a few minutes earlier, before Macauley started complaining. "Anyway, I've been thinking about what we can do to make it even less likely that anybody will come after us."

"What's that?"

"There's a good chance the Pawnee will set the town on fire." Fraker smiled. "And if they don't, we will. I'm gonna make sure we get away with this, Luther . . . even if it means burning Redemption to the ground."

Costigan rolled his shoulders in an attempt to ease the aching weariness that gripped them. He put his hands on his saddle horn and arched his back, feeling bones pop and muscles stretch.

He had been in the saddle too long, no doubt about that.

What he really needed right now was to crawl into his tent, stretch out on his bedroll, and sleep for twenty-four hours straight. Probably wasn't going to happen, though, and he was resigned to that fact.

He peered off to the west and squinted against the afternoon sunlight. Was something moving out there? He thought he had caught a flicker of motion.

After a minute he shook his head. Nothing. Maybe he had imagined it. Maybe it was just a trick of the light, or his eyes letting him know that they were too tired to keep this up.

Or maybe whatever he'd seen had gone to ground.

Just to be sure, Costigan turned his horse and rode in

that direction. He didn't think he was particularly nervous, but he realized that his hand was gripping the stock of the Henry tighter than before.

When he had gone a quarter of a mile, he saw more movement in the corner of his eye. He reined in and looked to the north.

No mistake about it this time. A rider was angling in from that direction. After a moment, Costigan's keen eyes recognized him as Dave McGinty.

Costigan raised a hand, just in case McGinty hadn't already seen him. He thought that was unlikely. McGinty was an observant man . . . at least most of the time.

Costigan stayed where he was and waited for McGinty to come to him. When the bearded man rode up, he reined in and asked, "Did you see something out this way, Ward?"

"Thought I did," Costigan replied. "You, too?"

"Yeah. Just a hint of something. Never could figure out what it was."

Costigan reached inside his saddlebags for his spyglass. "Let me take a better look."

He extended the telescope and lifted it to his eye. He swept the glass slowly along the horizon from north to south and then back.

Costigan lowered the telescope and shook his head.

"Nothing. Just empty prairie."

"Damn it, I'm sure I saw *something*." McGinty licked his lips. "You reckon I'm goin' loco, Ward? Seein' things that ain't there?"

"If you are, then the same thing has happened to me, and I don't think being crazy is contagious."

Although the way men acted sometimes, it was hard to be sure. The war was proof enough of that.

Costigan nodded toward the west. "Let's ride a little farther out."

McGinty looked over his shoulder toward Redemption and said, "We're gettin' a pretty good ways from the settlement."

"I know. We won't go much farther."

"All right," McGinty said, but he sounded like he thought it might not be a good idea.

Costigan wasn't sure it was, either, but if there was anything out here to worry about, the people back in Redemption would need all the warning they could get.

The two men rode side by side, scanning the landscape around them. Costigan didn't see anything, didn't hear anything, but still his skin crawled. He knew his instincts were speaking to him, trying to tell him that something was wrong.

Costigan wasn't the only one who felt that way. McGinty said, "Aw, hell, Ward, I'm startin' to get a mighty bad feelin' . . ."

"So am I," Costigan said. "Let's get out of—"

The dozen or so riders seemed to charge out of nowhere. As soon as Costigan saw them erupt into sight, he knew they must have been hidden in some arroyo or coulee. The ponies' hooves pounded the earth, but that was the only sound. The Pawnee warriors attacked in silence, instead of whooping and yipping, and somehow that made them even more frightening.

McGinty yelled a curse and yanked his horse around. Costigan hauled on his mount's reins and brought the animal around, too. They kicked the horses into a desperate gallop.

"We were right!" McGinty yelled over the hoofbeats as he held his hat on.

"Yeah!" Costigan said.

He would have rather been wrong.

Now it was a race. The Indian ponies were lighter and might be fresher, but the two white men had a lead. The Pawnee had jumped them a little too soon, thought Costigan. If they had waited until he and McGinty were a little closer, the two of them wouldn't have had a chance to get away.

But they had already slowed down and were thinking about turning back, and the Indians might have sensed that and figured that if they were going to attack, it had to be now.

The important thing was going to be maintaining that gap, and Costigan didn't know if they could do that. When he looked back, he saw that the pursuers had already closed in a little.

"Give it all you've got, Dave!" he shouted.

McGinty slashed his horse with the reins. "I'm tryin'!"

Costigan saw an arrow fall about ten yards to his right. He hadn't thought the Pawnee were within bowshot yet, but obviously he was wrong.

They were just firing wildly, though. At that range, and firing from galloping ponies, any sort of real accuracy was out of the question.

No sooner had that thought gone through Costigan's mind than McGinty yelled and jerked forward in the saddle. Costigan's head whipped toward him. He saw the arrow shaft sticking out of McGinty's back. The arrow had struck him just below the left shoulder and lodged there.

"Hang on, Dave!" Costigan shouted. He brought his racing horse a little closer to McGinty's mount and reached over with his left hand to grab his friend's arm and steady him.

McGinty let out a groan and clutched at the saddle horn. "God!" he said. "It hurts!"

"I know! Just hang on!"

Side by side, a single misstep away from disaster, they raced on toward the settlement with the Pawnee closing in on them from behind.

With Oscar Kipp locked up and not giving any trouble now except for the droning curses that came through the window in the cell block door, Bill gave in to his exhaustion and yawned.

"Why don't you go home and get some real sleep?" Eden asked as she paused in the office doorway.

Bill shook his head. "No, there's too much to do. If I stretch out and get comfortable, I'm liable not to wake up for ten or twelve hours." He motioned toward the old sofa that sat against the front wall of the office. "I'll just catch a nap here. I won't sleep as long that way."

"I don't like to see you wearing yourself out."

"Goes with the job, I reckon," he told her with a smile. He stepped over to her and bent to give her a kiss.

At the desk, Mordecai Flint cleared his throat.

Bill looked back at the deputy with a grin. "As old as you are, I'd have thought you'd seen a husband kiss his wife before now."

"Just remindin' you two youngsters that I'm still here," Flint said. "I know how the hot blood o' youth gets carried away sometimes."

"I'm going back to the mercantile now," Eden said with a smile. She slipped out of the arm that Bill had slid around her and was out the door before he could stop her.

"I'll go take a turn or two around town," Flint said as he stood up. "That way you'll have some peace and quiet in here." He looked at the cell block door. "Except for that varmint's cussin'. Want me to go knock him in the head and shut him up?"

Bill shook his head. "As tired as I am, I reckon that cussin' will sound just like a lullaby to me."

That prediction proved to be true. As soon as Bill stretched out on the old sofa, Kipp's curses faded away. So did everything else. Bill was asleep in moments.

He didn't dream, at least not that he remembered. But he came awake with a gasp, the same way he would have if a nightmare had jolted him out of his sleep.

It was no nightmare . . . or maybe it was. Mordecai Flint stood beside the sofa, leaning down with his arm extended. Bill realized that the deputy had just shaken him awake.

"What is it?" Bill asked as he sat up. He didn't know how long he had been asleep, and at the moment he didn't care. The worried look on Flint's whiskery face had banished all such thoughts.

"Riders comin' toward town, movin' fast," Flint reported.

"From which direction?"

"West."

That was bad. Of course, the Pawnee could circle around and attack the town from any direction, but they had been west of Redemption the last time they'd been seen. That made it more likely the war party was here at last.

Bill swung his legs off the sofa and stood up. He had left his boots on, so all he had to do was grab his hat from the nail and he was ready to go. As he started out the door, he asked, "Who spotted the riders?"

"Spotted the dust, you mean," Flint said. "The riders were too far away to make 'em out. But it was that Ramsey fella, the newspaperman. He's standin' watch on top of the bank."

Phillip Ramsey had been one of the volunteers right from the start. That kept him in the middle of things, and Bill had a hunch that played a part in him agreeing to stand guard. Scared though he might be, Ramsey wanted to be where he could get the best story for his paper.

As he and Flint hurried toward the bank, Bill looked around. Not many people were on the street, but that wasn't unusual these days. With the threat looming over the town, most folks stayed pretty close to home.

The few people he saw moving around didn't seem to be panicking, though. Bill asked Flint, "Ramsey didn't spread the alarm, did he?"

"Not yet," the deputy replied. "He wanted to let you know first. He saw me passin' by and called down and told me to fetch you."

Bill nodded. "You did good. This might be a false alarm."

"You really think so?"

Flint didn't sound like he believed that, and to be honest, neither did Bill. His pounding heart told him this was the real thing at last.

A ladder was propped against the side wall of the bank, in the alley that ran next to the brick building. Bill went up the ladder in a hurry with Flint following him.

The roof was flat, with a short wall around its edge.

Phillip Ramsey stood at the western wall with a pair of field glasses at his eyes. He must have heard Bill and Flint coming, because he lowered the glasses and turned to meet the two lawmen.

"Thank God you're here, Marshal," he said as he held out the glasses. "You'd better have a look."

"Got your big story, eh, Mr. Ramsey?"

"I wish I didn't," the newspaperman said, and somewhat to Bill's surprise, he believed him.

Bill lifted the field glasses and peered through them. He had already spotted the dust plumes west of town with his naked eyes, a mile or so out and coming closer with every second. He pointed the glasses in that direction and tried to find the riders.

After a moment, he was able to focus on them. His breath caught in his throat as he recognized Ward Costigan and Dave McGinty. The two buffalo hunters were riding close together. It looked like Costigan was trying to hold McGinty in the saddle, so Bill figured the smaller man must be hurt.

As fast as they were riding, they had to be running away from *something*. Bill took a deep breath to steady himself and raised the glasses so he could look beyond Costigan and McGinty at whoever was chasing them.

That breath seemed to stick in Bill's throat. "Dear Lord," he choked out.

"What is it?" Flint asked.

Bill answered the question honestly. It was too late for anything else.

"Looks like the whole blasted Pawnee nation."

Chapter 25

Bill handed the field glasses back to Ramsey and hurried toward the ladder. "Stay up here," he called to the newspaperman as he swung a leg over the wall around the edge of the bank roof. "You'll have a good vantage point for your story."

Ramsey put the glasses on the roof and picked up the Winchester that lay there. "I don't care about that, Marshal. I'll be ready to help fight them off when they get here."

Bill nodded and started to descend the ladder. Flint came down after him.

When the two lawmen reached the ground, Bill said, "Ring the fire bell and start gettin' folks organized, Mordecai."

"Where are you goin'?" the deputy asked.

"To meet Costigan and McGinty. I'll start spreadin' the word along the way, too."

It was too late now to worry about preventing panic. The town had to be alerted. As Bill ran toward the western edge of the settlement, he called to everyone he saw, "Get off the street! Indians comin'! Get off the street!"

Behind him, the loud tones of the fire bell began to peal out as Flint rang it.

The two buffalo hunters reached the edge of town at the same time Bill did. Dust swirled around them as they reined in. McGinty struggled to bring his horse under control. He sagged forward in the saddle with an arrow sticking out of his back.

"The Pawnee are close behind us, Marshal!" Costigan yelled as he leaped to the ground. He turned and reached up to grab McGinty as the smaller man started to topple out of the saddle.

"Take him to the mercantile," Bill said. "My wife can get that arrow out of him and patch him up."

He hoped Eden could manage that. He didn't suppose she had ever removed an arrow from anybody before.

But there was always a first time for everything, as the old saying went.

This was his first Indian attack, after all.

Grunting with the effort of carrying his friend, Costigan hurried toward the mercantile. Bill looked around the street and saw at least a dozen men running for positions behind the barrel barricades.

That false alarm when the buffalo hunters arrived in Redemption had proven to be good practice, Bill thought. Although the citizens looked upset and scared, they weren't panicking.

He tilted his head toward the roofs where the guards were posted and saw Ramsey and the other men in place with their rifles ready. That was another good sign.

Not only that, but Colonel Bledsoe and the members of his party were coming on the run from their camp at the other end of town. Gus Meade and his teamsters and bullwhackers, tough men each and every one, appeared as well, ready to take part in Redemption's defense.

They might have a chance to get through this, Bill told himself. It all depended on how big that war party was.

Unfortunately, judging from the size of the dust cloud

the Pawnee ponies were kicking up, the answer was pretty damned big.

Judge Dunaway was at one of the barricades, clutching a shotgun. Bill raised his voice to be heard over the hubbub in the street and addressed the men at his barricade.

"Judge Dunaway is in charge at this position," he told them. "Everybody hold your fire until he gives the word."

Dunaway nodded. "We won't let you down, Marshal."

Bill put Josiah Hartnett in command at another barricade and motioned for Mordecai Flint to take over at a third pile of barrels. Confident that this line of defense was in good hands, Bill hurried on down the street to check on the other preparations.

He glanced at the dust cloud. It was closer now. The Indians were still charging across the prairie at breakneck speed.

He stopped in at the mercantile long enough to see that Costigan had placed McGinty facedown on the counter at the rear of the store, where Eden was working to try to remove the arrow from the buffalo hunter's back.

Costigan and Perry Monroe were at the front of the store, rifles in hand.

"Why don't you stay here, Mr. Costigan?" Bill suggested. "That way you can watch over your friend."

And over my wife and her father, too, he thought.

Costigan nodded. "I'll do that."

It made Bill feel a little better to know that a reliable man would be here to protect Eden. He wished he could stay and do that himself, but he would be needed elsewhere and his duty to the town came first, whether he liked it or not.

"They're almost here, Marshal!" somebody yelled from the street.

Bill turned his head toward his wife just as Eden raised hers from her work on the wounded man. Their eyes met for a second, and while a moment like that could never be enough, it was better than nothing. Eden gave him a determined nod.

Bill smiled at her, then he was gone, hurrying along the street toward the western edge of the settlement.

Something was different now, he realized immediately. Something had changed in the last few minutes, and as he gazed toward the west, he realized what it was.

The dust cloud had thinned somewhat, and it no longer appeared to be coming closer.

Flint waved him over to the barricade where the deputy had taken charge.

"They've stopped!" Flint said. "I think they're just sittin' out there!"

That was what it looked like to Bill, too, but he wanted to be sure.

"I'm goin' up on top of the bank to get a better look," he told Flint. "Stay here."

By the time Bill reached the top of the ladder in the alley, Phillip Ramsey had put his rifle down again and taken up the field glasses. He stood peering through them with one foot up on the short wall at the edge of the roof.

Excitedly, he turned toward Bill, extended the glasses, and said, "You need to take a look at this, Marshal."

"That's why I'm here," Bill said.

He took the glasses and squinted through them. More of the dust had blown away, so his vision was only partially obscured by it as he focused the lenses on the riders who had come to a halt several hundred yards from the edge of town.

His heart thumped as the painted faces of the Pawnee warriors sprang out at him with sharp-edged clarity. He saw the claw necklaces some of them wore, the eagle feathers that stuck up from hair slick with animal grease, the lances with feathers and beads and strips of rawhide tied to them. Every face was set in grim, determined lines.

Slowly, Bill turned so he could scan the ranks with the glasses. He tried to make a rough count but gave up when he reached two hundred.

According to what Captain Stone had told them, this was a much larger party than the one that had been reported leaving the reservation. Either those numbers had been wrong to start with or else Spotted Dog and the men with him had joined up with other renegades to form this war party.

"What are they doing?" Phillip Ramsey asked.

"They're just . . . sitting there," Bill said, his tone edged with disbelief.

"I thought they were attacking the town."

"So did I. But they're just sitting there," Bill said again.

Not all of them. Bill stiffened as he caught a glimpse of movement through the lenses. He focused again and saw one man riding forward, away from the others and toward the settlement.

This warrior wasn't any bigger than the others, but he carried himself with such haughty pride that he seemed larger. His craggy face was lined with age. He wore several feathers in his hair instead of just one, and the front of his buckskin shirt was decorated with beads. Bill realized after a moment that the beads were sewn on in a pattern that formed the head of a buffalo.

He had a hunch he was looking at Chief Spotted Dog, the leader of these Pawnee.

And there was only one reason he could think of why Spotted Dog would be riding alone toward the settlement like that.

Bill tossed the field glasses back to Ramsey and cupped his hands around his mouth. He leaned over the wall and shouted, "Mordecai! Josiah! Judge Dunaway! Hold your fire! Nobody shoot! Hold your fire!"

Ramsey called, "What's going on?" as Bill ran toward the ladder, but there was no time to explain. Bill rattled down the rungs in a hurry. When he reached the ground he ran toward the barricades at the western edge of town.

Redemption was utterly silent, but the air of tension that gripped the town was so thick it was stifling. Bill knew it wouldn't take much to break that tension. A single shot would be enough to start the killing, and there was no way of knowing if it would stop before everyone was dead.

Flint hurried to meet Bill. "What the hell's that redskin doin'?" he asked.

"It looks to me like he wants to parley," Bill said. "I don't know of any other reason he'd ride in alone like that."

"He stopped!" Judge Dunaway called from the other side of the street.

Bill looked and saw that the judge was right. The lone warrior had brought his pony to a halt about halfway between the line of Pawnee and the edge of town. That was just further evidence his hunch was right, Bill thought.

He took a deep breath and said, "I'm goin' out there."

Flint shook his head. "You can't do that. If those varmints jump you, you're a goner."

"We may all be goners if we don't talk to that fella. If I go out there by myself, they won't have any reason to get spooked." Bill looked around for Hartnett. "Josiah, can you go saddle my horse and bring him to me?"

"I agree with Deputy Flint," Hartnett said. "It's too dangerous."

"Y'all put me in charge of defending this town. That's what I'm tryin' to do. Now go saddle my horse, Josiah."

Bill wasn't sure where the tone of command in his voice had come from. He wasn't even sure he liked it. But he had to do what he thought was best, and this was it.

Hartnett gave him a grudging nod. "All right. I'll be back as quick as I can."

The liveryman trotted off. Flint asked, "What're you gonna do now, Marshal?"

"I figure that's Spotted Dog his own self," Bill said. "I want him to get a good look at me before I ride out there to meet him."

Before the others could argue, he strode out into the middle of the street and then walked toward the waiting Indians, stopping when he was just past the edge of town. He hooked his thumbs in his gun belt and waited there. Across a distance of a hundred yards or so, he and Spotted Dog stared at each other.

Bill hoped the war chief didn't think he was being defiant and daring the Pawnee to attack.

The four minutes that it took Hartnett to get back with his horse were some of the longest minutes Bill had ever spent in his life. When he finally heard the thud of hoofbeats behind him, he didn't turn around. He waited until Hartnett led the horse up beside him and handed him the reins.

"They haven't budged, have they?"

"Nope," Bill said. "I'm hopin' that's a good sign."

He put his foot in the stirrup and swung up into the saddle. He was about to nudge the horse into a walk when Hartnett said, "Bill . . . you don't happen to speak Pawnee, do you?"

Bill managed to keep himself from saying, *Oh, hell*, but he thought it. He swallowed and said, "We'll have to hope ol' Spotted Dog savvies English. He lived on a reservation for a while, so he might."

"Yeah. We can hope."

Hartnett didn't sound convinced.

Bill heeled his mount into motion. He didn't get in any hurry as he rode toward the chief. He kept both hands in plain sight so Spotted Dog wouldn't think he was reaching for his Colt.

Bill had considered leaving the revolver behind, but the Pawnee chief carried a lance, so he thought it was all right for him to be armed, too. They would meet on equal terms.

The closer he came, the harder his heart pounded. He forced himself to take deep, regular breaths. It wouldn't be good for this war chief to know how scared he really was.

When less than twenty feet separated him from the Indian, Bill reined his horse to a stop. He figured it would be a good idea for him to be sure who he was talking to, and also to find out right away if the man spoke English. He said, "You are the war chief known as Spotted Dog?"

"I am," the man replied in a deep, guttural, but understandable voice. "And you are a cripple!"

The scornful words lashed at Bill. Spotted Dog had keen eyes for an older man. He had noticed Bill's limp.

Bill wasn't going to let it bother him. He said, "I'm the marshal of Redemption, and that's all that matters here. What do you want of me and my people?"

The phrase came out easily. He hadn't realized until just now how much he really thought of the citizens of Redemption as "his people."

"There are evil men among you," Spotted Dog snapped. "Murderers. We want them."

Bill frowned for a second, then tried not to let the war chief see that he was confused.

"There are no murderers among us," he said.

Then he thought about what had happened to Aaron Wetherby, and he realized he was probably wrong.

But how in blazes had this Pawnee chief known about that?

He realized a moment later that Spotted Dog wasn't talking about Aaron. The chief said, "We pursued them here. They murdered our young men who were hunting buffalo in peace. Slaughtered them as if they were animals."

Bill breathed a little harder. Spotted Dog had to be talking about Bledsoe and the rest of the buffalo hunters. They'd said all along that the Pawnee were behind them.

"I don't know anything about that. But you and your men have murdered, too. You raided ranches and attacked a train west of here."

This time it was Spotted Dog's turn to look a little confused, and even more angry.

"We raided no ranches," he declared. "We attacked no train."

"You left the reservation."

Spotted Dog nodded. "We did this so my people could go on one last hunt, so our young men could know what it was like when the Pawnee lived free in this land!" Bitterness crept into his voice. "Now our young men know only death."

Bill felt a stirring of horror inside him. He had no reason
to believe what Spotted Dog was saying . . . except that the
chief's words carried the ring of truth. He knew how people could get carried away where Indians were concerned.
He had seen it with his own eyes. Maybe the reports were
wrong.

"The cavalry says you raided those ranches."

"We watered our horses, that is all. Men shot at us, so
we left."

Bill could see how that could get blown up into an Indian attack by panicky settlers. He asked, "What about the
train?"

"We rode alongside the steel rails while one of the iron
horses passed by. Nothing happened."

If Spotted Dog was telling the truth, the only crime
committed by the Pawnee was leaving the reservation without permission. And they had done that in an attempt to recapture for a short time the past glory of their people.

"What about the buffalo hunters?"

A bleak look settled over Spotted Dog's rugged features. "One boy escaped the massacre. He told us how the
hunters killed all the others. Our young men were few.
They could not have harmed anyone."

Bill wasn't so sure about that, but he knew he'd have to
talk to Bledsoe and maybe some of the other men to get to
the bottom of this.

"What do you want, Chief?"

"Give us the men who killed our children," Spotted Dog
said with pain in his voice. "Give them to us, and we will
leave the rest of you in peace."

Bill had no intention of turning Bledsoe and the others
over to the Pawnee, but he figured it wouldn't hurt anything
to stall a little more.

"If we do that, you'll go back to the reservation?"

"We cannot do that. We fought with the yellowlegs
when they tried to stop us from seeking justice for our
young men. They are all dead now." A faraway tone entered
Spotted Dog's voice. "And so are we. It has gone too far.

More soldiers will come. There are too many of you white men. You are like ants on the carcass of a dead animal. You bite and bite and bite until there is nothing left. There will be nothing left of us." He squared his shoulders. "But before that day, we will have justice for our murdered young men. That is the only way you can save your town. Go back and tell them that." Spotted Dog pulled his pony around. "You have until the sun is one hand above the horizon! No longer!"

Chapter 26

Bill turned and rode back to the settlement at a deliberate pace, restraining the urge to kick his horse into a gallop. When he got there, dozens of tense, armed men surrounded him.

"What'd that painted varmint want?" Flint asked as Bill dismounted.

Bill didn't answer the deputy's question. Instead he looked at Bledsoe and said, "Colonel, I need to talk to you in private. Now."

He knew from the way that Bledsoe turned pale and got an angry, stubborn expression on his face that there was something to what Spotted Dog had said about the massacre.

Bledsoe was going to try to brazen his way through it, though. He said, "I don't know any reason we should do that, Marshal."

"I do," Bill snapped. "Because I said so. Come with me." He remembered where Ward Costigan was and thought it might be a good idea to get him in on the conversation, too. "We'll talk at the mercantile."

He headed in that direction without looking back to see if Bledsoe was following him.

A moment later the colonel came up alongside him. Even with Bill's limp, Bledsoe's shorter legs had to move fast to keep up with the marshal's determined stride.

"Listen, I don't know what that savage told you," Bledsoe said, "but it was a lie. You know you can't trust anything those redskins say."

"We'll talk about it when we get to the store," Bill said.

Costigan stepped out onto the porch and loading dock as Bill and Bledsoe came up the steps. "You went out and parleyed with the Pawnee?" the tall, lean buffalo hunter asked.

Bill nodded. "I talked to Spotted Dog. He had some pretty interesting things to say."

"Lies, I tell you!" Bledsoe blustered.

His reaction just convinced Bill more than ever that the Pawnee war chief had told the truth.

"Inside."

Costigan and Bledsoe followed him. At the rear of the store, Dave McGinty was sitting up on the counter with bandages wrapped thickly around his left shoulder, covering the arrow wound on his back. He was pale but looked stronger than he had earlier.

Eden hurried up the aisle between the shelves to meet Bill. She put a hand on his arm and asked, "You're all right?"

He nodded. "For now. Looks like you did a good job on McGinty."

"The arrow didn't penetrate too deeply. He lost some blood when I cut it out . . ." Eden was pale, too, and Bill figured that had been ordeal for her, as well. "But I think Mr. McGinty will be all right."

"What's goin' on out there?" McGinty asked. "The Pawnee ain't attackin' the town?"

"Not yet." Bill looked at Bledsoe again. "Spotted Dog has given us until an hour or so before sundown to turn over the hombres who slaughtered the young braves from his band."

Bledsoe's control finally broke. He yelled, "They attacked us, damn it! We didn't have any choice but to shoot them!"

"Yeah, we did," McGinty said. "Hell, Colonel, we out-numbered 'em two to one, and there wasn't a rifle among 'em, only bows and arrows. If we'd held our fire, they prob-ably would've turned and run after they made that little dash at us to save their pride."

Bledsoe jabbed a finger at McGinty. "You don't know that! You might've got an arrow in the guts, McGinty, you ever think about that?" He swung toward Bill and glared. "You think you're so damned high and mighty because you've got that star pinned to your shirt! You're nothing but a small-town badge toter! Don't you dare tell me what we should have done!"

"I'm not tellin' you anything, Colonel, except what Spotted Dog told me," Bill said. "He wants you and your men, and he intends to have you, one way or another. He doesn't have anything to lose anymore, either, because from what he told me, he and his warriors wiped out a cav-alry patrol a few days ago. The army's gonna hunt them down no matter what they do now, so they might as well go ahead and attack the town if it comes to that."

"Well, what do you expect *us* to do?" Bledsoe asked. "You think we should go out there and surrender to those savages so they can torture us to death? You'd condemn us to that in order to save your town?"

"Don't push me too hard, Colonel," Bill warned. "You might get an answer you don't want to hear." He sighed. "But no, I don't reckon I expect you to do that." He looked over at Costigan. "What do you have to say about this, Mr. Costigan?"

"Leave Ward out of it," McGinty said before Costigan could answer. "He's the only one who's not to blame for any of it. He wasn't even there when it happened."

Costigan smiled. "Thanks, Dave, but I have sins of my own I've been carrying around. I reckon we all do." He turned to Bill. "I'll stick with my friends, Marshal, no mat-ter what happens."

Perry Monroe had been listening the conversation. Now he spoke up, saying, "Bill, we can't let those savages wipe out the town, whether they were wronged or not. Even if we manage to fight them off, innocent people will be killed."

"More than likely," Bill agreed.

Bledsoe crossed his arms defiantly over his thick chest. "We're not going to turn ourselves over to the Indians. That's final. And if you try to run us out of town so they can kill us, then you're not men. You're cowards! Craven cowards!"

Bill looked at the clock on the wall. It was after noon, but several hours still remained until the deadline Spotted Dog had given him.

"Get out," he said to Bledsoe.

"I just told you—"

"Not out of town. Just out of here. I've got to think about this. Maybe you should go talk to your men and see how they feel about it."

"I make the decisions for my party."

Bill shook his head. "I reckon maybe it's gone beyond that. Get out and let me think."

Bledsoe looked like he wanted to argue some more, but he turned on his heel and stalked out of the mercantile. Mc-Ginty slid down from the counter and started to follow the colonel.

"You comin', Ward?" he asked Costigan.

"I'll be along," Costigan said. "I want to talk to the marshal, if that's all right."

Bill nodded. Costigan seemed to have the coolest head among the buffalo hunters. Maybe he could come up with some way out of this.

When Bledsoe and McGinty were gone, Costigan went on, "Nobody in Redemption is going to blame you if you turn us over to the Pawnee, Marshal."

"I wouldn't be so sure of that," Bill said. "I'd still have to live with myself."

Perry Monroe said, "Maybe we should put it to a vote."

Bill shook his head. "I'm not gonna make people vote to save themselves by sacrificing somebody else. There's got to be some other way."

Eden put her hand on his shoulder. "You can't take it all on yourself, either," she said. "That's not right. You're not responsible for . . . for . . ."

"For the whole town?" Bill asked with a faint smile. "I sort of am. And that's the hell of it, right there."

Fraker stood just inside the entrance of Smoot's Saloon, peering out over the batwings and holding a mug of beer in his left hand. He sipped from it now and then as he looked along the street.

From here he couldn't see the barricades at the western end of Main Street, but the muzzles of numerous rifles and shotguns sticking out of windows were visible. In the hour or so since the Indians had shown up, nothing had happened, but nobody in town was relaxing.

Macauley came up beside Fraker and said, "Anything going on out there?"

"Nope."

Quietly enough so that no one else in the saloon could overhear, Macauley said, "This is it, Jake. Our last chance to hit that bank."

Fraker nodded. "I know. But right now all we can do is wait it out."

"I'm sick and tired of hearing that."

Fraker jerked his head toward his partner. "Then why don't you go out there and do something about it?" he said. When Macauley didn't rise to the challenge, Fraker sneered. "That's what I thought."

"I'm tired of putting up with you, too," Macauley said. "When this is over, we're going our separate ways."

"Fine with me." Fraker took a long swig of the luke-warm beer. The tension of the past few days had driven a wedge between him and Macauley. He knew it, and he didn't particularly care.

Everything ended, including partnerships.

But not until they had looted that bank.

If the damn redskins would just go ahead and attack, thought Fraker, then he and Macauley could make their move. For now, though, the Pawnee seemed content to just sit out there and make nearly everybody in town scared enough to shit their drawers.

Fraker had tried to nudge things along once before, and it hadn't worked.

But maybe if he tried again, this time it would turn out better.

He was mulling that over when a commotion suddenly broke out at the western end of the street. Fraker leaned forward eagerly as he heard the swift rataplan of hoofbeats from that direction.

Maybe this was it at last.

Bill was in the marshal's office with Mordecai Flint, Josiah Hartnett, Judge Dunaway, and Mayor Fleming. They had spent the past hour hashing out every possible solution they could think of.

The problem was they had only two real options: surrender the buffalo hunters to the Indians, or refuse and defend the town against the inevitable attack.

Flint said, "Maybe one of us ought to go out yonder and talk to the chief again, see if there's anything he'd accept short of turnin' over Bledsoe and his bunch. I don't mind doin' it if you want me to, Marshal."

"I appreciate that, Mordecai," Bill said, "but if anybody goes to parley with Spotted Dog again, I reckon it ought to be me. I'm the marshal, and I'm the one he talked to before."

Roy Fleming said, "You may be the marshal, Bill, but I'm the mayor of Redemption. Maybe *I* should ride out there."

Bill was surprised that Fleming would volunteer to place himself in danger like that. He could tell from the look in the mayor's eyes that Fleming was mighty scared. But he had made the offer anyway, and Bill respected him for that.

"Sorry, Mayor," he said. "You're needed here in town."

"So are you," Judge Dunaway said. "You may not realize it, Bill, but you've won over pretty much the whole town, first with the way you handled that outlaw gang a while back, and now with the steady hand you've displayed in this crisis. Everybody looks to you for leadership now."

Maybe the judge was right, but Bill couldn't help but wonder how the hell such a thing had happened to a shiftless Texas cowboy.

"We're just goin' around and around in circles—"

The rapid thud of running footsteps interrupted him. One of the townsmen appeared in the open doorway of the marshal's office and reported breathlessly, "Somebody's ridin' out to the Indians! Looks like one of those buffalo hunters!"

Bill had been leaning against the desk. He straightened and hurried out onto the boardwalk, followed by the other men in the office.

"Who is it?" he asked. "Colonel Bledsoe?"

"No," the man replied, not surprising Bill at all. He knew better than to expect the colonel to sacrifice himself. "I think it's that fella called Costigan."

Bill stiffened. He hadn't seen Costigan since leaving him at the mercantile with Eden and her father an hour or so earlier. He had supposed that Costigan either stayed at the store or manned one of the defensive positions.

Bill ran out into the street so he could peer past the barricades at the western end. He saw the lone figure on horseback that was now several hundred yards away from town.

He had left his horse saddled when he came back from the parley with Spotted Dog. The animal's reins were looped around the hitch rail in front of the marshal's office. Bill jerked them loose and swung up into the saddle.

Flint grabbed the horse's bridle. "What the hell are you doin', Marshal?"

"That's what I figure on askin' Costigan," Bill said. He jerked on the reins and pulled the horse loose from the deputy's grip. His heels dug into the animal's flanks and sent it leaping forward.

He didn't know how Eden had realized something was going on, but she stepped out onto the mercantile's porch as he galloped past.

"Bill!"

Her cry tore at his heart, but he didn't slow down. He heard more yelling behind him but didn't look back.

Costigan must have heard him coming. The buffalo hunter reined in and half turned his horse before Bill reached him. Dust swirled as Bill brought his mount to a halt a few feet from Costigan's.

"What are you doing here, Marshal? Go back to town."

"What are *you* doin' here?" Bill demanded. He glanced at the grim line of Pawnee warriors not much more than two hundred yards away. "You're liable to get yourself killed."

"That's the idea," Costigan said. "I'm going to offer myself to Spotted Dog in the hope that he'll spare everybody else."

"That's loco!" Bill burst out. "You didn't even have anything to do with killin' those kids!"

Costigan shook his head. "Spotted Dog doesn't know that. He wants vengeance. Maybe I'll provide enough. If I don't . . ." Costigan shrugged. "It was worth a try, anyway."

"No, it's not." Bill glanced at the Pawnee again. His heart jumped as he saw that Spotted Dog had started his pony toward them, trailed by a couple of warriors. "Damn it, he's comin' out to see what this is all about. We got to light a shuck for town right now if we're gonna have a chance to get back!"

Even then, it would be close, Bill thought. Costigan's play might have cost them both their lives.

"You go on back," the buffalo hunter said. "I'll stay here. That'll keep Spotted Dog curious enough he probably won't come after you until he finds out what I want."

"Why? Why in the world would you do this?"

"I told you I've got my own sins, Marshal. I've been running away from them for a long time. I'm tired of running."

Bill shook his head. "I don't know what you did, Mr. Costigan, but it's not worth givin' up your life for Bledsoe and his bunch."

"Dave McGinty's my friend. He's worth it," Costigan insisted. "And so are all those innocent people in Redemption."

Bill couldn't argue with that.

Actually, he couldn't argue with anything.

Spotted Dog was there.

Chapter 27

Fraker and Macauley made their way along the street, listening to the hubbub of conversation around them. It didn't take long for Fraker to realize what was happening. That kid marshal from Texas and one of the buffalo hunters had ridden out to talk with the Indians again.

"You think they came up with some way to get the red-skins to leave, Jake?" Macauley asked. "That would ruin everything."

"Yeah, I know," Fraker said. "Come on. I want to get up there where we can see what's goin' on."

As they approached one of the barricades, Fraker could see that the two riders were stopped several hundred yards from the edge of town. He asked a heavyset older man, "What are they doing out there?"

"I'm not certain," the man replied, "but I'd wager it's something incredibly foolish . . . or incredibly brave. Perhaps both."

The marshal's pretty blond wife ran up to the barricade, trailed by her father, who was puffing for breath.

"Judge," she said to the older man, "has Bill gone crazy?"

"That buffalo hunter Costigan rode out there first. The marshal went after him, to try to bring him back, I suppose."

"What's Mr. Costigan trying to do?"

The judge shook his head. "I don't know, but I can venture a guess. I think he's going to offer himself to the Indians as a sacrifice, in hopes that they'll ride away and leave everyone else alone."

Eden Monroe's hand went to her mouth. "Dear God," she said. "And Bill's out there with him. What if the Indians take both of them?"

The same possibility had occurred to Fraker, and he didn't like it one damned bit. If the Indians rode away without attacking the town, it would ruin everything he had planned. He had to stop it from happening somehow.

His mind returned to the idea he had been pondering earlier. He caught Macauley's eye and motioned with his head. While everybody else at the barricade was concentrating on what was happening out on the prairie, Fraker and Macauley began drifting back away from the barrels.

"What do we do now?" Macauley asked in a murmur.

"We make sure this turns out the way we want it to," Fraker said. "Come on."

"Keep your hand away from your gun, Marshal," Costigan said as he and Bill faced Spotted Dog and the other two Pawnee warriors.

"You're not tellin' me anything I don't already know, Mr. Costigan."

"I take it the chief speaks English?"

Before Bill could answer, Spotted Dog said, "I speak the white man's tongue." His scornful tone indicated what he thought of it, too. "You look like one of the men we seek."

"I'm a buffalo hunter," Costigan said.

He glanced over at Bill, who understood the meaning behind the look. Costigan was warning him not to say anything about how he hadn't participated in the slaughter of the young Pawnee braves.

"You killed our young men. Their blood cries out for vengeance and justice."

"And that's what I'm here to offer you. Take me, Spotted Dog, and spare the others."

"All must die!" the war chief thundered.

"And to get that you'll sacrifice many of your other warriors? The town is well-defended. There are almost as many men with rifles as you have in your party, and they will fight."

"Many will die on both sides," Spotted Dog declared, "but justice will be done. And as I told this one"—a contemptuous nod toward Bill—"I and my people are doomed to die for what we did to the yellowlegs."

"Maybe, maybe not. But if you take me and ride away to fight another day, who knows what will happen in the future?"

Spotted Dog sat there glaring at Costigan for a long moment. Finally, he turned and spoke in Pawnee to the two men with him, who replied in the same tongue. They were older men, too, and Bill figured they were the war chief's most trusted lieutenants.

The discussion was an animated one. From the corner of his mouth, Bill asked Costigan, "You savvy any of what they're sayin'?"

"Not a damn bit," Costigan answered, tight-lipped.

At last Spotted Dog turned back to the two white men. "You know you will be going to your death?" he said to Costigan.

The buffalo hunter nodded. "I understand."

"And your dying will be long and painful."

"I wouldn't expect anything else," Costigan said.

Spotted Dog's eyes narrowed. "You are a brave man."

"No. Just a tired one."

The war chief took a deep breath and squared his shoulders. "All men must die," he said. "But the fortunate ones choose the manner of their deaths. My warriors would rather die fighting the hated yellowlegs than farmers and shopkeepers."

Anger welled up inside Bill. Spotted Dog didn't have to make it sound like the citizens of Redemption were beneath contempt. But he kept the feeling under control, not wanting to disrupt what was happening.

At the same time, he felt sick . . . because he knew that if Spotted Dog agreed to the bargain, he would let Costigan go with the Indians. The guilt over that might haunt him the rest of his life, but he had to think about Eden and everybody else back in the settlement.

"You will come with us," Spotted Dog continued. "We will leave this place, and you will die in agony and dishonor. This is the bargain you would make, buffalo hunter?"

"This is the bargain I would make."

Costigan's voice trembled. Just a little, but enough for Bill to hear it.

Of course Costigan was scared. He had to be, unless he was insane. But it appeared that he wasn't backing down.

"The other men who killed our children, justice will come to them in its own time," Spotted Dog said.

"It always does, sooner or later."

The war chief lifted his pony's reins. "Come."

Costigan glanced over at Bill. "Say so long to McGinty for me, will you, Marshal?"

Bill had to swallow hard before he could answer. "Sure."

Costigan smiled and said, "I'm glad you decided to be reasonable about this."

"I've got a whole townful of people back there to protect. There's nothing else I can do."

"I know the feeling," Costigan said.

The two Pawnee who had ridden out with Spotted Dog parted so they could flank Costigan as he rode forward. The buffalo hunter nodded to Bill and hitched his horse into motion.

"What are we . . . doing here?" Macauley panted as he and Fraker came to a stop in the alley beside the bank. "Shouldn't we be . . . around back?"

"Not yet. We'd never get away. There's something else we need to do first." Fraker grabbed the ladder and started up. "Go get our horses and tie them in the alley out back. Then wait for me here."

He climbed as fast as he could. When he reached the top, he was glad to see that the man posted up there was still alone. No one had joined him to help in the possible fight against the Pawnee.

The townie was a brown-haired man wearing spectacles. He glanced back over his shoulder as Fraker hurried toward him.

"Did you come to give me a hand? You'll need a rifle."

"No, you've already got one," Fraker said as he came up to the man. He brought his fist up and smashed it into the man's jaw, taking him completely by surprise. The man went down hard onto the roof, out cold.

His rifle clattered at Fraker's feet.

Fraker reached down and picked it up.

"And you don't know it, but I'm a hell of a shot with one of these," he said, even though the man was no longer conscious to hear him.

He dropped to a knee, worked the rifle's lever to make sure there was a bullet in the chamber, and then stretched out on his belly. The Winchester's barrel rested across the short wall around the roof's edge. The gun needed to be as steady as it could for this. A miss might achieve the same result, but a hit would mean there was no turning back.

Fraker rested his cheek against the smooth wood of the stock and peered over the barrel. He shifted the rifle until its sights rested squarely on the back of the Pawnee war chief who had just turned away to ride back to his men. The shot was a long one, but Fraker had a clear field of fire.

He squeezed the trigger.

Bill didn't hear the shot, but he saw the way the bullet's impact drove Spotted Dog forward over the neck of his pony. Blood spouted from the hole in the war chief's back.

The crack of the shot sounded then, just catching up to the slug that had smashed through Spotted Dog's body.

Costigan twisted in the saddle, obviously thinking Bill had gone crazy and gunned down the chief. He yelled, "No!"

Bill didn't know what had happened, but he saw what was about to. Face twisting with rage, one of the subchiefs lifted his lance and sent his horse plunging toward Costigan's mount, clearly intending to impale the buffalo hunter.

Instinct took over. Bill whipped his Colt from its holster and fired. He wasn't blindingly fast on the draw, but he was quick and accurate. His bullet caught the Pawnee warrior in the shoulder, shattering it.

Costigan still had his Henry rifle. He brought it to his shoulder and blew the other subchief off his pony as the man raised his bow with an arrow nocked.

Bill yanked his horse around and slashed at it with the reins. The animal lunged into a run toward the settlement.

Costigan fled, too. Bill glanced back and saw him following. They were closer to the rest of the war party than they were to town, but they stood a slender chance of reaching Redemption alive if the defenders gave them some covering fire.

Shots rolled out from the town. Bill hunkered low in the saddle as bullets whistled past from one direction and arrows rained through the air from the other direction.

The old saying about being between a rock and a hard place flickered through his mind. This was more like being between lead and a sharp place, but that was just as deadly.

Horror filled him at the way he and Costigan had gunned

down the two men with Spotted Dog. They'd had no choice, though. If they had turned their backs on those Pawnee, it would have been the same as committing suicide.

And no matter how tragic and unfair this situation was, Bill wasn't ready to die yet. He wasn't like Costigan.

Now that the battle couldn't be avoided, it appeared Costigan wasn't going to throw his life away for no reason, either, Bill realized. The buffalo hunter's horse drew even with his. Costigan was riding low in the saddle, too, to make himself a smaller target.

Over the pounding hoofbeats, Costigan yelled, "Why did you—"

Bill didn't let him finish. "I didn't! The shot came from town!"

"But who—"

The wind whipped away the rest of Costigan's words, but Bill didn't need to hear them to know what the man had said. He didn't have an answer.

But he hoped he lived long enough to find that answer. Whoever had fired that shot likely had doomed innocent people to death . . . and Bill intended to see that the varmint paid for that.

Fraker left the Winchester on the roof and scrambled back down the ladder to the alley. When he got there, Macauley stared at him in disbelief.

"What did you *do*?" Macauley asked over the roar of gunfire that had erupted in the wake of Fraker's shot.

"Killed that Pawnee chief," Fraker said. "There's our distraction." He pulled his Colt from its holster. "Come on. We don't have much time. They'll be herdin' women and kids in there pretty soon."

He led the way to the bank's back door. It was locked, but with all the shooting going on in town already, nobody was going to notice one more gun going off. He aimed the revolver at the lock and pulled the trigger.

It took two shots to shatter the lock, but then the door flew open when Fraker kicked it. He charged into the building with Macauley right behind him, also with gun in hand.

They found themselves in a short hallway with an open door at the other end that led into the bank's main room. Fraker's gaze landed immediately on the huge, squat safe that sat next to the bank president's desk.

With the threat of a Pawnee attack looming over the town, nobody was conducting any bank business this afternoon. The banker, who was also Redemption's mayor, Fraker had learned, wasn't here, and there weren't any customers, either.

In fact, only one man was in the bank: a slender, bespectacled teller. He had been standing in the open front door, watching what was going on outside, but he swung around as Fraker and Macauley charged into the room, and from the way his eyes widened, he grasped right away what was going on.

That was too damned bad . . . for him.

Fraker shot him in the belly.

As the teller groaned, doubled over, and collapsed, Fraker said to Macauley, "Get to work on that safe!" Fraker ran over to the door, grabbed the wounded man's collar, and dragged him away from the entrance so nobody passing the bank would see him.

"You think anybody heard that shot?" Macauley asked as he knelt in front of the massive safe.

"Hell, it sounds like the Battle of Gettysburg out there!" Fraker said. "Nobody knows what's going on in here. Just get that safe open!"

He pushed the bank's front door up but didn't close it all the way. He wanted to be able to keep an eye on the street. Holding the Colt close by his head, he leaned over to peer through the opening he had left.

The wounded man at his feet was still groaning. The sound got on Fraker's nerves after a moment. He reversed the gun in his hand, bent over the teller, and slammed the butt of the gun against the man's head as hard as he could three times, feeling bone splinter with each blow. The man got quiet and stopped writhing around.

It was merciful, thought Fraker. A man who was gut-shot generally took a long time to die, and it was a hard way to go. It was a lot quicker and easier having your head stove in.

"How's it comin' along?" Fraker asked as he straightened from the dead man.

"Getting there," Macauley said. "Don't distract me."

Macauley might have worse distractions in a minute, Fraker realized. He could hear the Indians howling and yipping now, even over the gun thunder.

The battle was about to spill into the very streets of Redemption.

Chapter 28

Bill never would have dreamed that it would take a year to ride a few hundred yards at a full gallop, but that's what it felt like as he and Costigan raced toward the settlement.

The air was dark with arrows around them. One of them struck the cantle of his saddle and glanced off. The shaft slapped his thigh and bounced away.

Lucky for him and Costigan, the Pawnee had been so shocked to see Spotted Dog gunned down that they hadn't reacted immediately. Bill and Costigan had already put more distance between them when the Indians charged. That swift reaction might have been enough to save them. The edge of town was close now.

Costigan's horse screamed and broke stride, leaping wildly as an arrow drove deep into a rear haunch. Costigan kicked his feet free of the stirrups just as the animal collapsed. He sailed over the horse's head and slammed into the ground, rolling over a couple of times before he came to a stop.

Bill reined in and yelled, "Costigan!"

The buffalo hunter came up running. An arrow skewered his right thigh. He cried out in pain and tumbled off his feet again.

But somehow he found the resolve to get up and limp toward Bill's horse. Bill extended a hand. Costigan reached up and gripped Bill's wrist. With a grunt of effort, Bill heaved the man up onto the back of his horse behind the saddle.

"You should've left me!" Costigan said as Bill kicked the horse into a run again.

"And abandon another gimpy-legged fella? I don't think so!"

Bill hoped the delay hadn't cost both their lives. The barricades at the end of Main Street were only fifty yards away now.

But the Pawnee were even closer.

Another volley of shots ripped out from the settlement's defenders. The hail of lead tore into the front ranks of the charging war party and slowed the Pawnee for an instant as several of their ponies went down. That gave Bill and Costigan the chance they needed to cover the last of the ground.

Nearly stumbling from exhaustion, the heavily burdened horse ran past the barricades.

Bill reined in and dropped out of the saddle. He turned quickly to grab Costigan as the buffalo hunter fell more than dismounted. Josiah Hartnett appeared at Bill's side to catch hold of the wounded man, too.

"Let's get him behind one of the barricades," Bill said.

"Somebody give me a rifle and prop me up where I can shoot," Costigan insisted.

Hartnett asked, "Are you all right, Bill?"

"Yeah, but don't ask me how! Pure luck, I reckon. Come on."

They helped Costigan over behind the piled-up barrels. They had been stacked so that there were gaps between them where the defenders could stick a rifle barrel and fire.

Costigan said, "Lean me against that hitch rack and give me a rifle. I can shoot from there."

Extra Winchesters were lying on the boardwalk. Bill picked up one of them and put it in Costigan's hands.

"You sure you're all right? You're losin' some blood from that arrow!"

"Go on, Marshal," Costigan said. "Don't worry about me."

Under the circumstances, Bill had no choice but to do what Costigan said.

The Pawnee were almost on top of the defenders at the edge of town. Bill yanked his Colt from its holster and ran to join the fight.

The plains just outside the settlement were littered with the bodies of the Pawnee and their ponies. At least half the war party had been cut down by the withering fire from the defenders.

But that left scores more, and now they were racing past the barricades, screaming their war cries, firing arrows, and thrusting iron-headed lances at the citizens of Redemption. Bill twisted, triggering the Colt again and again as he tracked its barrel from left to right, and blew a couple of the warriors off their mounts. As his hammer clicked on an empty chamber, he had to throw himself aside to avoid one of the lances.

He rolled up against the boardwalk and struggled to his feet. His bad leg ached like a rotten tooth, but that was the least of his worries now. He plucked fresh cartridges from the loops on his belt and thumbed them into the revolver's cylinder, snapping it shut just in time to squeeze the trigger and send a slug blasting into the chest of a Pawnee who was about to fire an arrow at him.

It was chaos in the street, a hellish melee of blood, gunfire, and death. Bill glanced toward the hardware store, knowing that Eden and her father had probably taken shelter there. His heart leaped in alarm as he saw one of the warriors bound onto the building's porch.

The Pawnee had barely taken a step toward the door when the store's front window erupted outward in a shower of glass. The bullet that drove into the warrior's chest threw him backward off the high porch.

Inside the broken window, Eden worked the lever of the smoking Winchester to throw another round into the chamber, then leaned forward to search for another target.

Bill felt a surge of relief, along with admiration for the courage his wife displayed, but it was tempered with fear for Eden. By getting into the middle of the fight, she was putting herself in danger.

Then struggling men surged between him and the hardware store, and he couldn't see her anymore. There was no time to worry, because another Pawnee lunged at him with a lance. The tip ripped Bill's shirt as he twisted aside. His Colt roared and bucked, and the warrior collapsed with a slug through his middle.

At least this was one battle in which it was easy to tell friend from foe. Bill found himself backed up against the barrels, shoulder to shoulder with Costigan, as more of the Pawnee swarmed around him and forced him to give ground. The two men emptied their weapons. Bill was able to reload again, but Costigan didn't have any more shells for the rifle. He turned it around and heaved himself to his feet, even with his wounded leg, using the rifle like a club and flailing back and forth with it as warriors closed in around him. Bodies with crushed skulls began to pile up around him. Blood dripped from scratches on his face, giving him a fearsome aspect.

Bill fired his last shot and saw the slug tear through the throat of a Pawnee who was screeching practically in his face. The man collapsed at Bill's feet, blood fountaining from his ruined neck. The lance he had tried to ram through Bill's body rattled to the ground beside him.

Bill shook his head as he realized that the shooting was beginning to be sporadic. The horrible tumult in the street was dying down. Only a few of the Pawnee were still mounted, and as Bill watched, riflemen on the roofs blasted them off their ponies. Here and there men on the ground still struggled, but Bill's heart leaped as he realized the fight was just about over.

Redemption had paid a price . . . but it was still here. The defenders had won. The war party was on the verge of being wiped out. That was a terrible, tragic thing, Bill thought as he reached down and picked up the lance that had fallen at his feet, considering that all the Pawnee had wanted at first was to recapture, if only for a short period of time, the way of life they had always known.

But that had led to the slaughter of their young men, and the thirst for vengeance that had brought them here, where Fate had presented them all with the choice of life or death. The people of Redemption had fought for life.

The Pawnee, in their own way, had embraced death.

But now, Bill thought as an overwhelming weariness washed over him, it was finished.

He looked along the street and saw smoke billowing up from the back of the bank.

"Fire!"

The shout ripped itself involuntarily from his throat. He broke into an awkward run toward the bank, weaving between bodies of Pawnee and the town's defenders. He saw Colonel William Bledsoe lying on his back, chest pincushioned with arrows. Bledsoe hadn't survived, but some of the other buffalo hunters had. They joined Bill in hurrying toward the bank, along with the townspeople who were still on their feet and relatively unhurt.

Frontier towns feared fire above almost anything. Flames could wipe out a settlement in almost the blink of an eye.

As Bill reached the bank, two men on horseback burst from the alley beside it. He caught a glimpse of them, recognized Fraker and Macauley, and saw the heavy canvas bank bags they had tied to their saddles. In that instant, Bill knew what had happened.

He also knew his gun was empty and Fraker was bearing down on him. The outlaw had a Colt in his free hand. Flame spouted from the muzzle as he fired. Bill felt the wind rip of the bullet past his ear as he thrust up with the only weapon he had.

The Pawnee lance.

The iron-tipped shaft caught Fraker in the belly and tore through his body at an angle. Fraker screamed as the impact drove him backward out of the saddle. He crashed to the ground. The lance had gone all the way through him. The blood-smeared tip stuck out a couple of feet from his back. He had dropped his gun, so he used both hands to paw feebly at the shaft lodged in his belly.

His fingers fell away from it limply as a shudder went through him. After that, he didn't move again.

Bill was vaguely aware that he had heard a couple of shots ring out from a rifle as he was thrusting the lance at Fraker. He turned away from the dead man and saw Macauley sprawled motionless on the ground a few yards away. Mordecai Flint prodded him with the smoking barrel of a Winchester.

"You got him, Mordecai?" Bill asked.

Flint snorted. "I know a damn bank robber when I see one, even if I ain't ever been a lawman before!"

"You are now," Bill told him. "You're a lawman for sure."

Now they had to worry about the blaze, but as Bill turned back toward the bank, Josiah Hartnett came up to him and said, "We've got the fire under control, Marshal. The brick walls stopped it from getting out. I don't know how it got started. The Indians never reached the bank."

Bill nodded toward the two bodies in the street. "That's how it started. Those two figured they could rob the bank while everybody was busy fightin' off the Pawnee. Reckon they started the fire as an extra distraction. They almost got away with it, too."

"They just didn't figure on Redemption havin' such good lawmen," Flint said, a note of pride in his voice.

"I think we're all mighty lucky that we do," Hartnett said, then he grabbed for Bill's arm as the marshal swayed. "Whoa! You all right, Bill?"

"Yeah, just mighty tired." He straightened. "But I'm all right now."

And he was, because he had just caught sight of Eden running toward him, unharmed and with an eager smile on her face.

The buffalo hunters' camp on the eastern edge of town was a subdued place when Bill visited it that night. Half of the men had been killed in the battle with the Pawnee, and several of the survivors were wounded.

Bill found Ward Costigan sitting on the lowered tailgate of one of the wagons. Costigan's right leg was heavily bandaged.

"You're gonna have trouble gettin' around with that," Bill said as he nodded toward the wounded leg.

Costigan smiled in the light from a campfire. "Between the two of us, Dave and I will be all right, I reckon. He has two good legs, and I have two good arms."

"Are you goin' back to buffalo hunting when you heal up?"

"No, I reckon I've had enough of it," Costigan said. "You smell that, Marshal?"

Bill frowned and shook his head. "I smell a lot of things . . . woodsmoke, bacon frying, coffee boiling . . ."

"No, I'm talking about the smell of death. I've been carrying it with me ever since the war. There's no sense in staying in a business that just adds to that stink."

Bill nodded. "Buffalo hides are pretty potent, all right." He hesitated. "You know, I don't have any idea what you did in the war that you've been carryin' around with you, Mr. Costigan, but you helped save some folks' lives today. Maybe that's a start on getting rid of that smell you talked about."

Harshly, Costigan said, "A lot of people died today on both sides who didn't really deserve to."

"That's true. But it wasn't your fault. You did what you could to save lives. That's got to count for something."

"Maybe. We'll see." Costigan looked up at him. "Did you ever find out who fired the shot that killed Spotted Dog?"

"As a matter of fact, I did," Bill said. "Sort of had to

piece it together from talking to Phillip Ramsey and that prisoner we've got locked up in jail, Oscar Kipp. That fella Fraker killed Spotted Dog. He saw that by you turnin' yourself over to the Pawnee, the fight was about to be headed off. Fraker didn't want that. He figured a battle with the Indians was just the distraction he needed to get away with robbing the bank."

"A bank robbery?" Costigan said. "That's why all those people died today? Greed?"

Bill shrugged. "That was part of it, all right. A simple thing. So's bein' afraid, and wanting things to be like they used to, and bein' proud. All of it came together in the worst way, seems to me."

Costigan shook his head. "I don't envy you your job, Marshal. You've got to pull the town back together and try to make sense of things."

"You'd be surprised," Bill said. "We'll bury our dead, and we'll mourn for 'em, but Redemption will be all right. There are too many good people here for it to be any other way."

"If you had put it to that vote, those good people probably would have turned us all over to the Pawnee in order to save their own skins," Costigan said.

"Don't reckon we'll ever know," Bill said. He put out his hand. "If I don't see you again, Mr. Costigan, good luck to you. I hope you find what you're lookin' for."

Costigan gripped his hand. "I won't forget that you saved my life out there, Marshal. I think maybe I owe it to you not to throw the rest of it away."

Bill smiled. "If you ever pass this way again, you can stop and buy me a drink. We'll call it square."

"I might take you up on that," Costigan said.

Bill left the camp and walked back toward the office. Redemption was quiet tonight . . . so quiet, in fact, that he could hear the weeping coming from some of the houses, including that of Mason Jones, who had been murdered inside the bank, probably by Fraker. There would be a lot of crying for the next few days, a lot of funerals and burials.

They could even have a funeral now for Aaron Wetherby, who had also been murdered by Jake Fraker. That was
another thing Bill had found out by questioning Oscar
Kipp. The big man had told everything he knew, including
how they had left several other members of the gang outside of town, in hopes of escaping a hangman's noose. He
probably would avoid that fate, too, because even though
he had known about Fraker's plans, he hadn't really taken
part in any of them, the way it turned out.

Once he was able to ride, though, Kipp would be wise to
put Redemption a long way behind him and take the rest of
the gang with him, if the Indian threat hadn't already made
them light a shuck. Bill intended to suggest that very thing
to Kipp, as strongly as possible. If they tried anything else
in these parts, they would be sorry.

Mordecai Flint pushed through the batwings and
stepped out of Smoot's Saloon as Bill walked by. He said,
"Sorry, Marshal. I was makin' my rounds, and I got a mite
sidetracked."

He wiped the back of his hand across his whiskery
mouth.

"That's all right, Mordecai," Bill said with a smile. "I
reckon most of us who lived through this day feel like gettin' a little . . . sidetracked."

Flint chuckled as he fell in step beside Bill. "Hell of a
thing, wasn't it?"

"Yeah," Bill said. "A hell of a thing." He brightened as
he went on, "Are you still thinkin' about settling down
here? Still want that deputy's job?"

"The badge kinda suits me. And even though the past
few days have been a mite hectic, I got to believe that in a
peaceful little town like Redemption, things have got to be
pretty quiet most of the time. Don't they?"

"You'd think so, wouldn't you?" Bill said.

Don't miss the best
Westerns from Berkley

LYLE BRANDT
PETER BRANDVOLD
JACK BALLAS
J. LEE BUTTS
JORY SHERMAN
DUSTY RICHARDS

M10G0610